DISCARD

DISCARD

Dirty Heat

Dear Reader:

Cairo has delivered yet again. This time it's book fourteen and it's as fast-paced and erotic as all of his titles. In these six lustful tales, he brings the heat showing a host of "dirty" ways to cheat between the sheets.

From titles like "All Three Holes" to "Phone Bone," Cairo takes readers on a wild ride bringing sexual heat in any way imaginable. Characters have hidden desires and explore their fantasies at full speed in this anthology driven by scandal and deceit.

As always, thanks for the love and support shown to me and the authors that I publish under Strebor Books. We appreciate each and every one of you and will continue to strive to bring you cutting-edge, exciting books in the future.

Blessings,

Zane

Publisher
Strebor Books
www.simonandschuster.com

Dirty Heat

CAIRO

SBI
STREBOR BOOKS
NEW YORK LONDON TORONTO SYDNEY

Strebor Books
P.O. Box 6505
Largo, MD 20792
http://www.streborbooks.com

ISBN 978-1-59309-596-3
ISBN 978-1-4767-7581-4 (ebook)
LCCN 2015934964

First Strebor Books trade paperback edition November 2015

Cover design: www.mariondesigns.com
Cover photograph: © Keith Saunders/Keith Saunders Photos

10 9 8 7 6 5 4 3 2 1

Manufactured in the United States of America

For information regarding special discounts for bulk purchases,
please contact Simon & Schuster Special Sales at 1-866-506-1949

The Simon & Schuster Speakers Bureau can bring authors to your live event.
For more information or to book an event, contact the Simon & Schuster Speakers Bureau at 1-866-248-3049 or visit our website at www.simonspeakers.com.

This book is dedicated to
Dara "MizPain" Williams & Zanetta "Ziggy" Davis,
two down-ass chicks who know how to be ladies in the streets,
but turn up the heat in them sheets. Mad luv, much respect!
Keep wavin' them freak flags!

ACKNOWLEDGMENTS

I am forever in awe at the mad luv I continue to get with each joint I drop. This is what, book number fourteen—and once again, it feels like my first release. You, my juice lovas, make the long hours of typing and racing to get to the finish line before every deadline so worth it. Yeah, I write the heat. But it's all of you who go out and drop ya paper on my joints, spread the word, wave ya freak flags, and keep me inspired to keep bringing you the kind of hot, nasty erotica you've all come to crave, and expect from me.

I am turned on by every keystroke knowing I'm about to turn *you* on in some creative, sexy way. I will never stop thanking you. So, here goes: Thank you for being open-minded enough, bold enough, and adventurous enough; and for allowing me to share my love of hotness in the sheets with you. All that I do is for you!

Some things change, some shit will forever stay the same. And this holds true for all the Facebook beauties 'n' cuties and cool-ass bruhs who make this journey mad fun: Real spit. Y'all my mutha-effen peeps! Too many of you to name, but YOU know who you are, godddammit!

Special shout-out to the best literary agent in the game: Sara Camilli. I am forever indebted to you for all that you do.

To Zane, Charmaine, Yona and the rest of the Strebor/Simon & Schuster team: As always, I hope you all know how much ya boy appreciates the never-ending luv!

To the members of *Cairo's World*: Thanks for the mad luv!

And, as always, to the naysayers: What would I do without you, huh, niggah-boos, huh? Y'all keep me wanting to turn up and get real nasty with it; just so I can fuck with you. I whack off knowing I'ma catch you in ya feelings. But fuck what ya heard, coon-muh-fuckas. The Cairo movement is here to stay! Thought you knew!

One luv—

Cairo

P-Spot
Under Siege

W*ell-hung, happily married black man seeks an extremely open-minded woman for no-strings, stress-free freaky fun. You must be kinky and willing to kiss, lick, finger and eat my ass til I explode. I want a babe who loves eating a man's hole. I know you're out there, baby, so come tongue me good. I'm looking for you to alternate between licking my hole and cock and balls. Please know how to suck dick! Lick it up and down and all over. Not just licking up and down and ignoring my balls. I don't want my dick in an empty mouth. You should be wrapping your tongue around my dick and licking it like it's your favorite ice cream. You should be licking my balls and the crack of my ass lovingly. I would love for you to finger your pussy while you play with my ass. Then, if you want, let me dick you down real good. To make sure you've read this carefully, put in subject line "ass play" so that I know you are not spam. I'm not looking to pay for sex or subscribe to any websites. I'm looking to get this dick sucked, ass licked, prostate stroked and pop a good nut. ***Women only** Repeat, this ad is for real women. I am not gay, bi-curious or confused. Don't even bother hitting me up. I will not reply back.*

I read and reread and edit the ad on my laptop multiple times before finally pressing the PUBLISH tab. In the last five years, this is like my fourth or fifth time placing an ad on Nastyfreaks4u. com—a sex site specifically for individuals looking to explore all of their wildest, kinkiest fantasies. There are lots of perverts up on here, but every now and then, you luck up and connect with some pretty decent freaks who aren't just looking to collect pictures, or get pissed or shitted on, or fucked raw, but really trying to get into some clean discreet, sexy, freaky fun.

The last two times I've posted I received over a hundred responses back. And only thirty-five were legit. Out of those, fifteen were halfway serious to meet up. But only six were remotely worth considering. The others had some type of handicap, were extremely hard on the eyes, had missing teeth, or were about the size of a Sumo wrestler.

Definitely not something I'd roll around in the sheets with, let alone allow anywhere near my dick or my ass.

However, after about an hour of sifting through ridiculous emails, then playing the back 'n' forth email game, I finally ended up connecting with this sexy Spanish chick who had a tongue like a lizard. No, on second thought, it was like a serpent's. Goddamn. I miss that tongue. That mouth. Them lips. Them fingers.

Elena was her name.

She was as sexy as she was freaky. And she loved to please me. She was patient. She took her time. She was generous with her tongue, her mouth, and her slender fingers. She sucked this dick and licked this ass with a whole lot of spit. Kissed and sucked on that spot between my balls and rectum while she stroked my dick. Then slid her finger in my asshole and caressed my spot until I shot my nut all down in her throat. I literally felt lightheaded and saw stars. That's how powerful the nut was. That's how it always is. Strong. Forceful. Toe-curling.

With loads of hot, sticky cum.

And that's exactly what coming had been while Elena had my dick in her mouth and her finger in my ass. Even while she continued sucking and stroking my prostate, milking the last of my nut out of me, my body convulsed. Hands fisted at my sides, head arched into the pillow, hips surged upward, dick jerking wildly, Elena and her heated tongue had taken me to the outer banks of nirvana. Then tossed me over the edge.

Then—after she finished washing my dick and balls with her tongue, and the shudders subsided—I rolled on a condom, flipped her over on her back and stroked her deep, getting lost in her wetness.

"Shit," was the only thing I could mutter when her pussy squeezed my dick and I exploded, emptying my balls inside the condom.

Feeling my dick harden at the memory, I plop back in my leather computer chair, and take a deep sigh, grabbing my erection.

Damn, I need to nut. Bad.

I log into my AOL account and the "You've Got Mail" instantly greets me. Already, I have six new emails. I immediately open the first one, hoping like hell I can connect with someone decent with a long tongue and wet, juicy mouth. It's from SugarWalls8908.

Hey, boo. What are your stats? How big is your dick? your ad doesn't say. I know you're looking for someone to lick up in your asshole n finger you in it, but I need to know how big that dick is. I can't see struggling to pull a little dick to the back to suck. It'll be a waste of time, energy, and good spit. And I like big balls too! I'll stuff your ass with my tongue, boo, but I have a big wide mouth and I need it filled to the rim with a big hard dick and lots of cum.

I shake my head, and type. *Hey. Thanks for the response. I'm like 6'1, 210. And my dick is 8.5. And real thick! Is that big enough for you? And I cum a lot. Now what are your stats, baby? What does that mouth and tongue look like? Let's not waste time!*

I open the next email. *Can I see a pic of your asshole? I need to be sure you don't have any hemorrhoids. I like cauliflower, but on a plate. Not in an ass.*

Delete.

I open the next email. *Sup yo. Dl nigga here. Let me beat dat shit up for you. Tongue game iz da truth. Dick stroke straight fire. Real nigga here bout dat real nigga shit yo. I'll fuck your gutz inside out. Lmk what's good!*

What the fuck? Didn't I say I'm not with that DL shit! Obviously this stupid-ass mofo didn't read the ad!

Delete.

Most people simply don't pay attention or follow basic instructions. I shake my head. The next three emails are spam. Not surprising. I delete them as well. It's been almost six months since I've been on the prowl for some prostate play, but one of the downsides of posting ads on a website is, you never know who or what you're going to encounter so there's a real possibility I won't connect with anyone. Still, it's a chance I take in hopes of meeting someone relatively sane, stable, sexy, and freaky enough to want to meet up and not play games.

Unfortunately, there are a lot of game players, psychos, and flakes up on this site. Lonely, miserable fucks with nothing else better to do than waste other people's time with their bullshit.

I open another email.

Lies!!!!!! How the fuck are you calling yourself a "happily-married" man when you on here looking for some nasty bitch to lick you in your ass? You sound confused and like ur some undercover gay man hiding behind a wedding band. It's nasty motherfuckers like you fucking over a good woman with your cheating ass ways!! Go find yourself a man to fuck you in the ass and stop fucking over your wife! Bastard!

"Yeah, okay. Good luck with that," I mutter to myself, deleting the email, shaking my head. *Miserable broads are always looking for someone else to blame for their misery!*

Let me just put it out there, now, before I get too far into my story. Yes. I'm a married man. Happily married, I might add. Surprising as that might seem. And, yes, Krista and I have—for all intents and purposes—an active healthy sex life. We have sex about three, sometimes four, times a week. And, on a good week, we often have it twice in the same day.

Is the sex explosive? No.

Is it mind-blowing? No.

Still, in many ways, it's pleasurable. And I enjoy making love to my wife. Her smooth, velvety walls feel good wrapped around my dick. But, for me—as good as the pussy feels, it's not enough. Not always, anyway.

Being honest, the foreplay is mediocre at best. I mean, don't get me wrong. There's some foreplay here and there—a lick here, a suck there…not on my part, but hers. But it isn't enough. Where I'm always willing and ready to slow lick and French kiss her down below before giving her this hard, thick wood, she's a little less—okay, okay…a whole lot less—uninhibited when it comes to orally pleasing me. All right, all right. I'll say it. Krista is orally challenged. Don't get me wrong. She'll give it her best go at it. Sucking dick that is. But, she's not as energetic, or as enthusiastic, in the dick-sucking department as I'd like her to be. She'll complain, after about five or ten minutes into it, that her jaws hurt, or that she's getting tired. Or she'll rush me to either hurry up and nut, or fuck her.

And I do.

Fuck her, that is.

Real good.

But sometimes, I need, want more. Sometimes I want them lips, that tongue, to go lower. Need my smooth-shaven balls in her mouth, her tongue sweeping around my asshole. Dipping in it. Tonguing it. Sometimes, I want her to slip a finger inside my ass and massage my prostate.

But that'll never happen. Not with Krista. Not the way I need it.

Now, hold up. Let me finish before you start twisting your lips up and passing judgment. I already know what some of you lames are thinking: What the fuck? Ass play?

Yeah, I'm a man—a *straight* man, be clear—who wants, nah, loves, ass play. It's my fetish, my deep, dark secret. One I wish I didn't have to keep from Krista. One I'd rather share *and* enjoy with her, my lover, my wife.

But I can't. I won't. That particular desire happens to be some shit she's not into. Not that I've flat out asked her to slide her tongue, or her finger, inside my ass. But I've asked her, numerous times, to lick my balls, to gently suck them into her mouth. And she's failed miserably at each attempt.

She tells me my balls are too big, that her mouth can't fit them in. Or she sucks them too roughly, grazes them with too much teeth. So I've stopped asking her. Shit. My thing is, after almost twelve years of marriage, I shouldn't have to ask her, or coach her, or teach her, how to suck this dick and lick on these balls. Hell, I shouldn't have to tell her how to please me, period. She should already know! She should want to explore more. Should want to be more adventurous. Should want to freak me. And allow me to freak her.

But she doesn't.

She can't.

She won't.

Sadly put, Krista doesn't know how to let go. My wife's painstakingly conservative when it comes to sex. She believes firmly in what roles—and positions—there should be in the bedroom. Missionary, doggy-style, spooning—those are her three positions. Anything else is too much for her. So in a word, my wife's a prude. Like I said, the pussy's good. But that's it. Creativity and openness are nonexistent.

So there's no way I can ever ask her to let down her guard and allow her tongue and fingers to explore my ass. Freak and Krista just doesn't go in the same sentence. And it damn sure isn't going to ever exist in the same room.

Hell, the one time I gently broached the subject to test the waters by—hypothetically speaking—asking her, her thoughts on men who enjoy having their ass licked and fingered, I thought she was about to hit the floor. I'd stretched the truth and told her some cat was talking about how he loved having it done to him and only dated women who enjoyed doing it.

Krista's eyes almost popped out of her head. "Ohmygod! He's a real nasty freak asking his woman to do some shit like that," she snapped. "What kind of nastiness is that? A man wanting his ass licked *and* fingered."

Yeah, a man like me, I thought as I calmly stated, "He claimed it feels good."

She tilted her head. Frowned. Gave me a questioning look, then said, "He must be gay then, because no *real* man's liking a tongue in his ass. And he's definitely not going to openly admit some shit like that feeling good. And then turn around and say he wants a finger stuffed up in it. Oh, no. He's down low and nasty. Sorry. But a real man is never letting *anyone* or *anything* go anywhere near his ass." She grunted, frowning up her face while shaking her head. "I don't know not one woman willing to be nasty enough to lick up in some man's ass like it's a vagina."

Inwardly, I cringed. But outwardly, I laughed. "Come on, baby. You really think a man's gay if he wants his woman to tongue him back there, or insert a finger inside him?"

She grimaced. "Yes, I think he and any other man wanting that nasty mess is gay. And if he isn't, then he's damn sure on his way to being gay."

Her tone rang with so much conviction and disgust that I thought my ears would start bleeding. I always knew Krista could be rigid in her thinking, but hearing those words solidified exactly how closed-minded my wife really was.

My body tensed.

"Damn, baby. Don't you think you're going a bit overboard? They say the prostate is a man's version of a woman's G-spot."

She gave me an incredulous look. "Oh, I'm hardly exaggerating. You asked me my opinion, and I'm sharing it. And who in the heck is *they?*"

Shit.

I hadn't meant to say that. Trying to educate Krista on how a man's prostate is called his sacred spot, like that of the G-spot in a woman and how tantric philosophy describes it as a man's emotional sex center would have turned the conversation into an ugly fight filled with accusations, leaving her doubting my manhood and questioning my masculinity. So there was no way I could enlighten her on the joys of prostate stimulation—of how the lobes of the prostate are highly sensitive and when stroked through the rectal wall can cause ecstatic, mind-blowing pleasure—without sounding like a man who'd had a few fingers wedged in his ass over the years of our marriage.

"Someone asked him what he got out of being fingered," I lied, masking my own hidden desires, "and licked back there and he said it was one of the most intense, most pleasurable orgasms he'd ever had."

That was my reality. One she would never know about.

She gave me a blank look. "You're joking, right? Sounds like he was trying to recruit him a few good ass lickers and some hard dick. I've never heard some mess like that. And I don't know if it's true or not. All I know is, the prostate and a man's ass aren't there for fingering. A straight man's pleasure is not coming from having a tongue or finger anywhere near his asshole." She narrowed her eyes. "Is there something you're trying to tell me here?"

I gave her an incredulous look, repeating in my head what she'd just asked me. *Is there something you're trying to tell me?* "Where is that coming from? There's nothing to tell. How did this all of a sudden become about me?"

She tilted her head, seemingly unconvinced. "I don't know. You seem a bit animated about some man getting his ass tongued."

I forced a laugh. "Oh, you have got to be kidding me. Krista, come on. I ask you your thoughts on something I overheard, and all of a sudden, you think I have some hidden agenda." I shake my head.

"Well, do you?"

I frowned. Stared her dead in the eyes. "Hell no. I'm not gay," I said defensively, feeling as if I'd opened up a box of chocolates covered in shit. "You know that."

"Well, that's a relief," she said, looking me over. "I mean, I don't think you are. But nowadays, you never know. You see what happened to Latrice and Herbie. After all those years together, she catches him in some motel room with a tranny. And here she thought he was as straight as an arrow. Then come to find out, he likes men in wigs and fishnet stockings and nasty-ass kitten heels. He didn't even look like he'd go that way. So you never know."

I cringed. *Here we go with this shit.* Herbie is her sister's husband. And the fact that she was bringing that sordid shit up at that moment was like comparing apples to oranges. They were two separate things. But not in my wife's eyes. Apparently, I'd hit a nerve with her.

I let her vent her dismay with how he hurt her sister. Still, at the end of the day, that shit had nothing to do with me, or my question to her. Hell. I wasn't interested in same-sex nothing. He was. And, shit, the question I'd asked had nothing to do with me... directly, anyway. Well, as far as she knew.

Yeah, it was my indirect way to gauge how she'd react to the idea before I broached the subject of her possibly trying it with me. However, all that extra shit she was talking wasn't necessary. But truth be told, she had her opinion. And I had my own. And for me, ass play had nothing to do with sexual preference. It was about pleasure. Period.

However, I kept my true feelings to myself.

"Well, that's not me," I assured her, keeping my eyes locked on her. "I'm not into any of that. You know that."

She smirked. "Oh, really? Do I? I mean, since when you start asking me about men wanting to be fucked in the ass? That sounds a little suspect to me."

"C'mon, Krista. Let's not turn this into something more than what it is. First of all, it was a theoretical question, baby. And, secondly, I thought you and I were able to talk about any-and-every-thing."

She eyed me, long and hard. "We can. But that kind of talk—ass licking and fingering—makes all kinds of red flags go up for me."

I sighed. Told her not to let her imagination run wild. That she had nothing to be worried about, or anything to doubt. I was completely heterosexual.

"Well, then, since you're asking—*hypothetically*, that is, is that something you want, someone to poke around in your ass?"

Hell yeah.

I swallowed. "Nah. I was simply sharing some shit I overheard down at the barbershop, that's all."

"*Down at the barbershop?*" she scoffed. "Oh hell no. You mean to tell me a man getting an ass licking was some open discussion being had by a bunch of so-called straight men?" She shook her head. "Mmmph. Sounds like somebody's up in there trying to have themselves some kind of booty-fest. And, if not, I'd be looking at him, or any other man side-eyed for even entertaining that conversation, especially in the company of other men."

I let out a nervous chuckle. "Whoa, baby. Hold up. You're blowing a simple question all out of proportion. This was about a man letting a woman finger and tongue him. Not another man. The question was simply, 'do you think he's gay for letting a woman do it?'"

"Mmph. You already know my answer to that. Like I said, any man who wants to be played with back there is suspect, period. And, all I know is, if you ever came home and asked me to lick your ass, or to stick my fingers, or anything else, up in it, I'd be hurt. And I wouldn't be able to trust you."

I gave her a look of disbelief. "Are you serious?

"As a heart attack. I love you, Kendall. But I know me. I'd always be thinking in the back of my mind that it'd only be a matter of time before you'd be on all fours glancing over your shoulder, looking to get some dick."

My jaws tightened. I shook my head. "Now you're talking real crazy."

"How am I talking crazy, huh? I'm telling you how I'd feel about it."

"And I'm telling you I'd have to be attracted to another man to want *dick*, Krista. Trust me, baby. Another mofo's dick is the last thing I'm interested in."

"Well, I'm not saying you are. I thought we were speaking hypothetically."

"We were. I mean, we are."

"Then, *hypothetically* speaking, it'd still be in the back of my mind. And I'd always be looking at you sideways, looking for signs that maybe you were bisexual." She shook her head. "It'd be too much for me. I'd have to divorce you."

I scoffed. *"Divorce?* See. Now you're letting this spin way to the left. It was a simple question."

She glanced meaningfully at me. "And I gave you my answer; *hypothetically* speaking; remember? I'm not accusing you, Kendall, of any sketchy wrongdoing. I'm simply stating a fact. And now I'm asking *you*, again, is that what you want? Your ass fucked?"

No. Licked. Fingered.

I considered her question. Considered her very visceral reaction to the question I'd posed about a man wanting ass play. "Come on, babe. I already told you. No."

"Well, since we're having this conversation, is it a secret fantasy of yours?"

It used to be. Now it's a reality.

"No. No fantasy of mine." I reached for her. Pulled her up from her seat, then pulled her into my arms, kissing her. "My *only* fantasy is *you*, baby."

She smirked. "Yeah, right. Every man has some secret desire."

Yeah, like you licking my ass and kissing this asshole every now and then.

I raised a brow, smirking. "Oh, yeah? And what secret desires do you have, baby? Do tell."

"I only have one. I don't want my man desiring some nastiness with another man; that's all I desire."

I blinked. I couldn't believe what had come out of her mouth. Of all the things to secretly crave, or fantasize about, the only thing Krista could focus on was the idea of her man, *me*, wanting to get down with another man. Like damn. My dick would have jumped if she'd said she fantasized about having a threesome. That she secretly fantasized about being tied up and gang-fucked.

Or better yet, about pleasing her damn man. But, hell, no such luck! The only shit she could come up with was, her man not fucking, or getting fucked by, another man. Talk about creativity at its finest.

"Well, no worries there, baby," I said reassuringly. "Believe that." I kissed her again. This time, cupping her ass. "You feel that hard dick? Does that feel like a man wanting to be with another man?"

She relaxed and grinned. "Not really. But…"

"'But' nothing. I'm not looking to have nothing stuck in my ass."

Only a woman's tongue, a few fingers…maybe a small, thin vibrator if I'm horny enough. I couldn't believe Krista, my wife, was going there with *me*, of all people. I'd never been the type to knock what someone else did behind closed doors. Their likes, their desires, are none of my concern. I respect everyone's space and their right to their private moments. What they do sexually has nothing to do with me. So if Herbie has a thing for trannies on the side, that wasn't/isn't my cross to bear. It's his. And it's his wife's decision to either deal with it or not.

At that moment, Herbie was still out of the house. But let him tell it, he was still fucking her. So, what did that say? Either she was confused, too emotionally caught up in him to let him go, couldn't let go of that hard dick, was willing to work through it, or all the above.

Regardless, it wasn't my business. And the fact that Krista had the audacity to bring his transgressions with another man into a discussion that had nothing to do with same-sex cheating had me feeling some type of way.

That was far from who I was, or who I am. I wasn't interested in—or attracted to—other men. So I wasn't looking to sleep with one, period, point blank.

Hell, I wasn't even interested in being pegged by a woman wielding a strap-on, or fucked by a dildo. But I'd taken a finger back there.

And…

I was twenty-six. And it was a few months before Krista and I met. I was out in Vegas with a few of my frat brothers, popping bottles at another one of our frat brother's bachelor party being held at a private rooftop club overlooking the city.

There were about fifteen badass strippers there to entertain us however any one of us wanted it. And most of the bros there were in full swing taking full advantage of the free-access pussy and head.

Except me.

I had my sights on the sexiest one who stood out from the rest. She was the one who'd caught my eye. She had voluptuous red lips, honeydew-melon breasts, a flat stomach, and a big bubblicious-ass that bounced and shook in sync to the music. She watched me watching her. Licked her lips—exposing a long pink tongue, and swung her hips, thrusting her pelvis, her eyes never leaving mine. My dick stirred for the first time that night.

I wanted her. Bad.

Fortunately, I didn't have to wait long. Or make a move. She'd made it first. She liked what she saw and came for it. One foot in front of the other, back straight, pelvis thrusting, she cat-walked her way over to me.

"What's your name, baby?"

"Kendall." I extended my hand to hers. "And yours?"

"Peaches." She licked her lips, letting her warm hand get lost in mine. Before I could ask her how she got her name, she added, "'Cause I'm real sweet 'n' juicy."

I grinned. "I like that."

"You *like that?* Oh, no, sweetheart. You'd love it."

I eyed her, feeling everything inside of me overheat. "Oh, yeah?"

"Mmhmm." She wagged a finger for me to lean in closer. "I wanna coat your lips with my juices, then fuck you," she whispered in my ear.

"Damn. You suck dick?"

She threw her head back, and laughed. "Do I suck dick? Does Queen Elizabeth have a throne? Of course I suck dick. What kind of question is that? Sucking dick is the fastest way to a man's heart, or into his wallet."

I laughed. "Is that so? Well, good thing I didn't fly way out here looking for love, but how 'bout I buy you a drink, then see where the rest of the night takes us?"

She smirked, brushing up on me as she swished her hips toward the bar. I followed behind her, mesmerized by the sway of her hips.

Several drinks in and two hundred dollars later, I was ready to get butt-naked, and roll around on satiny hotel sheets. But my brain went on pause the minute she asked, "You ever had your ass licked?"

I almost choked on my drink. "Oh, shit." I coughed. "I can't believe you just asked me that. Is this some kind of trick question? If that's your roundabout way of asking if I'm gay, then the answer is hell no."

She grinned, then licked her lips. "That's good to know. But as fine as you are, I wouldn't care if you were. I'd still give you some. But, no, I wasn't asking for that reason," she assured me as she dragged her gaze up and down my body. "I wanna see how nasty I can get with you. Now answer the question. Have you ever had your ass licked?"

Although I could feel my dick stretching, my mouth went suddenly dry. I swallowed. "Nah. Never had that done."

She licked them luscious lips again. "Can I lick it for you?"

I frowned. "Hell, no, you can't lick my ass. That's some homo shit. I told you I'm not gay."

She laughed. "Silly man, there's nothing *homo*, as you say, about a man allowing a woman to please him in every way possible. But if you're not open-minded enough to let a woman explore you, then you're not the one for me. I was wrong for approaching you."

I watched as she slid off the barstool. She started to grab her drink, but I stopped her. "Hold up. Where you going?"

"To find me a man I can freak. I'm looking to get freaky tonight, baby. Not simply get fucked. I'm not like most women. I'm very open-minded about sex and about pleasing a man. And I like my men adventurous."

Damn. She's bold.

She had my dick hard, harder than it'd ever been. And there was no way I was trying to pass up a night with her, one which seemed filled with the promise of good pussy and a night I'd always remember. There was no way I was letting the opportunity slip through my fingers.

I took another sip of my drink and relaxed a little.

"Nah. I'm all the man you need tonight."

She eyed me. "You sure about that?"

I swallowed. "Yeah. I'm sure. You took me by surprise; that's all. I've never had a female ask me that before."

"Well, like I said. I'm not your average woman. Pleasure is mutual, baby. And I take pleasure in pleasing a man. And turning him out."

I grinned. "Oh word? Is that right?"

"Yes," she purred. "I like it all, baby. Sucking dick. Licking balls. Swallowing. Licking ass. I do it all. And tonight, I wanna do you. You look like you have some nice, juicy ass."

"Damn. Why me?"

"Why not you? You're fine as hell. And I wanna make you feel real good. That's if I haven't scared you." She pursed her lips, tilting her head.

I laughed. "Scared? Who, me? Never that. I'm always up for a challenge."

She slowly dragged her tongue over her lips. "I promise you. It'll be the best experience of your life.'"

My dick twitched in my boxers. "Oh, damn. It's like that?"

Heat flashed in her eyes as she slowly nodded her head. "Oh, you have no idea, baby. Now let's go to your room so I can show you just how nasty I like it."

Nothing else needed to be said. I paid my tab, then followed her to the bank of elevators. The minute we stepped inside and the doors shut, it was on. We started kissing and groping each other up. Between the gin and her eagerness to please, she had me horny as fuck. I pressed her back into the wall and shoved my tongue down in her throat, grinding my rock-hard dick into her. She spread her legs and allowed me to slide a hand up between her thighs. She wasn't wearing any panties. And her pussy was soaking wet.

Exactly the way I liked it.

"Fuck," I muttered. "I could fuck you right here if I had a condom with me."

She moaned against my lips. "Mmm. And I'd let you." She reached for my dick. "I hope you know how to use this. I love it big, baby. And I like it all night."

"Oh, I know how to use it," I promised, toying with her clit. "Wait and see."

The elevator doors opened, and we staggered out of it still pawing at each other. We couldn't get inside my hotel room fast enough.

The minute we stumbled inside, and the door slammed shut behind us, buttons flew open, shoes were kicked off, clothes were strewn about. Kissing, groping, bucking, our naked bodies finally made it to the bedroom.

I'd never eaten the pussy of a female I didn't know, but that night I had my face between her thighs. I ran the tip of my tongue over every inch of her thick lips, then up over her clit and teased around it. "Damn," I murmured between her thighs. I moaned as I licked and sucked her. She was right. She was juicy. And her juices tasted sweet, like peppermint.

"Mmm, baby, yes, yes. Right there. Lick all over my pussy. Get all of Peaches' sweet juices. My turn, boo," she said, breathlessly as she tried to move. "Let me suck that dick, then taste your ass."

My dick jumped.

I kept licking her with broad wet strokes.

"Mmmm...please. Let me get some dick."

I ignored her protests, sucking on her clit and pushing two fingers in as deeply as I could, then stirring them in and out of her until my fingertips swept over her. Her pussy juice splashed out of her, over my hand, on my lips, on my chin.

She was wetter than a river. Juicier than any peach I'd ever eaten.

A few more licks and then she was clasping her thighs around my head, squeezing the life out of me, bucking her pelvis up into me, fucking my mouth, my tongue, my fingers. And when she came, she shook and screamed as she came, squirting, soaking my face and the sheets.

I sputtered and gasped for breath. I'd almost choked on her orgasm, literally.

"Now, you're all mine." She sat up in bed, her eyes glowing. "Get on your knees," she ordered. "I wanna suck your dick from the back."

Oh, shit. This bitch wasn't lying. She really is a freak. I was liquored up. Drunk on recklessness, and my dick was harder than a steel pipe.

In the back of my mind, I knew the minute she asked if I'd ever had my ass licked that should have been my cue to spin off on her. But, after having a mouthful of her pussy, whatever inhibitions I might have had were now nonexistent. She had me open. And ready to freak. And get freaked.

Despite my nerves and apprehensions, I turned over, got up on my knees and hoisted my ass in the air. A shiver of excitement raced down my spine as I held my breath and waited for her to handle my dick with some unknown mouth tricks.

"I'ma turn you out," she warned as she knelt in back of me. "When I'm finished with you, baby, I promise…you'll never be the same." And with that, she reached between my legs and pulled my dick backward, licking the head, then licking up and down the back of my balls, before sucking the head of my dick into her mouth. She sucked me until I felt faint. I'd never gotten my dick sucked from the back. And the shit turned me on.

"Mmm. Nice big dick," she groaned into my dick as her lips worked their magic on my cockhead. She cupped my balls. "Mmm, big juicy balls." She licked up and down my shaft in long wet strokes, then blew on my balls before opening her mouth and slowly easing both of them into her wide mouth, soaking them at the same time with warm spit. Her juicy mouth was hot, her tongue extra wet. I'd never been sucked with such intensity the way she sucked me that night. It was the kind of head you only saw in porn— sloppy and wet and greedy, with lots of spit and a bunch of gagging and loud gurgling sounds.

"Oh, shit, yeah…aaah…fuckfuckfuck…oooh, yeah, suck that dick, baby…yeah, like that…aaah, shit!"

And, just when I thought things couldn't get any kinkier, she reached up, opened my ass cheeks, then…goddamn! Slid her tongue along my hair-lined crack, where it lingered. Her warm breath teased me. Then she inched its way to that sacred—"no entrance, exit only"— spot between my cheeks. She licked it, sensually. My toes curled.

"Aah, shit."

I felt the air around me go thin. I couldn't believe it. I was letting her play in my ass with her tongue. Licking, lapping, laving, she trailed wet streaks up and down my crack, then she licked my ass-hole and gently tugged on my balls.

Propping up on my elbows, blinking hard, my heart beating fast, I held my breath. Felt my stomach quiver. Felt the throbbing in my dick as it stretched. Felt the tightening of my balls as they filled with arousal. Felt the electric currents that shot through my veins as her luscious lips kissed my hole, as the tip of her tongue touched the rim, circling and licking and circling some more, then licking, licking, licking, and more licking until my body shook. She sucked on my asshole, blew into it, then drove her tongue inside.

"Oh, shiiiiit!"

My mind went blank.

Everything I thought, everything I believed, about an asshole... *mine*, in particular—being touched by someone, about it being something only gay men enjoyed; whatever insecurities or reservations I might have had prior to her lips, her tongue, touching me there—went up in flames the moment I felt my insides vibrate. And heat shoot through me.

Holy fuck!

The shit felt good, real good.

My body tensed.

Whack!

She slapped my ass.

Shocked, I blinked. Bucked my hips.

"Mmm. You have a beautiful, manly ass." She pulled open my ass, again. Flicked her tongue over it again. "Mmm, it tastes so good. I love your man hole."

There was something about having my ass on display for her that had me feeling strangely aroused. I glanced over my shoulder, to see what she was doing.

Whack! Her hand went down on my ass, again; heat flaring over my skin.

"What the fuck...?"

"Relax, baby," she cooed, smoothing her hand over the area she'd smacked. "Maybe I should blindfold you. Tie your hands behind your back."

"Nah, you good," I said, hoping like hell she didn't try to pull out a pair of shiny handcuffs. I definitely wasn't down with that. It was bad enough I had my six-two frame up on the bed on my knees, pushing my dick to the back of me for her to suck. The last thing I needed, wanted, was to have her cuffing me up, then leaving me there with my ass up.

How the hell would I have ever explained that?

She touched my ass again. This time softly.

I'd never experienced anything like that before. And the shit had me so turned on. Turned my dick into a faucet of pleasure, leaking streams of precum.

Peaches pressed her thumb against my asshole, and my heart jumped.

I flinched. "Oh, shit. Wait, wait. Hold up."

"Relax, baby." Her lips pressed into my back. "Let me in," she whispered. She sprinkled kisses over my shoulders, then trailed her lips down my spine to my tailbone until she had me relaxed. A fingertip burrowed back into my crack, causing me to tense. "Let Peaches have this sweet, musky man ass."

She then used her free hand to stroke my dick back into her mouth. She stroked it. Licked it. Kissed it. Then sucked it back into her mouth, again, this time harder.

Aah. Now that felt good.

I let out a deep breath. A mixture of moan and groan escaped me as her thumb skimmed around my asshole. I knew it was now or never. I'd let her go this far. The ache in my balls wanted her to go a little further. I rocked my hips back as she pressed the pad of her thumb, rubbing her fingertip over it until I gasped.

"Relax, baby," she murmured. "Let Peaches love this man hole. Mmm." Her finger skimmed my ass again.

And then…her hand left my ass. I'm not sure if it was relief or disappointment I initially felt. All I know is, when I glanced over my shoulder to see what she was doing, she was holding a small bottle of lube in her hand. I couldn't remember when she'd had time to grab it. Couldn't recall if she'd already had it in her hand when she climbed onto the bed. I pulled in a quick breath. Watched as she opened the tube. Squeezed some out onto her fingers, then pulled my ass cheeks apart. I tensed again.

She encouraged me to relax as she squeezed out more lube, smearing it slick over my hole. My hole clenched.

"Mmm. Look at that sweet man hole winking at me. You ready to feel Peaches' fingers inside you?"

I don't remember if I responded or not. But what I do remember is, her finger sliding into my ass. I remember the way my ass muscles clenched, unclenched. But she kept on gliding her finger in and out.

"Aah, shit…aaah, shit…goddamn, fuck…"

My dick was back in her mouth again. And she sucked on it harder. Faster.

That did it. Got me to relax more. I found myself really getting into it. I spread my legs wider. Slowly winded my hips.

"Oh, yeah. Suck dick that dick, baby. Aaah, goddamnshit… mmm…damn."

She pulled her finger out. And as I glanced over my shoulder again, I watched as she stuck her finger into her mouth. Slowly sucked on it, moaning.

"Mmm. Your ass tastes so good."

The sight of her sucking and licking her finger as if it were a dick had me so damn aroused. The vision was so sexy.

Totally surprising myself, I reached in back of me and opened my ass. "Put your tongue back inside me. Lick it some more, baby…"

She happily obliged, her tongue working a mile a minute, wetting me, licking me, loving me. "Ooooh, yeah. Fuck, baby. Lick it, lick it…mmmm. Lick it real good."

I pressed her face into me as she stuck her tongue in my ass again. She moved her lips over my hole. Her tongue delved deep inside me. And all I remember at that moment is the room spinning.

Her finger went in deeper. Then she stopped pressing in, replacing her thumb with her tongue. She licked over and over.

I moaned softly, feeling guiltily like a bitch in heat. The persistent flickering of her tongue was driving me over the edge. But I wanted more.

Fuck.

Instead, she licked inside my thighs. Nibbled on my balls. Licked around my hole again. Then trailed her wet tongue along the back of my balls before licking the underside of my dick. She used her tongue to tickle under my nut sac, then sucked my balls back into her mouth.

She gave my dick a long, deep kiss. Then, without warning, she caught me completely off guard by pushing her finger back into my ass while taking my dick to the back of her throat. I gasped, breathless as her finger worked its way into the outer ring of my asshole, then slid out. I clamped around her finger, and started to buck. Peaches slid another finger inside. I'm not gonna lie. She had me wide open, ready to climb walls.

"Aaah, shit…"

She pulled out. Then slid them back in; eagerly, she sucked my dick while curling her fingers upward. A rush of fire shot through me.

She'd found my P-spot.

"Ohshitohshitohhhshiiiiiit!"

The shit she was doing to me that night had me begging like a junkie needing his fix. It was a feeling like no other I'd ever experienced. It was beyond bliss.

She licked my ass and sucked on my balls and suckled on my dick like it was her last meal. My dick got harder than I thought possible. And I emitted a deep groan as she sucked and fucked and licked me like a porn star. And then...I was coming, faster and harder than ever.

The muscles slightly below my dick clenched over and over and shot out spurts of cum. My body juddered in extreme pleasure. Heavy squirts of nut blasted out of me leaving me lightheaded, hardly able to breathe, and clawing at the sheets. She kept sucking and stroking, and I kept filling her mouth and her throat with warm gushes of semen, groaning in ecstasy as her finger continued stroking inside of me.

I literally almost passed out from the intense sensation.

The next day, when the liquor wore off, the memory of the night before hung over my head like a noose. I felt guilty as hell for what I'd let her do to me. She'd licked my ass. Then fingered it. Yet, I had enjoyed it. And wanted to experience that feeling again.

Still...the shit had me feeling confused like hell. Had me doubting everything I knew and believed to be true about who I was, about who I thought I was.

I knew I wasn't physically or sexually attracted to other guys, but that experience had me questioning my own sexuality. Had me second-guessing my masculinity. Had me wondering if something was wrong with me for enjoying having a tongue licking my ass and a finger stroking in it.

But the intensity of that nut I'd popped stayed with me, ingrained in my brain. Etched itself into my DNA. I knew then, I'd never be the same.

That night in Vegas was where it all began for me. A new kind of freaky was unleashed in that hotel room. And I wanted more of it. The problem was, finding women who were open-minded enough I could trust with my secret to indulge me.

Anyway…

Krista looked up at me. "Are you sure?"

I blinked, bringing my attention back to her. "Huh? Am I sure about what?"

She rolled her eyes. "I asked you if you were sure about not wanting to get fucked in your ass because I'm not signing up for none of that kinky mess."

I blinked back the image of a warm wet tongue swirling around my asshole, and the heated sensations that followed every time the tip of it dips inside me. "Of course I'm sure. I'm not with that shit."

She let out a sigh of relief. "Good. After everything that happened with Latrice and Herbie, you never know. I don't ever want to be in her shoes and find myself blindsided like she was."

Here we go again. Back to Herbie and Latrice. "C'mon now, Krista," I said calmly, trying to mask my frustration and annoyance that she'd try to spin the conversation into something more than what it was. Was she fucking serious? Blindside her? The mere fact that she even remotely entertained some shit like that had me pissed off. But I bit my tongue. Arguing wasn't the plan. Getting some pussy was. "I'm not Herbie. And you're not Latrice. What he did was fucked up. She didn't deserve that. But trust me, baby. The last thing you'll ever have to worry about is finding me with another man. Not gonna happen."

"I hope not. All I want is for us to always have an honest relationship."

I gave her another kiss. "And we do." *Yeah, an honestly one-sided sexually stagnant one, if you ask me.* "After all these years, you should know by now what kind of man you have." I shook my head in disbelief. "I can't even believe I'm standing here having this conversation with you, like I have to defend my honor *and* my manhood to you."

"I don't want you to defend anything."

"Well, that's how it feels," I said tersely.

"Don't get defensive," she replied, hand on hip. "All I said was I don't want to ever be in Latrice's shoes. My heart breaks for her. That bastard put her through hell."

"Well, I'm not him. And you're not Latrice. That's their struggle, not ours. Now how did me asking you what you thought about a man wanting his woman to lick his ass turn into a conversation about Latrice and Herbie, and you practically questioning my manhood?"

"I wasn't questioning your manhood, Kendall. I was only stating an opinion. But if your sexuality came into question for me, believe me, I'd be confronting you."

I frowned. "And so you should. But you don't have to. You know that."

"I only know what you tell me. Anything else is left up to fate and speculation."

I sighed, shaking my head. "You can't be serious."

"I know what kind of man you are with me, when we're alone behind closed doors. But questions like that make me wonder…"

"It was a question about *me*."

"I know it wasn't. Still…"

"And, again…not that I should have to say this, but I will so that we're very clear. I'm not some DL cat living a double life. And I'm not Herbie or any other man who does."

Yeah, it wasn't exactly the God's honest truth. But it wasn't a complete lie, either. I mean. The fact that she'd never have to worry about me being attracted to—or wanting to be with—another man was true.

But, creeping every now and again with a freaky babe was a whole other story. So yeah, I lied, sort of—by omission. But. Out of necessity, it had to be told. Still, I hated doing so.

I let go of her, feeling like shit for not being able to be straight up with her about my hidden desires. I felt like such a fraud for not being able to man up and tell her what I enjoyed.

That I loved my ass licked.

That she was married to a man who loved a finger stroking inside his ass.

That I loved having my prostate massaged, milked.

That it was the most intense, pleasurable experience, ever.

No. I couldn't tell her any of that. Her reaction to what was only a hypothetical question was proof of that. So what other choice did I really have? I could only imagine what her real reaction would be if I confessed my sexual sins. Divorce was (and is) the last thing I want. But does that mean I should deny my sexual urges? Am I supposed to deprive myself of pleasure simply because my wife isn't down with the program?

Hell no.

Why should I when I can have my cake and eat it, too? After all, isn't that what you're supposed to do? Eat the cake?

"Good," she finally replied. "Now that that's settled. I'm going to start dinner."

"Hey, hey. Not so fast." I gently grabbed her arm as she went to walk off. My mind still reeling from the conversation, I needed to be sure I'd heard her right. "So you'd really divorce me if I told you I wanted *you* to lick my ass?"

"No, I'd curse your ass out real good. Then give you the side-eye. I wouldn't end our marriage over you asking something like that. You're entitled to ask whatever you like. Just like it's my prerogative to either be down with it or not. But, yes. Trust and believe. I'd divorce you in a heartbeat if I found out you were out here on all fours with another man...*or* woman; but definitely if it's with a man. I'm not signing up for none of that. Back there is for exit only. Just like I'm not giving it up. I don't want a man who does, either. No real man should want any kind of anal play. And if he does," she paused, shaking her head, "you already know what my thought is..."

Yeah. Real closed-minded.

Krista's repressive ignorance to sex and sexuality was stifling, for a lack of a better word. And I'd be damned if I'd allow her thinking or that of society's to keep me chained to mediocre sex. It wasn't going to happen. Like I said, I loved my wife, but, unfortunately, not enough to be deprived of my own sexual desires.

No, I'd never leave her. My life with Krista is more than sex. Still, sex—fulfilling sex, that is—is very important...to me, anyway. So if Krista wanted to stay stuck in the dark ages of what sex should or shouldn't be between a man and woman, a husband and wife, then let her.

When the urge hit me, I'd find satisfaction elsewhere, in the sheets with another open-minded freak like me.

She continued eyeing me suspiciously. "I'm still wondering why you'd bring that nasty mess up, anyway?"

I shrugged off my true thoughts and said, "I didn't think it was a big deal. I simply wanted to know your feelings about it."

She raised a brow. "Oh. Well, now you know. It's nasty."

"Well, nasty or not, baby," I stated as a matter of fact. "Everyone's entitled to do what they do behind closed doors, in the privacy of their own homes and in their own relationships. To each its own."

She twisted her lips in disgust. "Mmph. Yeah, you got that right.

Not in my bed, though, and definitely *not* with me. I'm still trying to figure out what kind of woman is licking some man's ass…?"

A freaky one, I mused.

"Mmph. She's just as sick and nasty in the head as he is for wanting it. I wish the hell I would."

No surprise there. Tell me how you really feel.

"I hear you, baby," I said thoughtfully. I gave her a peck on the lips, then patted her on the ass. "I wouldn't want your pretty tongue anywhere near my ass, anyway. But I know somewhere else I'd love to feel it." I grinned, lightening the mood between us.

She smirked. "Oh, I bet you would."

"Yeah, right over the head," I teased, rubbing over the length of my erection.

She rolled her eyes, waving me on. "Oh, you might get it there." She glanced down at the bulge in my pants. She smirked, walking off. Then glanced over her shoulder, and said, "Maybe later."

Standing there with a semi-hard dick, I watched her swing her hips out of the living room, heading toward the kitchen to prepare dinner. I decided maybe I'd jack off to lighten the heavy load in my balls. Then thought otherwise and stalked behind her, grabbing her by the waist, then spinning her around.

"Kendall, what in the world?"

"I'm horny, baby. I want you. Now."

"What, all that talk about ass licking got you so turned on?"

I laughed. "See. Now you tryna be funny." *Hell yeah.* "The only thing that has me turned on is, *you.*"

"But I need to get dinner started," she protested, trying to wiggle out of my embrace.

"You can," I said, holding her tighter, then grinding into her. "Right after I get up in these beautiful hips." I cupped her ass with both hands. "Better yet, I'll just eat you."

She relaxed in my arms, and giggled. "Not now. Later."

I scooped her up in my arms. "No. Now."

She flung her arms around my neck, laughing. "Kendall Lamont Evans. If you don't put me down."

I ignored her, carrying her off to our bedroom, then tossing her on the bed. "I want you naked, baby. Take them jeans off," I ordered, pulling off my undershirt.

She must have seen the hunger flash in my eyes—or maybe she decided she wanted some hard dick as badly as I wanted to give it to her—because she didn't put up much of a fight. She quickly unfastened the button on her jeans, then pulled them down over her hips, kicking them to the floor.

"Lose them panties," I said next, slipping out of my sweats, then dropping my boxers. I stroked my erection in my hand. Watched as she watched it glide in and out of my hand.

"What in the world's gotten into you today," she said, only hesitating briefly before slipping her thumbs into the waistband of her pink cotton panties.

"Nothing. I want my wife," is all I said.

A moment later, her panties were fluttering to the floor. And she was spreading her legs. Surprisingly, her pussy was already glistening wet.

God, I loved fucking my wife. That was the truth. I wanted it from the back. Wanted to feel her pussy ripple along the length of my dick as I pushed and pulled, in and out. Wanted to see her ass pulled apart and her asshole puckered while I fucked her doggy-style.

"Get on your knees, baby."

Ass up, facedown, she did.

"God, I love you," I said, my voice low and reassuring. "I can't wait to be inside of you."

I inched up behind her. Smoothed my hands over the globes of her ass, then spread her cheeks open. My mouth watered at the sight of her asshole. I wanted to lap it, delve my tongue deep inside it. But restrained myself. Licking her asshole at that moment—right after having that bizarre discussion—probably would have sent her mind reeling into overdrive with all types of crazy homophobic scenarios. The last thing I wanted, or needed, was my wife thinking I was some down low motherfucker. Or that I might be curious to find out how the other side got down.

I know my wife. Once something gets planted inside her head, that's what it is. Doesn't matter if it's real or all made up in her little imagination. If she thinks it happened, then it did. And she loves to talk. Okay, all right…gossip is more like it. Krista can spend hours on the phone yapping about any-and-everything. No topic is off limits when it comes to her running her mouth. I could see her clear as day. On the phone or up on Facebook posing the same question to her girlfriends, sisters, and Facebook followers as to their thoughts on a man—her husband. *Me*—asking to have his ass licked, or for wanting his prostate stimulated. I could see all the bashing and obnoxious likes and comments going on in my head and wanted no parts of it.

So I settled my gaze on her tight, puckered hole instead, licking my lips. Then closed my eyes and imagined having another woman in back of me, her tongue probing my ass, her fingertips caressing my nut sac while I seesawed my way in and out of Krista's pussy, her juices soaking my dick.

I pulled out. Slapped her on the ass. Told her to get on her back. Then I spread her legs, and buried my head between her legs. "Mm, yeah, baby." I lapped at her juicy pussy and sank my tongue between her slick, swollen folds. I tongue-fucked her and teased her clit.

I loved the sight of my wife's wet pussy. Loved the taste of it. Loved the feel of it. Loved the smell of it. She knew it then. And she knows it now.

But that night, I was on a mission. And my only focus was on pleasuring her, allowing my own desires to go untouched as I always did with Krista. It was about Krista, as it always is with me pleasing her. And getting her to forget any silly notion of me being *suspect* to anything that she might have possibly conjured up in the back of her pretty little head was all that mattered.

I didn't need her trying to compare me to her sister's husband, Herbie, or any other dude who had a thing for other dudes in wigs and lip gloss.

I lapped harder. Tongued deeper. Sucked longer. And, then Krista cried out again, her hands gripping the sides of my head. "Yes, yes, yes…ooh, oooh, oooh…"

"Get that nut, baby," I urged. Seconds later—thighs shaking, body quaking, she climaxed, drenching my face. Then, without another word, I lifted her legs up and plunged into her with a quick force that had her gasping for air, and me groaning out her name.

Her pussy clenched. Legs wrapped around me, arm around my neck; she held onto to me as I fucked her hard. My fingers dug into her ass, massaging and kneading, holding her open as I pounded into her wetness.

Through gritted teeth, she grumbled, "Ohgod, yes! Yes! It feels—"

I leaned over her, covered my mouth over hers.

I stayed still inside of her for a moment, enjoying the clutch, and the feel of her satiny walls. Krista's eyes shut, then fluttered open. "Oh, baby, you feel so good inside of me."

"I know I do," I murmured, my dick basking in her inner heat.

Slowly, I pumped, my mind drifting to fantasies of her tongue… any tongue, probing me.

"Do you want your ass licked?"

I closed my eyes tight, fighting to block out her voice.

"I'd divorce you…"

I nuzzled my sweaty face against her. Nipped at her ear. "You feel so good, baby. So tight and hot…*Krista*."

My mouth brushed teasingly along her neck. I pulled all the way out, then sunk my teeth into the column of her neck and sucked as I plunged my dick back in deep, again. Krista gasped. Cried out.

"Oh, yes, baby…yesssss!"

My hips rocked against hers, my movements grew faster, each stroke brushing up against her clit.

I took her pussy, claimed it. Stole it. Fucked it deep. And fast. And slow.

Krista's hands slid up and down my sweaty spine, then she sank her nails into my back, marking her territory.

I groaned in pleasure as I reached a hand between our bodies and pinched her clit, causing tears to spring from her eyes as she dug her nails deeper into my flesh, this time into my ass cheeks.

"Aah, shit, yeah, baby…" My ass muscles tightened with each thrust. I was determined to make her forget me ever bringing the question up. *What do you think about a man wanting his woman to lick and finger his ass?*

Fire building up inside of me, I moved one hand from her hip to her clit, stroking and teasing her. I fucked Krista as if my life depended on it. As if I'd die if I didn't.

There was nothing gay or bi-curious about me. I loved pussy. Loved women. Loved my wife. But I loved having my ass licked and fingered, too.

What was so wrong with that?

"Kendall," she muttered as one of my hands reached up and found her breast. I fondled it, before lightly pinching her nipple.

She locked eyes with me. Tears sprang from her sockets. "Don't ever cheat on me."

Now that was some random shit.

Or was it?

My pulse quickened. And I hoped she couldn't feel my heart pounding in my chest. "You're all I need, baby."

"Do you want your ass licked?"

I pushed back thoughts of Elena's tongue snaking its way into the seam of my ass. Fought back the memory of Peaches and the way she used her tongue sensually to lick around my hole. I fought back the taste of my ass on her tongue when she slipped it into my mouth, and kissed me.

Krista shouted my name, pulling me out of my dirty thoughts, causing me to pull out, then slam back in. Hard, sharp thrusts. That's what I gave her. And another. And another. I fucked her hard and steady.

Her pussy tightened around my dick.

"That's it, baby," I coaxed. "Milk my nut out."

I pumped faster. Harder.

"Oh, yes…it's sooo deep. Mmm, Kendall, baby…"

Her eyes blurred with tears, but I could still see the storm rising inside. She was on the verge of another climax. She grew wetter. She arched up to me. Clenched tighter around me.

"Let go, baby. Give it to me. Come all over my dick, baby…"

I thrust into her again and again, wheedling her on, edging her closer to orgasm. "Let me come with you, baby…aaah, shit…I can't hold it any longer, baby…"

"Yes, yes, yes…"

"Give it to me. Explode with me. Let me feel it all over my dick."

As if those words were the key to her abyss, she came, bucking and shuddering. And I came in sync, my own moans matching her own.

"Damn, that was so good." I kissed her, realizing that I was clinging on to her as much as she was to me. I stared at her. Looked in her face, and saw her desire for me. It was deep and vivid as my own. Krista loved me with as much intensity as I loved her. She needed me as much as I needed her.

Unfortunately, I needed, wanted, more than what she was willing to give.

I brushed the wet tendrils of her hair away from her face, and with my dick still buried deep inside, I whispered, "Krista, I love you so much, baby."

And I meant it.

I still do, very much so.

So needless to say, that was over eight years ago. And to this day, I haven't said another word to her about ass play. For what? She made it very clear what her thoughts were on the matter. And I respected her position then as I do now. I still don't like it, but I definitely value my wife's boundaries.

But that hasn't stopped me from indulging my hidden desires from time to time. So I step out on my marriage…every now and again. Not because I'm not in love with my wife, or because she's stingy with the pussy. But because—like I already mentioned, I'm not always completely satisfied, sexually.

And I've learned real quick that sharing my deepest secret, or darkest fantasies with Krista is a pending death wish—or in my case, a divorce—waiting to come true.

And, contrary to what others might think, I'm not about to lose my marriage over my sporadic urges for ass play. But I'm not ready to completely ignore them either.

So I creep whenever I can, like now.

AOL alerts me that I have new messages. I click open the screen. Six new messages. *Let's hope it's not a bunch of bullshit.* I open the first email:

Damn. U sound sexy AF! No disrespect meant. I know you are only looking 4 real women, but if you ever change your mind, lmk. Discreet married guy here. Smooth shaven. Will dress up in women's clothes for u. i can be slutty behind closed doors. I love married black cock. Would love to lick your hole til u explode then let u blow a load on my horny tight hole. I promise u won't be disappointed.

What the hell? I frown, shaking my head and deleting the email. *Stupid-asses don't listen to shit!*

I open the next email:

Hi. I'm a sexy brunette. Married and also looking for some kinky fun. Love role play. Willing to be your little submissive ass licker. I love wearing fishnet stockings. I want to do everything you tell me to. Can I have your big black cock inside my tiny white pussy? Can I have it in me doggy style? I want you to twist my arm while you are inside me. I want you to leave bruises and a smile. Then when u are done fucking me, I want you to leave me tied to the bed with duct tape over my mouth and your sweet cum all over my face for my husband to find me, then pat me on the head and tell me how much of a good slut I am before you walk out the door. If this excites you as much as it excites me, please email back. Smooches.

I suck my teeth. "Hell no that shit doesn't excite me," I mutter, shaking my head. Role-play my ass. Next thing you know, she'd be screaming rape, then giving the police my description, trying to hem me up.

Delete.

The next three emails are all spam.

I delete them as well.

A few moments later, AOL dings again. Four more emails come through. I open the first one. It's an email from some calling themselves FreakOnWheels.

Hi. Saw your ad. Discreet wheelchair bound woman here. I'm 37, 5'4, 170lbs. Horny, lonely and looking for company. I've never licked a man's ass before but would like to try it. is your ass hairy? Smooth? Shaven? can you send me a picture of it?

I think to delete her email without a reply, but decide to send her a response back.

Hey there. Thanks for responding to my ad. I don't send pics. There's curly hair along the center of my crack. ☺ Hope that helps.

I open the next email.

Hey boo. If you're lookin for some wet pussy. I got a nice fat one for you. Bi freaky bitch lookin for a fuck buddy. Not the cutest chick. But not the ugliest either. But this pussy's real good. I'll ride you til your dick falls off and fuck you like a porn star! And my head n tongue work is heaven. U won't be disappointed. Love big dick niggas. love givin backshots. Doggystyle, boo. And I love love love it in my ass and have no problem strappin on a dildo n fuckin' my boo in his ass 2! i do it all boo! let me rock your world!!!!!

I shake my head. Either this chick is real young, or she's real ghetto. Either way, she's definitely not the one I'm looking to vibe with. A woman who is comfortable with referring to herself as a *bitch* is not someone I want to spend my time with on any level, one-time fling or not.

I move on to the next email.

Black ass licker here. I crave it all the time. I am addicted to it. Married white woman. Got a secret craving for black men. Sucking them. Licking them. Cleaning out their asshole with my long tongue. I'm 36, 5'7, 110 lbs, zero body fat. If you would like your own personal ass licker, then please contact me. I can host during the day while my husband is at work.

I frown. "Damn. How many dirty asses you licked clean?" I ask out loud. *This broad is all kinds of nasty and wrong. Who the fuck cleaning out a dirty asshole?*

I'm not one to judge, but that level of kinky is a no-go for me.

I delete those emails just as my cell phone starts ringing. I reach over and glance at the screen, then answer.

"Hey."

I click open another email. This one is from ChocolateBeauty3D: *Horny, sexy chick. High sex drive. Love my pussy ate...*

I shake my head. *Dumb-ass, did you fucking read my ad?*

"Hey," Krista says. "What are you doing?"

"Finishing up some work."

I keep reading: *And if you finger fuck my ass, you'll make my pussy squirt. I'd love to ride your face and tongue. I'm 5'2, 290lbs, thick hips, curvy with a nice fat pussy, big bouncy ass and 40DDD titties...*

There's a picture attached to the email.

"Are you on your way home?" I ask as I open the attachment.

"I'm on my way to Wegmans to pick up a few things, first. Do you...?"

I blink at my computer screen when the picture opens. It's a picture of a very short, round, light-skinned woman with a lazy eye and a double chin with no neck. She isn't lying. Her breasts are huge, but they hang like two fifty-pound air bags. They are practically resting on her even bigger stomach.

What the hell? Sorry, baby. Curvy my ass! You're a sloppy mess. I shake my head. I'm definitely into thick women. But, aside from the dead eye—and wearing what looks like a dirty head rag on her head, thick went out the window six chicken baskets ago for this chick. Sorry. But this babe is carrying around a little too much weight for me.

Delete.

"Kendall?"

I click open the next email. This one's from PassionPainPleasure.

"Huh? Yeah, baby?"

Hi. Finger fucking and licking your ass is my kinda freaky fun. Sounds real sexy. Reading your ad actually made my pussy wet.

"Kendall, what are you doing? I asked you if you want me to pick you up something while I'm out?"

"Oh, my bad, baby. I got caught up in something."

"Well…?"

I grin as I keep reading:

Sexy Scorpio here. I'm Black. Mid 30s, 5'8, 148lbs, small waist, pretty in the face, long tongue, and deep wet pussy for you to fuck when I'm done fingering your ass and getting you off. Very discreet. very freaky. No drama. No games. No sexual hangups. I'm happily involved but looking for something extra on the side. And I have a very high sex drive so I love lots of hot freaky sex. I love freaky men. And I love a man who loves his ass played with. I'm team ass-licking! Team-ass fucking! And everything else! Is your dick cut?

I lick my lips. "Oh, nah, baby." My voice dips a bit. "I don't need anything." *Except for a warm, wet tongue to lick up in this ass.* I press my legs together, trying to pinch off the ache in my swelling dick. Reading this email has me instantly horny.

I type: *Hey, what's up? I like your response. You sound like my kinda woman. I'm all for drama free & freaky. We definitely need to connect asap! Let me know what's good. Where u located? What county? Yes I'm cut.*

I attach a picture of my dick, then press SEND.

"What are you doing?" Krista asks again, this time sounding annoyed.

"Online."

"I thought you said you were finishing up work?"

Then why'd you ask?

I click open another tab and open Xfinity. "I was. But I'm done. Now I'm getting ready to catch up on the last two episodes of *Chicago Fire*."

Well, that's partially true. So no harm, no foul.

She grunts. "Mmph, I should have known. You and them TV shows."

I chuckle. "Hey, it beats running the streets. At least you know where I am. Home."

"Yeah, making a mess, I'm sure."

"Nah. Home, waiting on my baby."

I can practically feel her smiling through the phone. "Uh-huh. Good answer."

My computer pings, alerting me I have more emails. I open the AOL screen again. I have two more emails from PassionPain-Pleasure.

"Hey, hey," I say, opening the first email. "Watch it. It's the only answer."

Mmm. Damn, papi! Now that's a beautiful dick! Looks like it feels good deep inside some pussy and down in a throat too! ☺ Oh and I'm from Essex county. Hopefully we can coordinate a way to meet unless you end up having an inbox flooded w/emails of horny/freaky women like me.

I smile.

"I'll be home in about an hour," Krista says.

"Okay," I respond mindlessly. "See you when you get here."

I keep reading: *Just so u know. I'm classy in the streets. Freak in the streets. Probably a little too freaky for most. Love sucking dick, licking ass, balls and anything else you want done. But not too many men are into that. So I was surprised when I came across your ad to see that there was a black man who knows what he likes. And isn't afraid to ask for it!*

Goddamn.

There's an attachment of her tongue. And there's another pic of her from the neck down, wearing a sports bra and a pair of white booty shorts. My dick stirs in my sweats. That tongue is right. And she's full of curves and thick as hell in all the right places. Her body is right.

Damn, baby. I need that.

I quickly reply: *Damn nice pics. you real sexy from the neck down. Yeah I'm in Essex/Hudson county area a lot. I'm a freak too so hopefully we can be on the same page. So tell me what are you into? Fetishes? And no, my inbox as of yet hasn't been flooded. And i'm not looking for quantity, just quality. If you and I click, the ad will get deleted anyway. So tell me what floats your boat, sexy.*

I press SEND.

"What do you want to eat?" Krista wants to know, causing me to momentarily look away from the computer screen. I almost forgot she was still on the phone. And now I'm feeling slightly annoyed that she's disrupting my email time.

"You," I tease, bringing my attention back to the pictures of this sexy bombshell up on my screen.

"You had me this morning," she says softly.

I groan, opening another email. "Yeah. And it was good…"

Thanks! OK, that's great. Well, like I said in my previous email, I love sucking dick, deep throating; love licking a man's ass, but not many men are into that, but that's what I love to do. I love my pussy ate. Love to be fucked in the ass, again something a lot of men don't seem to be okay with. But it makes my pussy squirt. And I can actually cum out of my ass IF a man knows what he's doing.

I clear my throat. "But I want some more," I say to Krista. I lick my lips.

I love being fucked doggie-style and having my asshole finger fucked or with a vibrator. I like to fuck more than one round. Like I said, I stay horny. So to answer your question. What floats my boat? A man who is secure and confident in his sexuality. A man with good dick. a man who knows how to fuck and make love and knows when to do both. I love my pussy pounded so good that long after we're done and have gone back to our own lives/worlds, I can still feel his hard dick inside me. what about you? besides loving your ass played with, what else are you into?

Krista laughs, briefly bringing my attention back to our phone conversation. I swallow back a mouthful of drool.

"Greedy man. You always want more."

"You know me so well, baby," I say as I quickly type: *Nice. I like. I'm very much into anal…just the taboo of it all is arousing to me. Like you, I'm very reserved and conservative in the streets but am a total freak in bed. I'm down with eating your ass. I love to eat ass maybe more than I love eating pussy. And I have no problem fucking you in the ass either. I like passionate, sensual sex where we are both committed to bringing the maximum pleasure. I have a fetish for tights, spandex, leggings…love foreplay, feeling an ass and pussy thru them…licking it, then sliding them off to taste the real thing. I like doggy style too. Can get into role-play if that's your thing.*

"Uh-huh, I sure do," Krista says. "I'm going into the store now. I'll see you in a few."

I press SEND.

"Okay, babe. See you when you get home."

"Love you."

"Love you, too."

The call disconnects just as I get another email from Passion-PainPleasure. I lick my lips, opening it.

Oooooooh, yes! Yes! Yesssssss! I love my ass eaten! And the fact that you love getting yours eaten too is so damn sexy to me! Oooh two freaky ass eaters in one bed! Mmmph! I love the musky taste of a man's ass on my tongue. Mmm. I getting wet thinking about it! I love foreplay as well. I just love good hard black dick attached to a freaky man with stamina. I'm open to role-play as well. I'd love to tie a man up and blindfold him. Even spank him lightly before spreading open his ass and licking it, then sucking his balls into my mouth.

"Goddamn, baby," I murmur to myself. "Shit. I need you in my life. Right now!"

I ease my dick out of my sweats, then slowly stroke it, continuing to read the email. Precum is already coating my head. I use the pad of my thumb and smear it all over the head of my dick.

I'll also tell you this: if there weren't so many risks for diseases, I'd want raw sex. I love the feel of naked dick stroking my walls. There's something so sexy about a man nutting in my pussy, eating his nut out of me then kissing me. I also love cumming on a dick, then sucking my pussy juice off. I love the taste of my pussy.

Damn, this freak got me ready to bust a nut.

I glance at the time. *I can probably get a quick one off before Krista gets home.* I lean back in my chair. Close my eyes. Then stroke my dick. But it's not enough. I need my spot stroked. Bad.

I lift my hips up from my seat, then yank my sweats and boxers all the way down before reaching underneath me and massaging the area between my balls and ass to stimulate my prostate. But it's not enough.

I'm worked up for more.

Rising up in my seat, I unlock my desk drawer, then dig way in the back and pull out a bottle of lube I keep hidden.

Sitting back in my chair and leaning as far back as I can go, I spread open my legs. Then squirt out a generous amount of lube onto my index and middle fingers, and reach in between my legs.

Although massaging my perineum can stimulate my prostate, I prefer sticking a finger inside me and massaging it anally. The orgasm is more intense. Like I said earlier, like nothing imaginable.

With my dick in one hand and the other between my legs, I slide my lube-slick fingers up into my crack, skimming my hole, then pressing on it while stroking my dick and imagining my fingers are PassionPainPleasure's fingers, her wet tongue, her soft lips, her hot mouth.

I stare at her tongue up on my screen.

I groan. "Damn, baby. I can't wait to feel that tongue. Aah… can't wait for you to get all up in this ass with it."

Using a rhythmic circular motion, I start massaging my ass, then start pushing in as if I'm pushing on a button. I do this to relax my sphincter muscle.

"Aaah, yeah."

As I play with my dick, I concentrate on the sensation I feel when a tongue's back there; the wet lick-lick-lick that causes me to squirm in pleasure. I keep pushing inward, slowly pressing the pad of my finger in. I push inward and upward. And without much effort, I find my spot—about two inches in and toward my stomach; a small round bulb, about the size of a walnut.

"Yeah, baby…aah, shit…"

I gently massage it, my finger lightly sweeping its sides. My dick-head swells. Precum overflows out of my piss slit, coating my hand as it slides up and down along my shaft.

I grunt. Focus on the building heat as my prostate swells.

After a few toe-curling minutes, I feel it building, building, building. The pressure. The urge to piss. But I know it's the milking process. My arousal is evident in the abundance of precum running out of my dick slit and sliding down onto my hand.

"Aaaah, yeah. Aaah, yeah…oooh, shit. Uh, uh, uh…fuck."

It's coming, coming, coming, coming.

A loud grunt escapes from the back of my throat as my toes curl, my hand rapidly stroking my shaft.

It doesn't take much longer before my nut shoots out of my dick, splattering up on my chest and stomach. I growl out, my body shaking. My nut spurts out of me.

"Shit," I groan, feeling lightheaded as I squeeze out the last bit of nut before reaching for a handful of tissue and wiping my fingers. I grab more tissue and wipe my chest and stomach, before plopping back in my chair, spent.

Finally I reply back to PassionPainPleasure's email. *LOL, yeah it is extra sexy busting up in a woman's pussy.*

I am pulling my boxers and sweats back up over my hips as my computer dings, alerting me I have more emails. Quickly, I scan them until I see another one from PassionPainPleasure. I open it.

Yes, yes, yes it is! How tall are you? And what size shoe are you? I have a thing for a man's feet. I love sucking a man's toes, provided they're not looking like hoofs, LOL. Something else most men don't seem to get into. Having their feet licked and toes sucked. Are you?

I blink. Then reread her email. I can't believe it. A woman who is into what I'm looking for. Toe-sucking and licking my feet is a bonus. Hell, I've never had it done. But shit. I'm open to it.

I respond back. *Damn, baby. I hope you're real! you sound too good to be true. nah, I've never had my toes sucked or my feet licked. My wife won't go anywhere near my feet. Not even a foot massage. But damn! That sounds hot! At some point we will need to voice verify so I know you are real and not some dude tryna catfish, posing as a woman. I'm 6'1. Size 11.5 and I'm open to anything. The freakier the better. What else are you into?*

Although I'm not usually in for all the back and forth, there's something about her emails that I don't mind the ongoing exchange.

My computer chimes again. I have six more emails. I delete the first two since they didn't put what I asked in the subject heading. The third email reads: *Freaky bi-female here. 32, 4'11", 190 lbs, a few extra pounds in the middle. Big tits. Tight fat pussy. Very oral. Love to fuck and rim a man's ass. Real Horny here, baby. I host only. I once rimmed a man and he farted as I licked him and it turned me on. My pussy got real wet. Since then I've become addicted to having a man sit on my face and farting. Once you do that I become extra slutty. I'll suck you good, and even give up my tight, fat pussy too. I love nice hard dicks. Let me suck in your ass fumes while I tongue you.*

I frown. *Oh, this broad is nasty as hell!*

Delete.

When my email chimes again. It's another email from Passion-PainPleasure. It's officially decided. All other emails get ignored and deleted. She's the one I'm interested in freaking with.

I open her email. *Ohhhh lord! You are really really trying to have me confess all of my freaky sins. LOL. Oh, no catfishing going on here. I'm all woman here, boo. Real breasts, real pussy, real hair. So you have no worries. We can voice verify & skype whenever you're ready. Okay, so I told u that I'm into licking a man's ass. But I purposefully left out the fact that I enjoy using a strap-on and slow fucking a man's ass or inserting a small vibrator in his ass while sucking his dick...stroking his prostate. Mmm. I love hearing him moan and seeing his eyes roll up in the back of his head while I'm working his hole. The nut is always so much creamier, more intense. And for some reason thicker and hotter. I also like to suck the nut out of a man, then kiss him. And it's real sexy having a man sucking his nut off my tongue while I climb up on his dick.*

Damn.

I feel my dick stirring again. She's definitely my kind of freaky.

The kind I wish Krista were. I read the email again. Something about her using a strap-on sounds hot, even if I'd never actually let her run a silicone dick up in me. The thought of watching her fucking another dude in his ass is still a turn-on.

I reply back. *Nice! Not sure about sucking my own nut, or having a dildo in my ass. but I'm def down for trying a thin vibrator. That's been a recent fantasy of mine for a while. I've only had fingers in me. But I'm def open to giving it a try. If we click, then maybe I'd be down to eventually try a strap-on. Not sure though. Does your man let you fuck him?*

I'm surprised at myself for admitting that I'd be down to try getting pegged by her since up until now a finger and tongue have been the only two things I've ever wanted. But there's something about her emails that has me wanting to know more, experience more, to try something new, to take ass play to another level.

I smile when another email comes in from her. I quickly glance at the time in the upper right-hand corner of my laptop. It's 5:56 p.m. Krista should be walking through the door any minute now.

I open her email. *Nice. Riding a man's muscular ass with a strap-on and the base of it pressing up against my clit while I'm grinding inside of him and stroking his dick with a bunch of lube, soaks my pussy. Oh, hell no. My fiance is from the Caribbean. He's open to many things, but ass play is definitely not one of them. He knows I've done it with other men before him. But it's not his thing. I can't go anywhere near his asshole. Such a sinful shame too! Especially when I'm down there sucking his big juicy dick and licking around his balls. Oh well. What else are you into? Fantasize about? Oh, another secret fantasy of mine is riding a man's dick while he's sucking a dick. Sssssh! My little dirty secret. *hangs head* I think it's sexy. I've always wanted to be with a bi-curious man. OMG, I can't believe I am actually sharing this with someone.*

I quickly type back. *Damn, baby. You got my dick hard as fuck! Like I said, I've never been fucked with a strap-on, and I'm not sure if I'd actually go through with it. But it sounds hot. I'd like to watch you though. Maybe we could find another dude who'd be down to let me watch you fuck him. Anyway, but having a vibrator in my ass, pulsing up against my prostate is, like I said, a fantasy. And it does have me curious. So have you ever stepped outside of your relationship before?*

I shut my laptop the second I hear the alarm chirp. Krista's home. I stand. Readjust my dick inside my underwear. Then head downstairs to greet my wife with a hug and a kiss.

Krista stirs as I slip from underneath the sheets. It's almost five o'clock in the morning. She doesn't usually get up until seven to prepare herself for work. I lean down to kiss her forehead, then quietly slip on my underwear and a pair of lounge pants before easing out of the room, shutting the door behind me.

Last night I was so aroused from the email exchange between PassionPainPleasure and myself that I was on the verge of nutting in my boxers. Every time I pressed my legs together I felt like my nut would shoot out of my dick on the spot.

I ended up stepping into the shower with Krista and fucking her up against the wet tiles, and even that wasn't enough. Those emails had me horny as hell. I went to bed with a hard, aching dick. All I could do to squelch the burning heat in my loins was to sneak into my office in the middle of the night, lube a finger, then stroke my prostate while I jacked off.

I exploded, popping the cork to a hot, thick load in less than five minutes, then quietly eased back in bed. Krista stirred slightly, uttering a sleepy sound as I pulled her close, curling my arms around her, then hooking my leg over hers, molding her to my body before falling into sleep.

Shutting my office door, I step around my desk and sit, lifting open my laptop and powering it on. I type in my password, then wait for it to boot up. I glance at the time, thankful I have the rest of the week off from work.

Hopefully I can get in some freaky fun while I'm off. I log into AOL, then grin when I'm alerted I have new emails. Ten new emails, but the only one I'm interested in is from PassionPainPleasure. I open hers.

Nice. Yes I have. Three times. Honestly, I love my fiancé. He's much younger than me. But he's good to me. And he fucks me down like no other. Ooh, the dick is good! Still I sometimes need more. But I'm not leaving him. Yes, I'm greedy. But sexually, smh, he's not always as freaky as I'd like him to be. And he doesn't like fucking every day. I do.

What about you?

I reply back. *I understand. I've cheated a few times on my wife. I used to fuck this young chick…she had a daddy fetish and it was a turn-on. Like you, I love my wife but I have fetishes that I enjoy taking part in. things I'd never discuss with my wife…like ass play. She's too close-minded. she'd never understand me enjoying a finger or tongue in my ass.*

Surprisingly, there's another email from her in less than a minute. *Good morning, nasty man! Lucky for me, my fiancé isn't overly rigid in his thinking about sex. Just about some things, like ass play and fucking a man. So I definitely understand. My fiancé would lose his mind if he knew half the freaky shit I did behind his back.*

Damn.

I reply with: *Good morning, sexy. Yeah, I'm in the same boat. So sounds like we're both on the same page as far as discretion. And I'm definitely not looking for a one-time thing. Ongoing would be preferable…*

Moments later, an IM screen pops up on my screen. It's her. I grin. *Damn, baby, I see you aren't about the games.*

Passionpainpleasure: Mmm. That's sexy! The thought is making my pussy wet! You like wet pussy?

Harddick4assplay: Love it!! Who doesn't? Love licking and fucking it! I wish my wife could be as open as you are about my fantasies

Passionpainpleasure: Fantasies can become an important part of one's sexuality. Your fantasies don't make you any less of a man, baby. They make you more man than most. Mmm. I love a man who submits to me. My pussy is getting real juicy thinking about pulling open your ass cheeks and licking my tongue all in it. I can't wait to taste you

Harddick4assplay: Damn, stop! You're making my dick hard!

Passionpainpleasure: Mmmm…Can't wait to slowly suck it into my mouth then swallow it down in my throat! Hope you can handle a good dick suck ☺

Harddick4assplay: Hell yeah!!! Let's make it happen. All this talking has my dick hard! When r you free?

Passionpainpleasure: Today after 10am. And u?

Harddick4assplay: Anytime today. Just say the word.

Passionpainpleasure: Mmm. Nice! Let's get freaky! How's 11:30?

Harddick4assplay: Perfect! Here's my number 973-444-1212. U can block ur number if you want

Passionpainpleasure: Call now?

Harddick4assplay: If u can, hell yeah!

I check to make sure my phone is on VIBRATE, then delete the remaining emails from my inbox. I still have about an hour and fifteen minutes to play with before Krista starts stirring around the house.

My cell buzzes. PRIVATE CALLER flashes across the screen. "Hello?"

"Hey, freaky man," a soft voice drifts through the other end of the phone. "Do I sound like someone trying to Catfish you?"

"Nah. You sound sexy as fuck. Like a woman ready to get it in."

I close my eyes and imagine her licking her lips. "You sure you're ready for some freaky fun?"

"Hell yeah, baby," I say in a low, husky voice. "I need that. Bad."

"Mmm. You sound so sexy. I love a man with a deep voice. I can already feel my pussy starting to get wet."

I groan. "Damn, baby. Stop. You got my dick hard."

She moans. "Mmm. Wait until I wrap these soft lips around it and suck it into my hot mouth."

I rub my crotch. Grab my dick. "Damn. I want you now."

"Oooh, I bet you do," she coos. "And this mouth, these lips, these fingers want you, too. But all good things come to those who wait. Ooh, you lucky my two sisters aren't into man swapping anymore. We'd tag-team the shit out of you."

I blink. Ask her to elaborate. She tells me her and her sisters used to share men sexually. But that's stopped over the last few years. All I can think is, where the fuck have you been all my life.

She moans. "Those were the good ole days. It's all a delicious memory now. Oh, well. Anyway, boo. My mouth is so wet for you. I can't wait to tongue that ass."

My asshole clenches as I slide my hand down inside my lounge pants. Shit. She has my dick harder than a steel pipe. Precum is already seeping out of my dickhead. I tell her how horny she has me. Let her know I'm looking forward to linking up with her. Today. Then tell her our meeting spot. Residence Inn in West Orange. On Prospect Avenue.

"Don't stand me up," I say.

"Oh, no, boo," she assures me. "I don't play games. Trust and believe. I'll be there, waving my freak flag *and* my tongue. And ready to freak you all afternoon."

"Cool. What's your name? I'm Kendall."

"I'm Passion, Pain, and Pleasure, baby," she says in a seductive whisper. She then laughs. "Make sure you have your dick, balls, and ass freshly washed. I don't do funk, boo. Cheesy balls and a shitty ass is a no-no. I like my men smelling good."

I chuckle. "Oh, okay...Passion, Pain, and Pleasure. No worries there, baby. I'm always clean. And I'll be showered before you get there."

"Great. See you at eleven-thirty."

"Cool. I'll be ready. Hard dick and all."

She giggles. "Oooh, I'ma tear that ass up, boo. And suck the snot out of you."

The call ends, leaving me with precum drizzling out of my hard, throbbing dick.

Goddamn.

Shit.

Yeah, I'ma see just how high her freak flag flies.

Stepping out of the shower, I don't bother to robe. I wrap a towel around my hips, instead, and head toward the hotel's door, glancing into the peephole before swinging it open. Eleven thirty on the dot, she's right on time. The sight of her causes my dick to throb. Hand on hip. Head slightly tilted. She's wearing what looks like a swing coat and a pair of very expensive designer heels. Something tells me she's naked underneath the high-end material.

Damn, she's classy as fuck!

She's more beautiful in person than I imagined. She licks her lips, and heated anticipation thrums through my veins, along with something naughty. And more freaky.

So far, she's everything I hoped for. And then some. I catch her hand and pull her out of the hallway and into the suite, shutting the door behind her.

My hands claw the sheets, my stomach clenches as she leans forward and licks a slow circle around the head of my dick, before suckling it between her lips.

"Damn, baby, that feels so good," I moan.

"I'm glad you like it," she purrs, licking over my piss slit, catching precum with the tip of her tongue. "Mmm, you taste so good. Sweet."

She licks more precum, coating her tongue.

"Mmm…your dick is so thick. And hard." She licks up and down my shaft, then fists me at the base, milking me with her wet mouth and soft hands.

She runs her parted lips up and down the side of my shaft. "Fuck," I gasp as she licks along a thick, pulsing vein. She sucks my dick into her mouth, full of heat and lots of tongue and spit. Then eases my dick out of her mouth, gliding her lips along the shaft again. She's fucking with me.

"Stop playing, baby," I growl. "Suck that dick."

She ignores my demand, gliding her tongue up and down as if she's licking an ice cream cone, catching the precum as it drizzles out. She licks her way down to the base, then slowly back up to the head. My toes curl when she opens her mouth wide and swallows my dick, sucking it to the back of her tight throat. She starts humming.

"Oh, shit…"

She sucks, and sucks, and sucks, gulping down my dick, her throat clutching and pulling at it. It's been years since I've been deep-throated. But this beauty gives it to me deep and wet and sloppy, the way I love it, the way I've missed it.

Damn, why can't Krista handle this dick like that?

My neck arches, pressing my head into the pillow. "Oh, shit that's good. Mmm. Fuck, baby. You sucking the hell out that dick."

She moans, working her mouth wetly up and down on my dick, drooling everywhere, soaking my balls, the crack of my ass. The sight of her tongue as it lolls out and swirls all around my dickhead, causes me to groan in ecstasy.

My dick throbs against her tongue as she cups my balls, gently fondling them. As if sensing my impending orgasm, she pulls off me, her mouth stretched wide, her lips glossed with spit and precum.

My heavy-lidded gaze catches hers. "Damn, why you stop?" I sound almost like a whining kid.

She smiles, caressing one of her breasts, then pulling at her thick, chocolate nipple. She wags her tongue, then slides it over her nipple.

I swallow. "Come sit on my face and let me eat that pussy for you."

"Oh, I'm not done, yet. You'll get this pussy in due time. Get on your knees, motherfucker. Let Passion, Pain, and Pleasure get up in that ass."

As if she has more than one personality, I blink, surprised by her sudden change in demeanor. And even more surprised at how turned on I am by it.

I turn over on my stomach, then inch up on my knees, resting on my elbows.

"You have one of the most beautiful asses I've seen on a man," she mutters, her breath sizzling over my bare skin just before she presses her mouth into my crack, sliding her tongue in.

"Aah, yeah, baby...lick that shit."

She moans. "Mmm...nice hairy ass..." Her tongue sweeps over my asshole. "You like that...?"

The room slowly begins to spin.

I grunt, then let out a low groan. "Oh, yeah, baby." My dick throbs and bounces, hardens to the point of exploding. "Fuck, yeah!"

Whack!

She slaps my ass. Pulls it open. Blows a warm breath on my hole. Then her wet tongue slides up along the crack of my ass. She reaches for my throbbing dick, then pulls it to the back, suckling it between her pillow-soft lips.

"Yeah, baby, like that. Aaah, yeah…"

She has me clawing at the sheets, again and my stomach clenching as she reaches between my legs and pulls my dick back, sucking the head into her mouth. I can feel the precum streaming out of my dick coating her tongue as she sucks me.

Damn, she's nasty as fuck.

"Aaah, shit, baby. Yeah, suck on that dick."

Her tongue glides over the head, licks over my piss slit, then slides down over my balls, before wedging into the crack of my ass and nudging my hole.

I moan. "Yeah, baby. Get all in that ass."

Whack!

She slaps my ass, again. Pulls her soft lips, her hot mouth, her wet tongue away from my dick. Tells me to turn over onto my back, to spread my legs and bend at the knees.

Body trembling, dick bouncing in anticipation, I do.

I watch her as she reaches for the bottle of lube. Oozes the thick lubricant along her index finger, then slides it inside me.

Her gaze never leaves mine as she gently strokes each lobe. "Yeah, milk me, baby…" I grab my dick to stroke it.

"Don't touch it, you nasty fucker," she says low and breathy. "Let me watch it bob up and down."

"Aah, shit…" The way she says *you nasty fucker* brushes over my skin like heated silk. *You nasty fucker.* "Yeah, baby…yeah, I'm a nasty fucker…real nasty, baby. Let me bust this nut in your face…"

Her free hand slips between her legs. She pulls open her slick lips. "Look how wet you have my pussy, you freaky bastard."

My gaze drops down to her glistening cunt.

I lick my lips.

"You wanna fuck that?"

My dick bounces wildly.

"Yeah, baby..."

"I know you do, you freaky motherfucker. Your ass feels so hot, so tight, clutching my finger." She rhythmically moves her finger in and out, causing the sensitive nerve endings in my ass to spark.

She licks her lips. "Mmm, yeah, squeeze my finger. Look at that big, juicy dick swell."

She eases a second finger inside me and I moan, loud.

She moans. "You wanna see my pussy come?"

"Aaah, fuck...ohhh, yeah, baby...aaaah, goddamnmotherfuck... I'm ready to nut."

"No, wait for me. Wait for me...mmmm..." Her fingers click in and out of her wet pussy in sync to the thrust of her fingers in my ass. "You wanna feel that thick dick all up in this hot, juicy pussy?"

"Yeah, baby, yeah..."

Using varying pressure on my prostate, she keeps me on the brink of nearing ejaculation. The pressure keeps building.

I groan as she leans forward and covers my dick with her mouth. "Fuck! Ahh, shitshitshitshit!"

Then I cry out, her screen name. PassionPainPleasure. She's sucking my dick with so much passion, fingering my ass and stroking my prostate with so much intensity that my vision blurs.

"Aaaahhhhhh, shiiiit!" Within seconds, my stomach coils, my ass muscles tighten, my toes curl. The room spins. And...oh, oh, oh, aaaaah...

I nut, hard.

She moans. And comes on her hand, her warm juices squirting out of her, splashing on me as she swallows my nut, then licks up the rest, before pulling fingers from my ass and from out of her cunt.

I eye her as she presses the two fingers she had in my ass to her lips, then rolls her tongue over each finger before simultaneously slipping them into her mouth as she lifts her other hand and offers me her pussy-slick fingers.

I open my mouth, welcoming her sticky fingers. She slowly slides them in and out, watching me as I watch her, the both of us greedily sucking on her fingers.

When she is done sucking her fingers clean, she pulls her other set of fingers from my mouth and eases up over me and covers her mouth with mine. Her tongue slides into my mouth.

I've never tasted my own nut, my own ass, but here I am, kissing and sucking on her lips, her tongue, savoring my own scent, my own nut mixed with her juices. I groan into her mouth, feeling my dick slowly come back to life.

When she pulls her lips away from mine, I feel disoriented. It takes a minute for my vision to clear and my eyes to focus. "Damn, that was good," I say, collapsing on the damn sheets.

She wraps her arms and legs around me. I am surprised by the sudden gesture. "It sure was, boo." She stares at me, reaches for my dick and strokes it. "By the way, my name is Persia."

I grin. *Persia.* "Exotic name, for a beautifully freaky woman. I like that, *Persia.*"

She kisses me. Silently our tongues tangle and clash, twirling and swirling and rolling until we are both panting and breathless. She groans low in her throat, then tears her mouth from mine.

Without words, I know she wants to feel this dick inside her.

It's in her eyes.

I reach over, grab a condom, then tear the wrapper with my teeth, before rolling it down over my dick. She gasps as I push my dick into her pussy, hooking an arm under her leg and lifting it. Her nails graze along my back, her body arching up into my thrusts.

"Next time," she says, her lips just inches away from mine, running a hand over my chest, then pinching a nipple. "I'll bring my ball-gag and gag your mouth, then tie you to the bed and fuck your tight man ass with one of my vibrators. Would you like that? Me fucking your ass with a vibrator while I'm sucking your dick?"

My asshole clenches. I smile, my lips curving against hers. "Yeah, baby, I love the sound of that."

My hips move fluidly, my dick sliding in and out of her body, pounding her pussy into multiple orgasms, with dirty thoughts of creeping out on my wife again, and having my P-spot under siege.

Wet Pussy Gone Wild

Have you ever wanted something so bad, you couldn't imagine not having it?

Well, there are only three things in my life that I've ever felt that strongly about: being married to my husband, Sebastian; giving birth to my two sons, Dillon and Jacob; and now...deep breath—Kyree.

He's dangerously handsome, with thickly lashed eyes draped around light-brown, almond-shaped orbs that hold specks of amber when the light strikes them just so.

Six-foot-three.

Strong arms. Rippling washboard abs. Thick eight-inch, two-toned dick with a toe-curling, sheet-clutching curve. That I love sucking, that I love feeling stretching inside me, that I've fallen so recklessly in love with. Mmm. My mouth waters and my panties moisten every time I think about his delicious dick.

Kyree. Kyree. Kyree.

Dammit.

Just look at him, his beautifully hard and defined body on display for my pleasure. Goddammit! How did I ever let this nineteen-year-old, sexually aggressive man-child charm his way into my head, my mouth, and in between my quivering legs?

Everything about him screams trouble. However, here I am.

I hate the way the sight of him takes my breath away. Yet, love the way he makes me feel sluttier and sexier than I've ever felt. Everything about being with him is such a contradiction. My unnerving guilt overshadowed by demanding need. My emotional torment eclipsed by burning desires.

I stare at him, stretched out in the center of the bed, hands bound over his head and his legs splayed, his wrists and ankles tethered to the bedposts with silk scarves. He welcomes boundaries being pushed, which is why he's tied to my bed. His idea.

Besides having me, another fantasy of his.

My gaze dances over his muscular body, marveling over every inch of him; my mouth watering until it is as wet and juicy as my pussy.

Kyree grins at me, then licks those sexy, toe-curling lips of his. "Yo, c'mere and suck this dick."

My heart stutters a bit as I keep my gaze on him, lusty-eyed and trembling with unbridled need. He makes me feel so unanchored and out of control; yet, alive.

God help me.

When I'm with Kyree, I am so carefree and unapologetic—his youthful masculinity brings that out of me. I'm always so wet and wild and wanton. Every time he comes over—to hang out with my nineteen-year-old son, Jacob—wearing nothing but a crisp white wifebeater and basketball shorts with the waistband of his boxers showing, my skin flushes with heated need. Every time he steals a glance at me and winks slyly or licks his lips, heat blooms inside of me.

And all I want to do is be fucked by him. Bent over. Grabbing my ankles. Ass cheeks spread open, wide and ready. Kyree grabbing me by the hips.

But then I come to what's left of my senses, and I feel so shamelessly dirty. So, so, scandalously perverted. Fucking someone almost twenty-six years younger than me.

And, yet, I keep letting him crawl back between my thighs, plunging his hard, horny dick deep into my wet, trembling cunt.

Lord, help me.

I've always been a flamboyantly sexy and beautiful woman comfortable in her own skin, confident and seemingly carefree. And although, I am way much closer to forty-five that I am to ever being thirty-five, you'd never know it. And, yes, I'm about fifteen pounds heavier than I was ten, fifteen, years ago, but thanks to Pilates and a slew of yoga classes, I've painstakingly maintained my curves in all the right places. Despite the stretch marks that fan out over my stomach, I have a body better than some of the young women half my age.

And the way Kyree and the rest of the young men his age drink in the sight of me—with hot, hungry gazes—every time they see me, confirms what I already know. Like any man, those young horny boys are enthralled with big, bouncy asses, beautiful breasts, powerful hips and lots of wet pussy.

I briefly allow my mind to roll back to when it began. When I'd first discovered it. Felt it. The temptation. The stirring between my legs that undeniably made me feel weak. The looming desire that seemed to balloon from out of nowhere.

It was the week following the Memorial Day weekend. Both of my sons were home from college, and my husband, Sebastian, had flown out to Toronto on business earlier that morning and wasn't expected back until the following week.

My twenty-one-year-old son, Dillon, spent most of his time either working at a job he'd had every summer since his freshman year of college, or he was with his girlfriend, Paige, out in Brooklyn where she lived. So I rarely saw him.

Jacob, on the other hand, was another story. He preferred to stay close to home, particularly when his father traveled. And any girlfriends he had, he'd rather bring them home rather than spend his time at their places. He'd said he preferred to "freak them" in his own backyard. So basically he was telling me he was screwing his fast-assed girlfriends right here under my nose. My sons were very open—sometimes a bit *too* open—with me about their sexual conquests. Still, some things I simply didn't need to know, or hear.

Anyway, this particular day, I was in the kitchen preparing dinner when I heard the alarm chirp, alerting that the front door had been opened. A few moments later, I heard, "Hey, Mrs. Lang." It was Kyree. He and Jacob have been friends since second grade so he was like family, and pretty much always had free rein to come in and out without ringing the doorbell. Truthfully, he was practically like one of my own sons.

He walked into the kitchen where I was standing at the sink, washing a pot. I could feel his gaze on my back, my ass, my legs.

I craned my neck and smiled. "Oh, hey, Kyree."

He grinned as he stalked over wearing a V-neck tee and a pair of green camouflage cargo pants—one leg rolled up showing his bulging, heart-shaped calf—with a pair of wheat Timberland boots.

I tried not to stare at the way his T-shirt clung to his barreled chest or the way his biceps bulged under his sleeves as he made his way over and kissed me on the cheek.

"Dang. You smell good," he said, mischief glinting in his eye. "You're making me hungry," he said low and sexy for only me to hear.

I playfully rolled my eyes, waving him on. "Boy, stop. It isn't me that has you hungry. It's that barbecue chicken you smell baking in the oven."

He laughed, shaking his head. "Nah, it's *you*, for real. You smell real nice, Mrs. Lang." He paused, looking me over. "You always do."

The only thing I could do to keep from swooning was, smile and let the compliment float over my head. Kyree was known for always flattering me and for being flirty, so it wasn't anything out of the ordinary. He'd been that way since he was around eleven, twelve. His mother and I would always joke how he was going to be a real ladies man, and a heartbreaker. And from what I'd witnessed over the years, he'd slowly become just that.

Still…

When he was younger, his flirting was harmless. Cute. But he wasn't a little boy anymore. He was a young man growing into a man's body. He was bold. And direct. And knew what he wanted. His seductive charm was borderline cannibalistic. Untamed. Dangerous.

God help me, but I was enjoying it. I was enjoying *him*.

I swallowed back the rising thoughts of what he'd look like without his clothes on, of what it'd feel like with him between my legs. "How's Carla?" I asked, changing the subject to something safe.

He gave me a puzzled look. "Who?"

"Your girlfriend." I dried my hands on a towel, turning to face him.

"Oh, Kara. I gave her the boot."

"Oh." I smiled, shaking my head. He and Jacob were both notorious for showcasing a girl for a few months, sometimes for only a few weeks, before replacing her with someone *cuter* or *hotter*. Most times it was hard to keep up. It was always a revolving door of different girls. "She seemed like a nice girl."

He shrugged, grabbing a chair from the kitchen table and taking a seat. He stretched his long legs out, crossing his size fourteens at the ankles. "She was aiight, I guess. Just not for me."

I tilted my head. "Oh?"

"Yeah, she was too young-minded. Young girls bore me. I can't relate to 'em. And most of 'em can't handle me."

I bit into my bottom lip, trying to control my breathing.

"I need me a woman. Someone with lots of experience."

I swallowed, hard.

His lips curled up into a slow, sexy grin as his eyes skimmed over my body. This particular afternoon, I was wearing a short white skirt with a pink tank top that had WORLD'S SEXIEST MOM scrawled across the front in silver glitter. Toes painted pink, my pedicured feet were in a pair of sandals.

You couldn't tell me shit. I knew I was the world's sexiest mom alive. Hell, even my sons knew it, hence why they'd picked out the shirt I had on and bought it for me. But, then, would be ready to punch someone's admiring eyes shut for staring too long.

"Besides," he added, giving me a lingering look that made my skin tingle, "older women are real sexy to me."

I smiled, swiping a strand of hair from out of my face.

"Well, dating an older woman is every young man's fantasy. So I'm sure you'll have no problem snaring you a few cougars."

"True." He licked his luscious lips. Suddenly I felt like I was dancing with fire and quickly averted my eyes from his burning gaze. "Been there, done that. Now I have my eye on…"

"Yo, ma…?" my son Jacob called out walking into the kitchen. *Saved.* He frowned, stalking over and mushing Kyree in the head. "Man, why you always all up under my moms for? I just texted your ugly ass to see where you were."

"Jacob!"

"My bad, Ma."

Kyree sucked his teeth, pulling his phone from his front pocket. "Man, go 'head with that. Don't hate. Celebrate. You know I'm big on your mom."

"Yeah, well, you about to get a big lump upside that big-ass head of…"

"Boy, watch your mouth," I warned, grabbing a dishtowel and playfully swatting him with it.

He laughed. "I'm saying, Ma. This fool is always somewhere grinning in your face. You know I don't play that." He wrapped his lanky arms around me and kissed me on the side of my head. "And you know I'm not even about to share you with this clown."

Now it was my turn to laugh, trying to wiggle out of his embrace. "Boy, stop. You know there's enough of me to go around." That hadn't come out the way I'd meant it, but the only one who seemed to pick up on the innuendo was Kyree.

Lust seemed to glow in his eyes. Fortunately Jacob hadn't seen it. Otherwise I'm sure things wouldn't have turned out so great that day. Both of my sons were overprotective and liked to think they were my fathers at times, especially when their father was away on business for extended periods of time, like he was this particular day.

Jacob draped his arm over my shoulder as Kyree smiled.

"Yeah, aiight. I got your clown all right," he said, eyeing me. "Besides, you heard your mom. You gotta *share* her with me. Now we both have the *world's sexiest* mom."

My cheeks flushed.

"Man, you buggin'," Jacob said, shooting him a dirty look. "Get outta here with that."

"Kyree, are you staying for dinner?" I asked, shifting my weight from one foot to the other, feeling heat swell up inside of me from somewhere unknown, and so unexpected.

Jacob sucked his teeth. "You already know his greedy butt is. That's the only reason he comes over."

Kyree laughed, rising to his feet. "Hey, what can I say"—he rubbed his stomach—"I stay hungry. And I *love* to eat. So, yup, if you cooking, Mrs. Lang, I'm eating." His eyes twinkled when he smiled, flashing the dimple in his left cheek.

"Yo, come on, fool, before I have to punch your lights out." Jacob yanked him by the arm, dragging him toward the doorway. "Ma, we'll be down in the basement. Let us know when dinner's ready."

"Okay," I said, feeling somewhat relieved and flustered as they disappeared down the stairs, closing the door behind them.

I took a deep breath, then gasped.

Shit.

My panties were wet.

Later that evening, after dinner was long eaten and the dishes washed, Kyree sauntered out into the living room—leaving Jacob down in the basement, supposedly on the phone talking to his latest girlfriend. I was on the sofa finally watching the season finale of *The Blacklist* when he stood in the middle of the room.

There was about twenty more minutes left, and it literally had me sitting on the edge of my seat. And talking to me *before* a commercial break was a no-no.

"Awww, damn. This is my shit"—I shot him a scathing look—"oops, my bad, Mrs. Lang." He looked at me apologetically. "I'm sayin' though. Reddington is *that* dude; feel me?"

I didn't answer, but it didn't matter. I eyed him out of my peripheral vision as he sat down beside me. Breathed in his masculine scent as he eased back and stretched a muscled arm over the back of the sofa and spread his legs.

I nearly jumped out of my seat when Harold Cooper got attacked in his car.

"Oh, daaaayum!"

I lightly slapped him on his hard thigh. "Boy, I'ma put you up out of here, if you don't watch your mouth."

He grinned sheepishly. "My bad, Mrs. Lang." His knee lightly brushed against my thigh. "You know I'd never do anything to disrespect you."

"Then stop talking and watch your mouth," I said, glancing over at him.

He widened his grin. "I got you, *World Sexiest Mom*."

"Boy, hush. And quit flirting with me."

He looked over toward the archway that led into the hallway to see if the coast was clear. Then back at me. "Why? I'm only speaking truth. Am I making you uncomfortable?" There was defiance in the way he stared, smirking. He was testing me, trying to bait me. His mouth curved, revealing that scrumptious dimple.

I studied his tall muscled frame. Took in his boyish charm. God he was fine, too damn fine. I knew I was toying with fire, especially with Jacob being right there in the house. But who the hell in their right mind would dare to stick their hand in it?

Me, apparently. *Shit*.

Keenly aware of the arousal bubbling inside of me, I considered scooting away from him, but I wasn't going to give him the satisfaction of knowing he was unraveling me. Instead, I stayed planted in my seat, willing my racing pulse still.

"No, not at all. Should I be?"

Kyree's peering eyes stayed fixed on me when he said, very softly, "Nah. You mad sexy, Mrs. Lang. I wanna make love to you."

"Excuse me?"

He boldly repeated himself. And that time I heard the hunger in his voice, hot and greedy, like a starved lion circling its prey.

Instantly my pussy grew wet, and my throat dry. I snatched up the remote to the DVR and pressed PAUSE. Then met his eyes, clearing my throat along with the filthy thoughts pooling in the crevices of my mind.

"Young man, have you been drinking?"

He shook his head. "Nah. I don't drink."

I tilted my head. "Smoking?"

"I don't do that either."

I playfully popped him in the back of the head. "Then your horny behind must have been dropped on your head to think it's okay to play with me. I'm old enough to be your mother."

"Oww, oww." He feigned hurt, rubbing his head, then smiled. "And I'm old enough to know what sexy is."

"Well, sexy or not. You need to get your hormones under control."

"See. You still think I'm a little boy?"

"Oh, you're not?"

"Nah. I'm a man, Mrs. Lang. And I'm very much in control of my hormones. If I wasn't…" His voice trailed off as he licked his lips. Heat shot through my pussy, and I shifted in my seat, pressing my thighs together in hopes to squelch the fire slowly burning inside me. "Just know I'm mature enough to know what I want."

My brows rose. "That's nice. But, know this: in life—we *don't* always *get* what we want."

"Don't you know I'm spoiled? I *always* get what I want." And with that he grinned, showing his dimple again.

I rolled my eyes. "Yeah, I'm sure you do."

"I do, Mrs. Lang. And right now"—he leaned into my ear and whispered—"I want *you.*"

"Okay, boy. That's it. Out." I jumped to my feet, trying to mask being unnerved by him. But my mind was spinning so goddamn fast, I thought my head would twist right off my shoulders. I concentrated on breathing, while steadying myself from toppling over. Kyree stood to his feet as well. And it took everything in me to keep my eyes off the meaty bulge I noticed straining against the fabric of his pants.

"It's time for you to go."

He laughed. "Why? What I do? I'm only speaking the truth."

"You're too damn fresh." I walked over, hips swinging—a little harder than usual—and opened the door. "Bye, Kyree." I stifled a girlish giggle. *Shame on me.* "Tell your mom I said hello."

"I will." He stepped into my space. "If I tell you something, I need for you to promise me you won't get offended."

I tilted my head. My breathing quickened. "Will I need to wash your mouth out?"

He chuckled. "Nah, nah."

I eyed him, curiously, my mind reeling between excitement and wonder. "Go 'head." My voice went soft, and breathy.

"Not until you promise you won't get mad." His voice was low. Enticing.

I felt the impending waves of pleasure. The sexual tide was rising. And he was drawing me under, and—in a matter of time—I knew I was going to drown in the swell of whatever words he'd spoken. Everything about this boy—this, this man-child—was raw sensuality. And it had me toying precariously along the sinful edges of desire.

Primal heat.

I drew in my breath. "Boy, since when has anything ever stopped you from saying whatever you wanted to me?"

He grinned knowingly. Like my sons, the boy had no filter, so there was very little he could say—that he hadn't already said, or attempted to say—that would shock me. He stepped in closer and leaned into my ear. "I've been fantasizing about you since I was fifteen, Mrs. Lang. I'm tired of imagining what it'd be like." I felt the sensual brush of his lips against my ear as he spoke. "Tonight, I'm gonna go home and masturbate, imagining it's your pretty mouth instead of my hand. But I'm ready to experience the real thing."

I know, right then, I should have smacked the sexy smirk that followed clean off his handsome face. I should have drawn a deep line in the proverbial sand long before it'd gotten that far and made it clear as to where he stood and what boundaries he was never to cross. Goddamn him! But I didn't.

Stunned into silence, I watched as this cocky little bastard lightly brushed by me and strolled out with a smooth, sultry stride that made my toes curl, leaving the bait dangling—and me hot, flustered, and dangerously horny.

I couldn't deny it. Kyree had sparked something deep inside me. Something that made me feel naughty and exciting. Something that made me feel wickedly dirty and scandalous.

And I wanted a taste of him...forbidden fruit.

"Damn, babe," Kyree says, slicing into my thoughts. "You're driving me crazy."

I blink him back into view. I know I shouldn't enjoy this, him, but I so desperately do. I grin mischievously as I saunter over toward the bed, slowly sliding my tongue over my lips as I climb up onto the bed, and slowly crawl between his magnificent legs.

A hot coil of desire twists through me, making my flesh boil and my pussy go slicker than it already is. I lick the inside of his right thigh, then his left thigh, brushing my hand provocatively over his balls, then crawling up over his body. I lick inside his navel. Kiss his stomach. Trail my tongue up to his chest. Then suck his nipples awhile, twirling my tongue over them every so often, until they harden. Then I nip them, flick them, and lick them some more. The sensations are driving him wild.

"Ahh. Shit. Damn. Ooh, yeah. Fuck."

All politeness goes out the window, and the rules change, when Kyree and I are alone and he is naked. He talks dirty. I talk dirty. Cursing is allowed. It is welcomed. Wanted. Warranted.

I move back down his ripped body, raking my aching 36-C's across his chest and stomach before stopping at his dick, then rubbing my breasts all over his dick and balls. I tease him the way he teases me, flicking my tongue over the head of his dick, then grabbing my breasts and licking over each nipple.

"Fuck, yo. Stop fuckin' with me."

I grin, finally putting his dick between my breasts and titty-fucking him. My tongue laps at the slit of his dick each time its head pops out between my golden brown globes.

"Mmm. Look at that big hard dick sliding between my breasts. You like that?"

He grunts. "Yeah. But I'm tryna fuck, babe. Let me get some pussy. Shit, yo. Let me get up in you."

"Not yet," I say, taking the head of his dick and smearing it over my right nipple, soaking it with his precum. I suck my nipple into my mouth, moaning. "Mmm. Tastes so good."

"C'mere and let me suck them titties. That pussy. Something."

I smear more of his nectar over my left nipple, then lick it.

A few minutes more, and I free his dick from between my breasts, then lap at it. It bobs around, jerking away from my tongue. I fondle his balls, gently pulling at them, cupping them, then squeezing them.

Kyree groans. "What. The. Fuuuuck…?"

He's at my mercy. And he knows it. I possess him in this moment. He is mine. All mine.

I keep my gaze locked on his heavy-lidded eyes. "You heard the saying, 'be careful what you ask for,' *right?*"

"Yeah," he mutters, winding his hips. "And I want everything I've asked for. Give it to me. Fuck."

"Well, baby, tonight's your lucky night."

I inch my way back down his body, licking his thighs, his shins, the sides of his calves, his ankles, then slide my tongue over the top of his right foot, before licking over his toes. I switch to his left foot. He groans, then grunts as I suck his big toe into my mouth, my tongue sliding in between it. His head thrashes side to side.

"Aah. Shit. Aah. You killin' me. Suck me. Fuck me. Give me somethin'. I'm ready to nut. Aaah, shiiiit." One toe, then two, then three. My tongue laves each one, before sucking them back into my mouth. "Uhh, fuck, babe. Shit. I ain't never had my toes sucked. Aaah, damn."

Licking the bottom of his left foot, I eye his throbbing dick as it bounces wildly, streaks of his sticky man sap drizzling all over his abdomen. He's so hard and thick, so aroused that his nipples pebble harder.

Kyree allows me to do things to him that Sebastian would never consider. And I love it. I am so turned on by his adventurous streak.

I crawl back up between his legs. Grab ahold of the base of his shaft. I lick along a thick, pulsing vein. Run my parted lips up and down the side, teasing him.

"Fuck, baby. Shit. Aaah, shit. Suck my dick." His stomach clenches as I swirl my tongue around the plush head of his dick, coating my tongue with his precum. I slowly fist him, milking him for more of his sticky fluids.

He keeps his gaze on me, cursing and moaning. Watching every wet swipe of my tongue over his head, along his shaft. "Suck that shit. Aah. Fuck."

He throbs against my tongue, his scent, his tongue, intoxicating me. Filling my dripping mouth, I French-kiss the big, swollen head of his dick, slowly licking the precum as it oozes from its slit. I touch the tip of my tongue to it and swirl it around, spreading his sweet nectar over the head.

"Damn, baby," he says hoarsely. "Yeah, like that. Yeah. That's it. God, that feels good. Aaah, fuck…"

I place wet, warm, sticky kisses all the way down the underside of his throbbing shaft, then lick up and down before washing his young, tender, full balls with my tongue.

"Aaah, yeah…shit…oooh, fuck…"

My eyes flutter up at him. "You like that, little daddy?"

He grunts, thrusting his pelvis upward, his saliva-slick dick jabbing the air. "Untie me. Let me show you how lil I am."

I smirk, then cup one hand under his balls and run the tips of my fingers across his heavy sac while suckling on the head of his dick. His balls draw up.

"Aaah, shit. Aaah, shit…I'm getting ready to bust this nut, babe. Aaah, shit…let me get in that throat."

I happily oblige, sucking his dick into the back of my mouth, then quickly pulling back, teasing him, sending him further over the edge. His neck arches to press his head into the pillow.

"Aaah, shit. Aaaah, fuck, I'm gonna cum. Catch that shit…"

As his dick starts spurting out a stream of thick white cum, I seize most of it with my tongue and mouth. The rest shoots up in my face, then splatters all over his chest and stomach.

I lick my lips and moan as Kyree moans, sucking the last of his warm, creamy seeds out of his dick, then licking around his balls before sliding my tongue back up over his sticky shaft. I lap up the creamy puddles of pleasure splattered over his torso. His dick still pulses, hard and ready for more.

"Now it's my turn," he says, causing his dick to bounce faster. "Untie me so I can hit that shit from the back."

My pussy clenches in response.

My whole body is hot and sizzling.

Trembling, I breathe in. Once, twice. Then step into the flames. Not even God can help me now.

Ree-Ree: I want you sooo bad u jst dnt kno baby

Me: Aww. Stop.

Ree-Ree: Nah im deadazz. U got me open sexy

Me: Well you had me OPEN yesterday

Ree-Ree: ☺ *that shyt waz gud...ad juicy*

I smile, then text back. *Glad you enjoyed it*

Ree-ree: Nah luvd it!! My dik hard!! I want sum more asap!

My toes curl as I type. *Mmmm*

A few moments later, he texts back, *Freak me baby*, with a snap-shot of his hard dick. My mouth instantly waters.

Me: Mmm! Delicious!

Kyree and I have been messaging back and forth for the last twenty minutes while I prepare breakfast. I saved him in my phone as Ree-Ree. Each text message causes my pulse to quicken. I feel like a schoolgirl. Vibrant. Alive. I feel like I've found the fountain of youth on the tip of Kyree's young, hard dick and it's given me eternal life. No matter how sick it is, no matter how insane it all feels; I feel like I've caught my second wind. And I love the excitement of it all.

Several moments pass before my cell pings again. I swipe my fingertips across the screen and instantly become dizzy with want.

U make me cum so hard

My mouth waters. There's another picture attached to the text message. His fist wrapped around the base of his dick; a glob of white goo flowing out of its slit, dripping all over his hand. *I want u*

I lick my lips, and quickly type. *Ooo I want u too!*

I hit SEND just as Sebastian walks into the kitchen. I stuff my phone down into the front pocket of my robe. Although my husband isn't the jealous type and has never been the type to pick up my phone and go through it, I still have a passcode on it. And he has one on his phone as well. And neither of us is bothered by it.

Sebastian trusts me. And I've never given him any reason not to. And vice-versa.

"Hey, beautiful," he says as he leans in and kisses me on the mouth. He cups my ass and squeezes. He'd been away on business, again, for the last eight days, this time Venezuela and Curacao.

"Hey." I smile, breathing him in. He's wearing Kenneth Cole Black, one of my favorite colognes on him. "Good morning."

He kisses me again. Then wraps his arms around me, and I melt into him. "I missed you."

I feel a tinge of guilt. But quickly push it aside. "I missed you, too." He kisses me again, then lets me go. "I didn't hear you when you came home," I say. "What time did you get in last night?"

He reaches for a mug, and fills it with coffee before taking a seat at the table. "Yeah, I know. My flight didn't land until a little after midnight. I didn't pull up into the driveway until after one in the morning."

"How come you didn't wake me?"

"I wanted to, but—" He blows into his mug, taking a slow sip. "You were in such a deep sleep. I hated to wake you." He grins. "You had that look on your face you usually get right after a night of this good lovin'."

I swallow. "Oh? Really?"

"Yeah. But I wasn't here, so I know that couldn't have been why you were looking so peaceful." He eyes me as I flit around the kitchen scooping scrambled eggs and cheese onto two plates, then several pieces of turkey bacon. He chuckles. "You must have been exhausted. I could have had my way with you and you wouldn't have known it, or felt it."

Thank God you didn't.

After the three rounds of fucking Kyree put on me all afternoon yesterday, there is no way my pussy, or my body, could have handled having anything sliding up in me. After I untied Kyree, he became an animal in bed, ravishing every part of my body. Sucking my breasts, my clit, my pussy, licking my asshole, then flipping me over and slamming his dick inside of me, boomeranging my cunt walls with deep, fast thrusts. He fucked me long and hard. Punished me for torturing him. Then pulled out and watched as my hips thrust hungrily, my exposed pussy vacant, begging for more of him. I blink back the image of him pulling me toward the edge of the bed, cupping my ass, then lifting me to his mouth, sucking, slurping, lapping at my pussy, dipping into its wet folds as if it were a bowl of honey; his tongue fucking me swiftly, pushing me toward multiple orgasms.

I let out a nervous laugh, bringing my attention to Sebastian. "Oh, trust me. I would have felt you *and* it," I say, leaning in and kissing him on the lips, setting a plate down in front of him.

"Uh, not the way you were snoring," he says, teasing.

"The lies you tell. I was not. I don't snore."

He chuckles, picking up his fork. "Yeah, okay. Next time I'm going to record you."

"Whatever." I laugh. "You do that." I take a seat across from him. Lower my head, then say grace. But what I should be asking is, for God to have mercy on my horny soul.

"So how was Caracas?"

He chews a forkful of eggs, then swallows. "Very expensive. And flooded with robberies and murders. So we didn't get a chance to do much sightseeing on our own."

"That's a shame." I reach over and lift a piece of bacon from off his plate, biting into it.

He takes another sip of his coffee. "Curaçao, however, was peaceful. Got a chance to get out and tour the country a bit. I'd like to go back with you. It's a beautiful country. Besides, we're overdue for a vacation." He looks at me; his eyes filled with love and passion. And his heated gaze sends me skidding deeper into emotional turmoil. How can I love this man with everything in me, yet cheat on him—with our son's best friend, no less? How can I sit here—pussy pulsing and needy—looking in Sebastian's face and have the image of Kyree's hard dick still stained into my brain?

God knows Sebastian doesn't deserve my indiscretions. But when I'm with Kyree I feel powerful surges of excitement. And, frankly, I can't get enough of him.

Ping. There's another text message. Instantly, my walls clench at the thought of it being another naughty text from Kyree. Or maybe another snapshot of his cock.

I ignore the burning urge to look at the screen.

My stomach roils as Sebastian reaches over and gently strokes my hand. "It's been a long time since we've made love on a secluded beach."

I smile, taking my husband in. He's still as handsome as he was the day I fell in love with him. Aside from his graying edges and the sprinkles of gray in his goatee, he still has a youthful appearance. And he is still very much desirable. He just doesn't excite me with the same intensity as he once did.

God, I feel so horrible for saying that, let alone for feeling it. But I would never, ever, tell him this. Or make him feel any less loved or wanted. Loving Sebastian has always been easy. He's easygoing and has made being married to him uncomplicated. No drama. No disrespect. No second-guessing. He's always upfront, honest, and true to his words. And he's provided me with a wonderful lifestyle. And he's been a loving husband and father. Always.

Still…

Kyree—with all of his college boy charm and sexiness—has robbed me of the will to resist him. Having my panties *and* my control snatched away so quickly by him is as exhilarating as it is unsettling.

Damn him.

My mind wanders back to yesterday. Him tied to the bed. Me between his legs. And how he groaned long and low as I moaned against his balls, my tongue swathing against the ridges before sucking one into my mouth, followed by the other until I had them soaked. I swallow, remembering the way my mouth felt against his chest, trailing wet kisses toward each nipple. How I pinched both nipples. Hard. Harder. Tightening down on the chocolate peaks, causing his rock-hard abs to contract as he groaned out in pleasure. He'd been helpless to me as I've been to him. And I savored it.

Oh, God.

Shaking salacious thoughts of my sweaty, sex-filled romp with Kyree from my mind, I lean in and kiss Sebastian on the lips. "Yes, we are," I say rising to my feet, while removing the dishes from the table. "Say the word. And I'm packed."

He pats my ass. "You know what time it is when I get home tonight, don't you?"

Yes. Fifteen minutes of passionate sex. "You should have taken what you needed early this morning," I say teasingly. *Although I'm glad you didn't.*

My cell phone pings again for another incoming text. This time I pull it out of my pocket and glance at it as MESSAGING lights up on the screen. I don't punch in my passcode, though, to retrieve the message.

Sebastian rises and walks up behind me at the sink. "You know, baby," he slides an arm around my waist, kissing me on the neck, "it would have been great waking up to you all over me."

"I know," I say softly.

His hands slide over my breasts, where they stay. He cups them. "Your husband's been away for almost two weeks. You should have missed him." He presses his dick into my lower back. "And this."

I swallow. "Mmm. I do. I did."

Guilt creeps up into the pit of my stomach as I grip my cell in my hand. Maybe he's right. I should have pounced on him. Should have wakened him to a wet mouth full of his cock. Should have had my cunt hovering over his face as an early morning breakfast treat. I should be sex-starved and eager to be ravished by him. But we all know why I'm not.

Kyree.

Damn him.

But that doesn't mean I am still not turned on by my husband's touch. Sebastian grinds himself into me; the length of his arousal presses into my lower back, thick and wanting. He pinches my nipples and I hear myself let out a moan. Then somehow—I don't know, it happens so fast—I am spun around, my back pressing up against the sink as he steps between my knees, and he gently kneads my breasts.

"I've missed you, baby," he says, pinching my already sensitive nipples. He pulls me into him tightly, nestling my pussy against his thigh, and I can feel the thick bulge of his dick as it throbs against my stomach. "Where's Jacob?" he asks; his mouth is beside my ear, then his tongue is tracing my lobe, causing my already moist pussy to simmer in its juices.

"H-he's still asleep." My voice is low. Then it catches as he kisses along the column of my neck.

"Good," he mutters against my flesh.

"You b-better stop. Mmm." I squirm. My arms wrap around him, my free hand inching up and down along his muscled back. "You'll be late…for work."

His hands ease lower, sliding over my hips, then down over my ass. He cups it in his big hands. Squeezes it. Grinds his hard dick deeper into my belly. And instantly my pussy melts into a puddle. Yet, I'm torn. Unsure if it's because of Sebastian's smoldering gaze and his touch all over my body or if it's the lingering thoughts I have of Kyree's text messages that I am on fire. His persistent desire to fuck me, to taste me, to have me morning, noon, and night.

I feel my throat close with emotion. God, I love my husband. He is my heart. And, in spite of that, I am fucking him over. Unwilling—okay, not yet ready, to let go of my deliciously hung boy toy. His dick, his lips, his tongue, pops into my head. And I shiver, wondering if I am I really willing to risk everything I have with Sebastian for some young, hard dick?

"Work can wait," Sebastian murmurs, pulling me out of my seductive trance as his hand slides inside my robe, then between my legs. "Right now"—his fingers find my clit and lightly pinch it over my damp panties—"I want my wife."

I gasp.

"You're already wet." He cups my pussy, pressing his palm inward. "Ride my hand."

"Not here," I push out. Breathy. "Bedroom."

"No. Here. Now."

Slowly, I shake my head as my legs close, capturing his hand. "B-but, Jacob."

"He's asleep, remember?"

"But—"

"Now." His finger presses against my lip before skimming back down my body. I swallow. I've never denied Sebastian pussy. Never. No matter where he's wanted it. So right now will be no different, no matter what internal conflicts I have going on inside my head.

"We—"

"Let's live on the edge a little." My robe falls open. "Let's be adventurous, baby." The nightgown beneath rises above my hips. Sebastian's finger follows my wet seam, making me shudder.

"Oh, God, yes."

"You're so soft, baby. So wet."

My breath hitches in my throat, and I have to bite my lip to keep from crying out in ecstasy. Overlapping two fingers, Sebastian thrusts inside me and slides them in and out of my slickness.

"You're wet for me, baby."

"Yes." I gasp, tossing my head back. "Yes. It's all for you."

Liar!

Slut-ass!

You're wet for Kyree.

You let that young boy fuck you senseless.

U make me cum so hard

I moan. "Oh, fucking god, baby, please."

Sebastian presses his pelvis into me. "This dick missed you."

He's looking at me, through me, with a force that makes me shiver. I fear if I look at him too long that I'll get lost in the intensity of his deep, brown eyes and he'll see my lies, my truths.

I love my husband.

I love him. I love him. I love him.

But I am unfaithful to him.

I want you sooo bad u jst dnt kno baby

I shut my eyes—blocking out the heated text messages burning on my phone and squeezing out the imagery of Kyree's young muscular body and the tight lacing of muscle wrapped around his frame; his wet tongue, his soft lips all over my body—and focus my energy, my attention, my needs, on the sensations brought on by Sebastian. Focus on the feeling of being filled so deliciously. The sweet way his fingers brush against my spot. Hearing my juices slosh around his fingers.

Beneath my nightgown, my nipples are as hard as pebbles. My

pussy is as wet as a river, rippling with pleasure. I want more, need more. Now. Shamelessly. More Sebastian. More Kyree. More sex. More fucking. More deceit.

My cell hits the floor as I reach for the buckle of Sebastian's belt and unfasten it.

"I can't wait to slide up in you."

"Oh, yes," I breathe. "Oh, yes. Oh, yes. Yes, yes, yes…" My hand fumbles for the button on his trousers. I flip it open, then ease down the zipper and yank open his shirt. Buttons fly everywhere. I slip my hand inside his underwear, then yank them down his hips. Veined and thick as my wrist, his luscious ebony-colored dick springs upward from tight coils of dark brown hair and heavy balls. The mushroom head is so engorged, already wet, already pulsing.

I gasp. The mere sight of it is impressively breathtaking.

"You're my everything, baby," Sebastian says, cupping my ass, then lifting me up on the edge of the sink. My arms go around his neck as he thrusts hard, sinking deep in one lunge, wrenching a cry from me as I melt around him.

"Fuck me," I whisper, finally staring in his eyes. Seeing him, and only him. I say it again. "Fuck me." This time my voice is filled with more urgency. "Fuck me. Fuck me."

Sebastian's eyes light up with a mixture of surprise and fascination in them. He's never heard me talk this way. Just as I've never known him to want to fuck me out in the open knowing there's a chance our son, Jacob, could walk in on us.

Twisting fingers through my hair, Sebastian tugs, and bends to sprinkle kisses across my jaw, then laps his way up toward my ear, nipping. Heat fans from his breath along the sensitive skin along my neck as his dick slices into my pussy.

"Yes, yes, yes…oh, baby, yes…fuuuuuck meeee…"

"You feel so good, baby," he mutters against my skin. Then his mouth finds mine. He licks my lips, nips my bottom lip, enticing me to part them. I do for him.

For Kyree.

For Sebastian.

For the both of them.

Kyree.

Damn him.

Sebastian's tongue sweeps through my mouth, lingering, as if he's searching for something sweet to savor. And I let him, giving into the sweetness of his kiss.

I choke back emotions as my climax swells. I feel myself melting perilously fast.

Sebastian stretches me wide, and the heat of my betrayal rises with the tide of my orgasm.

I am on the verge of coming.

"Oh, oh, oh…"

Sebastian rasps, "Ah, yeah. Shit, baby."

He is on the verge of coming, too.

"Come with me, baby." He pants, covering his mouth with mine again.

Liquid fire dances through my core. Tears spring from my eyes.

I come.

He grunts.

I keep coming, my body shuddering.

Sebastian keeps grunting, his body shaking.

Inside me I feel him growing impossibly thicker, bigger, taking more of me, each stroke burning my pussy.

I dig my nails into his back. Urge him on. Beg him.

"Keep fucking me. Mmm. Mmm…yes, yes, yes…"

He growls. And comes. Flooding me with everything he is.

Three days later…

"We have to stop this," I tell Kyree in a breathy whisper. The roping of muscle in his biceps, thick and hard, as he hovers over me with his now semi-erect dick still inside of me. I reach up and trace his sweaty cheekbone with my thumb. He stares at me, searching my face for contradictions. There are so many. My guilt is eating away at me. However, not enough to keep me home. Once again, Kyree and I are at a sleazy motel three towns away—sneakily, catching our breaths from a round of sweet, sweaty fucking.

He grins down at me, slowly circling his hips, stirring his dick inside of my juices.

Somewhere stuck in my muddled thoughts is the possibility of his nut-filled condom slipping off his dick inside me; his little white-creamed soldiers swimming their way to the center of everything I am. I already feel like I've given him more than I should.

Yet, he keeps taking more of me.

And I keep letting him.

Screwing him is one thing. Getting pregnant by him is a whole other level of betrayal. But I don't express my concern about the chances of his condom slipping off inside of me. I'm not ready for him or his cock to vacate the warmth and wetness.

A long moment passes, his hips still slowly winding into me. He kisses the arch of my brow, then asks, "Why? Don't you like how I make you feel?" He kisses me on the lips. "I know I do. I love the way you feel on my dick. Don't you?"

I swallow. "Yes, yes. Of course I do." *Oh, God, how I love this dick.* "A little too much."

Sex with Sebastian is good. No, more than good. It's great.

But, but…*ohgod, but…*

Sex with Kyree is…breathtaking. It's like I'm having an out-of-body experience. I am not myself. It's like I'm possessed. I become this wild sexual beast with him, sinking my teeth into his flesh, clawing at his back, clutching the sheets, bucking and growling. He pulls this out of me. Fucks it out of me. Reaches into the core of who I thought I am—who I thought I was—and turns me into this sex-crazed being.

I knew I'd never be the same the first night I gave in to his advances and snuck him into the large shed out in my backyard late in the night—like close to two in the morning, when I thought Jacob was knocked out—and fucked him bent over Sebastian's work bench.

Kyree tore through my wet pussy, ravishing it with his mouth, his tongue, his cock. Heat blasted through me when the tip of his dick eased into me. He inched it in and out at a sweetly tormenting pace, pushing deeper and deeper until I was reaching in back of me—craning my neck, cursing him under my breath, while grabbing him by the thighs, pulling him in, clamping my muscles around his cock. The minute he nudged my cervix I cried out. Thankful for having the thunder and heavy rain to drown out my wails of pleasure.

I loved the way his curved dick scraped against my walls with each twist and thrust of his hips. I'd never experienced a curved dick before. Until Kyree. Ooh, it was sooo good. Hell, it still is. But, that first night I experienced it...my God. My thighs quivered. My stomach clenched. And then I felt his dick swell even more just as he pulled out, then slammed deep.

I watched him over my shoulder as I held open my ass cheeks for him—per his request, his chiseled face painted with pleasure as he spat on his middle finger. I had no idea what he was going to do with that finger until I saw droplets of spit descend from his lips and splatter onto my asshole.

My body stiffened. But he coaxed me to relax and whispered sweet nothings, daring me to let go and give in. And then he was pushing the tip of that long middle finger in my ass, while slow stroking my pussy. Slowly, push, push, push. Then out. Push, push, push. Then back out again. More spit. Then push, push, push. Then out again. More spit. Then push, push, push. He did that several more times—with his dick stoking the fires inside me—until I opened around his probing digit, and felt flames roaring up my spine.

I'd never had a finger in my ass. Not even a tongue lap there. Ever.

Not until that night.

And there I was slumped over, one knee up on Sebastian's work bench for support, my ass up and pulled open wide with a finger pumping in and out of it, while Kyree matched each finger thrust with the stroke of his dick. Pumping, pumping, pumping…stroking, stroking, stroking—a blanket of pleasure rolled over me. I was tumbling over into the maelstrom of an orgasm like no other climax I'd ever experienced.

I felt it. The rumbling. The whirl. It started at the tips of my toes, then rolled over the soles of my feet, then surged upward into the back of my calves, then spread fiercely through my ass-hole, then roiled over into the pit of my pussy. The sensitive tip of my clit pulsed and tingled.

I reached down between my legs, per Kyree's demand, and pressed on the slick, swollen nub, opening the floodgates to a powerful orgasm that shook my whole body, causing every muscle in my body to spasm.

My eyes stung with tears when that second and third orgasm hit, snatching my breath and causing white spots to blur my vision. I gasped. Felt my eyes cross. Then howled, dragging my nails across the metal bench as a bundle of throbbing, pulsing heat gushed out of me.

I'd experienced my first female ejaculation.

I'd squirted.

And I owed it all to Kyree.

Just like that. He managed to turn me into a mindless dick junkie.

He grins, that sexy dimple of his flashing. "Then what's the problem?" he says, pulling me out from my thoughts. "Sounds"— he grinds deeper into me—"*and* feels mutually beneficial to the both of us."

My legs open wider. Allowing Kyree's dick to possess more of me. I blink back the rest of those sordid images of that night inside Sebastian's shed, and focus on him. Lying here beneath him, my heartbeat quickening as I slowly melt under his warm gaze, I feel like I could become one of those needy women who'd empty out her entire savings, ruin her credit, and throw her whole life away just to keep getting this young hard dick. Good dick. Powerful dick. Addictive dick. That's what this is. Too damn dangerous.

And when I'm with this boy, this man-child, I am not myself. I don't know who this woman is; lying atop damp sheets, sprawled beneath this muscled body, legs spread open, pussy slick and well-fucked and still wanting more.

"You already know why," I say softly, my pussy still pulsing around his dick. "It's not right."

"But it *feels* right, Mrs. Lang."

I cringe. The fact that he calls me *Mrs. Lang* is confirmation in itself that this is all wrong, and it is a clear aide-mémoire of my age…and his. And it is a painful reminder that I am a married woman, having an affair with my son's best friend.

"My bad, babe. But you know what I'm saying. I'm big on you."
He kisses me lightly on the lips. "And this thing we got is good.
Real good."

I swallow.

Damn him.

"Who have you told? About *us?*"

He shakes his head. "No one." I raise a brow, unconvinced. "Nah,
for real. On everything, I'm real discreet about mine. Besides, Jay
is my boy. I could never dog him out like that. He's like a brother
to me."

My stomach tightens. I feel my insides churning. *Ohgod. I think
I'm going to be sick.* I swallow the bile rising in the back of my throat.
"But *you're* screwing *his* mother. And I'm married. So, you see how
ugly this could get. This puts us both in a very precarious position."

His dick finally slips out of me, and I immediately feel regret-
fully empty as he rolls over on his back, then swings his legs over
the bed and gets up, holding the cream-filled condom in place
with his hand.

"Only if someone finds out. And they won't. You just gotta know
how to move. That's all."

"Oh? And you know how to move?"

"Of course I do. Hey, I might be only nineteen," he says, carefully removing the condom, "but I'm not new to *this*." I eye him
as walks across the room and tosses it in a nearby trashcan. Then
saunters back over toward the bed, his skin glistening with sweat,
his dick covered in a wet glaze of cum.

Right then, realization hits. I'm not his first. Silly of me to think
I was. I should have known better. Should have known a boy with
as much charm and sexual energy as he would have plenty of older,
more evolved, seasoned women at his fingertips. Still, I can't help
feel a tinge of…*ohgod*…jealousy.

I drink in his curved dick as it bounces. "So who else have you done this with?"

He grins. "See. Now you doing too much." He leans down, cups my face in his hands and kisses me. "I told you I don't kiss 'n' tell."

And that may be true. But I still can't help wondering what other friends' mothers he's worked his magical charm on. Or how many of them bitches has he fucked senseless. Or am I the only one who's lost her damned mind?

He grabs his cum-sticky dick, shaking it at me. "Don't worry. I got this. And I got you."

I sit up in bed, swinging my legs over. "Well, that's good to know."

He gives me a quizzical look. "Um, where you going?"

"To shower."

He shakes his head, reaching for another condom on the night-stand. "Nah. I'm not done, yet. Lie back and lift open your legs."

I smile, doing as I am told. Allowing this man-child to dominate. Allowing myself to submit to his will. I spread wide, bending at the knees, displaying my wet cunt for his taking.

"Damn. You gotta *phat* pussy. I wanna cream-pie you so bad." I lift my head up from the mattress and give him a questioning look. He smirks. "Bust inside you, then eat you out."

My cunt clenches.

Ooh, he's one freaky-ass motherfucker.

A week later...

"Dang, Mrs. Lang," Kyree says in between bites of his food, "this lasagna is bangin'."

Kyree and Jacob have spent the most part of the afternoon out back entertaining a group of their friends, a mixture of horny males and giggling, bikini-clad sex kittens, lounging about our in-ground pool. Today had been a near-perfect summer day. A delicious breeze, warm sun shining down. Every so often, I found myself dashing up the stairs and peeking through slits of the blinds of my upstairs window, stalking the area as I eyed Jacob and…Kyree.

They were teen boys, for heaven's sake. Doing what teen boys do. But when Kyree stepped out of the pool—water cascading down his chiseled body—and caught some big-booty, platinum-blonde-haired hussy around the waist and pulled her up against his hard, wet chest, I froze.

She threw her arms around his neck, then eased up on her tip-toes and kissed him. On the mouth! *Fast-ass little ho!*

He whispered something in her ear, and she giggled. I rolled my eyes. "Bitch," I muttered as I watched. "I hope the chlorine breaks your edges off." I stepped back from the window. I'd seen enough. But fifteen minutes later, I found myself peering out of another window. "What the hell am doing?" I murmured, even as a rush of wetness trickled down my thighs and I slipped a finger inside my overheated pussy. I had to scold myself several times for not trusting my son and his friend enough to entertain their friends without prying eyes, for not being able to allow them a measure of privacy. They deserved that much. Didn't they? Hell no! Not under my roof. I had every right to know what the heck was going on right under my nose. After all, they were my responsibility.

So, why was I frozen in shock when Kyree's gaze lifted, and suddenly I was caught in his snare?

When he lifted his head and his lips curved upward, my knees nearly buckled. All the blood left my face. *Shit.* I was busted. He knew I was watching! He cupped the little hotbox's ass and kissed her back. My nipples pebbled and my pussy flooded with liquid warmth. I closed my eyes and an image of Kyree filled my mind. Suddenly I envisioned him thrusting his long, talented tongue in and out of me, licking me to orgasm. I could almost feel the brush of his tongue against my sensitive clit, laving my pussy with loving strokes. Each erotic image brought forth a moan. I pumped hard and fast, then climaxed. My juices soaked my fingers and my cunt clenched and unclenched, making me ache for a good fuck. My heartbeat sped up and I cursed myself for spying on Jacob and his friends—particularly for eyeing Kyree—and for being so incredibly turned on by my voyeuristic behavior. Shamelessly wet, I turned and headed back downstairs. I needed a hard dick and a stiff drink.

"I wish my moms cooked like this," Kyree says, tugging me from my thoughts.

I blink back the remaining images of him at the pool, and smile. "I'm glad you're enjoying it."

"I am," he says as he lifts his eyes up from his plate long enough to take me in with his gaze. "I enjoy *every*thing you cook. I love eating…" He pauses, mischief flickering in his eyes. *You. I love eating you*, I hear him say in my head. I shift in my seat. "Good food," he finishes, smacking his lips.

I swallow back a rush of drool as he swipes his wet tongue over his thick juicy lips, then licks his long, pussy-probing fingers.

I fight to shake the memory of how, just days ago, he had me clutching the sheets, moaning, digging my heels into the mattress as he cupped my ass and lifted me to his mouth and fucked me swiftly with his tongue; each shallow thrust of his tongue sending me spiraling closer to another climax.

"Ohgod, yes," I cried out as his growl vibrated against my clit. "Don't stop. Oooh…don't stop giving me that tongue…it feels so good, baby. Mmmm, yesss…"

"I'm going to make you come hard." He looked up just long enough to take in the expression of ecstasy etched on my face; my bottom lip pulled in tight, my eyes fluttering, my head thrashing side to side.

He pulled my lips apart, then followed his finger along my wet slit, making me shudder and my toes curl before replacing his finger with his tongue and running the tip of it over my clit, then delving in deep.

One finger entered me as he licked. My hips thrust hungrily.

"Right there," I said breathlessly. "I like that. Oooh, yes…oooh, yes…lick my pussy. Mmmm. Faster. Oooh…"

Kyree wedged a second finger inside. But he'd removed them too fast, too soon, only to dip them into my mouth for me to suck, to taste. And, then, he snatches them away and surges onto his knees, elevating me. My hips rose off the mattress. My legs spread wider, my cunt so hungry and greedy for more of him, all of him. The rapid-fire flicking of his tongue had me on the verge of combustion. I was so full from arousal that I could feel it building deep in the pit of my soul.

I thrashed anew, fighting to hold in the rushing wave of wet yearning roiling inside of me. I'd cast a hazy gaze at the beauty of his hardened biceps as they supported the weight of me. It was a beautiful sight to behold. This young man eagerly licking me, sucking me, fucking me with fingers and tongue; his face wet… from me; my pussy his meal, his nourishment, to enjoy.

In my frenzy, a low moan broke free from the back of my throat. "Jesus! Yes, God!" My clit, my labia, my open sex…all trembled from pleasure; his, mine. The tip of Kyree's tongue danced against my slit, then over my clit. He urged me closer to orgasm. Trilled his tongue against my pussy, causing my head to pound with the need, want, desire to climax.

My toes curled tight, my fists clenched. The things Kyree can do with his mouth and tongue are magical. Excruciating delight. Boundless pleasure. And almost unbearable. But I wanted more, so much more.

"Oh, God," I moaned as he sucked on my clit, then used his teeth to nip and graze it, before releasing it with a wet sound. "No, don't stop!"

He rasped, "You want more?"

I sputtered out spit and drool. "Yes."

He blew on my clit, his ragged breath heating my flared opening, then sucked it back into his mouth and sucked harder than ever before, tonguing me at the same time. My body twisted as my hips bucked wantonly to his mouth. *Fuck. Fuck. Fuck.*

Sucking me harder, faster, Kyree wrung from me one of the most powerful orgasms I'd ever imagined.

And, just as he promised, I came in a thunderous roar.

"Yeah, my mom can definitely cook," Jacob says, pulling me from the after-shudders of my reverie. "If a broad ever expects me to put a ring on it, she had better know how to throw down in the bedroom *and* the kitchen."

I laugh. "Boy, T-M-I."

He shrugs. "I'm just saying. The way to my heart is not only through my stomach, but through…"

"All right, all right. Enough. I get it." I shake my head. "And what about you, Kyree? What kind of woman are you looking for"

He looks up from his plate, the answer flashing in his eyes. "*A woman like you.*" "I'm with Jay, Mrs. Lane. I want a woman...like *you* and my mom combined in one."

Jacob frowns. "Man, what's up with you sweating my mom. I keep telling you, you need to chill with that."

Kyree grins. "Man, relax. Stop acting all jealous. You know I'm only speaking truth. Don't get me wrong. My mom is a good woman. And I definitely like whoever I marry to have a lot of her qualities. But she doesn't cook all that good. And I want a woman who does, like your mom." Kyree looks over at me. "Mr. Lane is one lucky man."

I shift in my seat, feeling heat spread through me.

"Man, whatever," Jacob says, oblivious to the fact that I've just wet my panties simply from sitting here across the table and watching Kyree practically make love to his food as if he were making love to *me.* He licks his fork, and that sends more chills rippling along my spine.

I know he is far too young for me. I'm old enough to be his mother, for crying out loud. Yet, I am sitting here undressing him with my eyes, reliving some of my most intimate moments with him. We steal glances at each other, our eyes openly saying what our mouths don't. *I want you. Tonight.*

Some would say age isn't anything but a number as long as he's legal. And he is. But others might say that fucking a nineteen-year-old is appalling, but that doesn't stop me from lusting him, from me wanting more of him, from me wanting him to have more of me.

And he will.

Wearing nothing but a pair of black stilettos—heels my own husband hasn't seen me in, desire swells through me as Kyree's gaze glides over my shimmering body, then clings to my hand as I spread my legs slightly and dip it in between my thighs.

Kyree is sprawled out in the center of the bed, his plump semi-erect dick lying to one side over his thigh.

"Damn," he whispers. "I bet you're so wet."

I moan. "I am. Real wet." My breath catches as I lightly brush over my clit with my fingertips. There's a slow ache pooling in my cunt, a burning need to have him see me spread open to him—for his throbbing cock, my wet, juicy offering to him.

"You teasing me. I want that pussy. Now."

"What do you wanna do with this pussy?" I spread my legs wider, open my slick, pouty lips, revealing my pink, wet insides. "Fuck it?"

Slowly sinking two fingers between my lips, I gasp.

He grabs his dick, strokes it in his fist. "Yeah," he rasps. "I wanna fuck it."

I lick my lips. Watch his manhood come alive. "Mmm. Ooh, yes." My fingers plunge in and out of my warmth. "What else you wanna do to this wet pussy?"

"Lick it." He tightens his grip on his dick. "I wanna taste you, baby. Fuck you with my tongue."

My eyes flicker over into his as my finger lightly grazes my clit. A tremor ripples through me. He watches as I lift my finger to my mouth and slip it inside, tasting myself, savoring my warm, wet, sticky juices.

"Damn." Kyree crooks his finger at me, motioning me over to the bed. "C'mere. Let me taste it."

I feel so liberated. Feel so empowered. Feel so alive. Every nerve ending in my body is ablaze. And it's all because of Kyree. He does this to me. Makes the cream in my cunt churn for him.

I moan. "Mmm. Your wish is my command."

I crawl up on the bed. Squat down low over his face, and allow him to behold my glistening sex before clamping my knees on either side of his head. His heated breath kisses my pussy lips, and then he sticks his long tongue out, curling it up, then down, then up again in slow, sensual motion. He tells me how pretty my kitty is and how he loves its taste before burying his tongue between my slick folds.

Oooh, yes, yes, yes! My heart flutters, as my pussy grows wetter with each lick. His tongue works me into a mindless frenzy, sending me hurtling toward the edge of one of the sweetest climaxes.

His thick, banana-curved cock bounces. It beckons me to taste it. To make love to it with my mouth, lips, tongue and hands. The tip glistens with precum. Oh, God! I feel a terrible yearning to suckle the head of his dick. I lick my lips. Reach for it. Lean in to lick it. Take it deep into my wet, greedy mouth. But Kyree catches my wrist, and stops me. He wants me to look. Not touch. He wants to torture me.

I reach for it, again.

"No," he mutters against my burning flesh, "watch."

I swallow back hunger and want, eyeing his nectar as it drizzles out of his piss slit like melting donut glaze. He reaches for his dick. Shakes it. Strokes it. Strings of precum streak across his stomach.

I groan my displeasure, but my disappointment is quickly replaced with an overwhelming sensation that pulses through me as his tongue sweeps over my clit, then circles around my cunt. When his sticky tongue goes from my pussy to my asshole, my whole body shakes with unexpected pleasure. My knees almost give out.

"Oh, God!" I cry out. "Yes, baby, yes…oohhh!"

Kyree masturbates, his rhythm matching the strokes of his tongue over my pussy, over my clit, then inside my slit. My mind buzzes, wondering where the hell someone his age mastered the art of cunnilingus.

He licks again, long and hard, right over my clit, then against my cum-soaked hole.

Dear God…

"Aaaaah, yes, baby, yes…"

He pushes a finger into my ass.

Sweet holy Jesus…

My cunt goes into spasms. I buck and writhe, wanting more of his tongue, more of his finger. He strokes his dick with rapid speed, groans into the slit of my pussy. Then comes all over his hand, his dick pumping out waves of hot cream.

Instinctively, I lean forward and greedily lap at his hand, sweeping my tongue all over his fingers. Mmmm. Wanting those wicked fingers. Wanting every creamy drop of him. I squeeze my eyes shut as heat surges through my veins. Then come all over his face.

Heart racing, I flop over onto the bed, turning onto my side and facing him. I prop myself up on one arm. His lips are glossy from my sweet juices. "Boy, where'd you learn to perform oral sex like that?"

He grins. "Books. Porn. And lots of practice." He wiggles his brows up and down. "And I'm not a boy, babe. I'm all man. Or do I need to remind you?"

I lean over and kiss him on the lips, tasting myself on him. Mmm. I swipe my tongue over his top lip, then suck his bottom lip into my mouth.

His warm hands roam over my body as I crawl up on top of him. Slide my hot pussy up and down over his dick. I am always impressed at how quickly his dick springs back to life. When I have him slick with my juices, I reach beneath me and take him deep into my cunt.

I slowly work him inside of me in a slow steady rhythm, swiveling my hips around and around, bringing my plump ass up high every time I rotate up his shaft, to the top of his dick, the head slowly peeking out from between my luscious folds before slipping back in, wetting him, keeping him slick.

Kyree moans loudly. "Aaah, shit. Mmmhmmm…damn, baby…"

I lean forward, my pussy quivering and tingling. "You wanted a woman," I say, sliding my tongue into his ear, "you got it. Now remind me, again"—I slam down on his dick, taking him deeper, pushing him into a wet river of pleasure, fueling the fires of his lust, and my own—"how much of a man you are."

Kyree grabs my hips, flips me over, pulls my legs up over his shoulders, and responds with a low growl, then begins to coat the walls of my pussy with warm semen.

Several days later, I'm curled up on the sofa reading Allison Hobbs' latest novel with a glass of white wine, unwinding from my day while Sebastian's upstairs taking a shower. We spent the early part of our Sunday working in the yard, before driving into the city for a bite to eat at Taramind Tribeca, an Indian restaurant with towering windows and Brazilian teak located in the heart of Tribeca. I really enjoy my husband's company, so spending the day out with him was a nice treat. I even surprised myself, and him, when I leaned over in his lap, unfastened his jeans, then fished out his dick and sucked him deep into my wet mouth. He was so taken aback by my brazenness that he'd climaxed within minutes, coating the back of my throat and filling my mouth with his thick seeds.

"Damn, baby," he said breathlessly. "Whatever you're reading in those nasty books, please keep reading it." He took his eyes off the road, and grinned. "I love this new nasty you."

I said, "Me, too." Then slid my tongue over my teeth for any remnants of his man milk, and settled back in my seat, fastening my seatbelt, smiling inside.

It was a nice way to end not only the evening, but the weekend as well.

Now all I want to do is read a few chapters of this book, then crawl into bed and lie in my husband's arms until sleep claims me.

Ping. An incoming text. I reach for my phone. Swipe my finger across the screen. And open the message. *I want u tonight*

I smile, staring at the message. Slowly, my insides come alive.

Mmm. I want you too, I type back.

A minute later: *I wanna tongue u*

My walls clench.

I want u sooo bad u just dnt kno baby. Sneak out?

Heat sweeps through me. I swallow hard, glancing over at the crystal clock on the end table. It's a little after ten p.m.

My shaky fingers itch to type back to tell him yes. But I stop myself. The rational part of my brain screams for me not to do it. This thing between us has gotten out of hand. It has me lying to my husband. Has me pretending to be someone I no longer am.

Faithful.

Trustworthy.

Grounded.

Worthy.

Of my life with Sebastian.

Deserving.

Of his love.

Yet...

In a matter of one heated text message—*I wanna tongue u*—my pussy aches and pulses, and I am contemplating defying every logical reason as to why I should turn off my cell and ignore Kyree's texts. I am literally sifting through a laundry list of rational-

izations as to why I shouldn't hop in the shower, then crawl into
bed with my husband, where I belong. There is no need for me to
sneak out to be with anyone else when all the hard dick I need is
right upstairs waiting on me.

But the moment I climb the stairs, step into my bathroom,
squeeze a dollop of Dial Coconut Water Refreshing Mango body
wash onto a rag, then run it under warm water, I am aware of my
decision, certain of my destination. I slip into a short skirt and
tank top. Slide my feet into a pair of sandals. Then clip my hair in
a haphazard twist that leaves skeins of highlighted tresses caressing the sides of my face.

Let's meet, I quickly text.

Less than a minute later, Kyree texts back. *Fuck U outdoors?*

My mouth waters as I read the text. *Yes, I type back. Where?*

A few moments later, my cell pings. *Eagle rock?*

Mygod! He wants to fuck me in a park! Eagle Rock Reservation is
a wooded, red oak forest laced with paths and hiking trails. Perfect
for in-the-middle-of-the-night fucking.

See u in 20mins, I type before tossing my cell inside my bag.

With keys in hand, I find Sebastian sitting in the den watching
the sports channel. I lean in and kiss him on the lips. Tell him I'm
running out to the store. For milk. Then head out the door.

It takes me less than fifteen minutes to get to Eagle Rock. Kyree
is already here, waiting along a secluded trail, smiling.

Tonight, I'm not a wife. A mother. A homemaker.

I'm a dick-crazed tramp.

A greedy cougar whore.

A cum-slut.

A filthy cradle-robber.

For Kyree's dick. Young and hard and curved. And so very good.

He locks eyes with me, his dick hanging out over the waistband
of his sweats, already in his hand. He jerks it.

There's a strong demanding need pounding through my body as I watch him watching me. Kyree with his young, hard dick has done this to me. I reach up and release my hair from the ponytail, shaking my hair out. I warn him, "I'm wet. I'm horny. And ready. So fuck me fast. I only have twenty minutes."

He licks his lips when I reach under my skirt and shimmy out of my red lace panties. "Damn, baby."

My eyes alight with desire, I toss my panties at him and match his lusty gaze when he catches them. "Fuck me now," I urge, my voice hoarse and heated and full of lust.

There's no time for dick sucking.

No time for pussy licking.

Just fucking.

Quick. Hard. Raw. Animalistic.

I bend over, and grab my ankles.

"Damn, you gotta phat ass," Kyree says, stepping up behind me, smoothing his hand over my cheeks.

"Slap my ass," I say over my shoulder. "Then ram your dick up in me."

"Aww, shit." He laughs. "You wanna talk smack, I see."

"Yeah. Now less talk, and more action, little daddy," I say real sassy as I shake my hips and cause my ass cheeks to clap.

My insides quiver anticipating him sinking his dick between my wet pussy lips, but Kyree wants to tease me instead, tracing his dick along my slick slit.

"C'mon. Fuck me."

Slap!

His hand strikes my ass, hard.

"Again."

Slap!

This goes on for five or six pussy-dripping minutes before my knees feel like they're about to buckle. And then he finally gives me what my pussy yearns. I yelp when he plunges inside me, harshly, sliding all the way in until his balls are smacking the back of my pussy.

"Oh, yes!" I gasp as I lurch back toward him, my plump ass cheeks crashing against his pelvis. "Take this pussy, Kyree, baby... mmmm...oooh...that young dick is so gooood."

Kyree groans loudly, grinding his hips against me, before pulling out, then slamming back in over and over again.

I reach between my legs, skidding my fingers over my puffy clit. It's so engorged and sensitive.

He slaps my ass again. And every time his hand heats my flesh, I buck back harder, faster, greedily sucking in his dick. Kyree catches me by surprise, slapping into a newfound sweet spot—the underside of my ass. He slaps his hand upward, making my ass shake as he rams his dick in and out, burying himself deep inside me.

Each thrust, each slap, pushes me closer to orgasm.

Sparks of pleasure shoot through me, causing my pulse to pound in my cunt and my blood to heat in my veins.

Ohgod, ohgod...this man-child, this young stud and...his dick... oooh. He is everything I shouldn't want and everything I know I don't need, and yet right at this moment—open and wet, my body hot and needy, while being fucked outside in the woods in the middle of the night—there's no denying that he is my sweetest taboo.

Kyree grunts. "You like this dick...?"

"Yes, God, yesssss."

Three more deep strokes, my body clenches tight around him. I melt with pleasure. Then, with the stars twinkling overhead and the New York City skyline in view—my orgasm bursts through me.

I mewl out.

And spasm.

A half-hour later, I walk back through the front door. Sebastian is sitting in the kitchen, the *New York Times* in his hands, folded in sections. He looks up from the paper, then narrows his eyes, searching, studying me. Right now, I can only imagine what he sees. Hair disarrayed. Face flushed. Lips glazed. Clothes askew. *Ohgod, I must look a mess.* I immediately feel self-conscious and start to wonder if he can smell my soaking sex. Paranoia starts to set in, and I question if he senses my indiscretions?

He frowns.

Ohgod!

Subconsciously, I touch the side of my neck. My fingertips absorb the subtle heat still radiating from my skin. I swallow. I can still feel Kyree's soft lips skimming over my flesh. His fingers slipping down my crack, sweeping my asshole, then slowly moving lower until he grazes my deliciously wet sex; his fingertip teasing my slit. I swallow again. Slide my tongue over my teeth. Then swallow the lingering taste of Kyree's sweet man meat.

Sebastian's voice slices through my dirty thoughts. "Baby, you all right?"

I blink. "Huh?"

"I said your face looks flush."

"Oh, uh…didn't hear you." I feel my forehead. "I don't know why. I haven't done anything out of the ordinary, except go to the store." *Yeah, and get fucked outdoors.*

He chuckles. "Well, you're practically glowing."

I push out a nervous laugh. "Must be the new face cream I've been using."

He smiles and folds the paper as he rises from his seat. "Well, keep doing what you're doing, baby."

You don't really mean that.

He pushes his chair in. "You're more beautiful than ever."

Ohgod. Help me. He walks up on me and pulls me into him, brushing a gentle kiss over my lips. "Wait," he says, then pauses. "I thought you said you were going to the store."

"Uh?"

He repeats himself.

"Oh, I did," I quickly lie. "They didn't have what I needed."

"I thought you wanted milk."

Mmm. Yes, Kyree's sweet, thick dick milk.

I quickly sidestep him, avoiding his gaze skimming over me. "Yeah, I wanted buttermilk for this new recipe I want to try." I walk over to the sink and run the water. "But they were all out."

I consider saying more, but then decide otherwise. Less is sometimes best, especially when you know it's going to be a lie added onto another lie.

Sebastian eyes me, then slowly raises a brow.

"What?" I ask, feeling increasingly uncomfortable.

"So are you going to tell me, or keep me in suspense?"

My pulse quickens. "Tell you what?"

He smiles. "What's this new recipe that had you rushing up outta here for *buttermilk?*"

Guilt swirls around me. I want to turn away from his gaze. Want to confess my dirty sins and beg for his forgiveness. But I don't. Instead, I straighten my shoulders, and swallow, before forcing a small smile to touch my lips. "It's a surprise."

"I like the sound of that." He reaches for me. Pulls me into him by the waist. "Speaking of surprises." He leans in and pecks me on the lips. The kiss is quick, but ever so sweet. "Meet me upstairs. I'll have one waiting for you."

His smile teases. And when he steps back, I can't help but glance down at the bulge in his pajama bottoms. No other words are needed. I smile back at him.

Then pray to the high heavens that my still-throbbing cunt can handle another pounding.

It's a little after ten o'clock in the evening, three days later. And, once again, like a schoolgirl with raging hormones, I've snuck out to be with Kyree—this time under the guise of needing to pick up a *friend* from the airport. Sebastian asks no questions; he allows me the freedom to do whatever I need to do. Besides, I left him home, smiling, after sucking his dick down to the gristle. I gave my husband the best blowjob of his life, unprompted, unsuspected, unwavering. I took Sebastian by surprise. Something I don't do often when it comes to giving him head. Performing oral sex on my husband has never been an issue for me. I suck him without pause. It's simply not an act performed as often as he'd like. But since being with Kyree, I've become surprisingly more spontaneous when it comes to pleasing him orally.

Sebastian says he loves this new orgasmic me.

I tell him I love this new me, too.

He's asked me again, what's gotten into me. Of course I dare not tell him that it's the result of being fucked by a young, horny college stud. So I show him a few erotica books I've since bought, and allow him to believe that they've awakened this sexual beast inside of me.

Kyree kisses my forehead, then brushes a kiss over my lips. "Whatchu thinking about?"

I smile. Take his face in, then lightly kiss him. "You."

He grins. "You're so fuckin' sexy. You know that, right?"

I blush. "Boy, stop. You're just saying that."

"Nah, for real." He takes my hand and raises it to his lips, kissing my fingers. "So, so, sexy, baby."

I close my eyes, guilt flooding my heart.

He reaches between my thighs. And I spread them open, allowing his fingers to find the edge of my panties. He brushes his heated palm over the front of my pussy. I shiver with burning want. And then his fingers slip inside, and I gasp, relishing in his touch. My cunt, slick and wet, clenches in anticipation.

My eyes glisten. I know what I'm doing is wrong. Lying to Sebastian. Lusting after a teenaged boy. No matter how mature he is for his age; no matter the fact that he's over the legal age of consent, I know this thing between us has to stop. All he is, all he will ever be, is a good fuck.

Oh how good of a fuck he is.

A bittersweet memory of what is, of what shouldn't be. He has quickly become my addiction. Sometimes in the still of the night, I lie awake at night, with Sebastian snoring lightly beside me, and fantasize about the way Kyree feels inside of me, the way his dick strokes my walls. The way he kisses me and nibbles on my bottom lip with lips and teeth, stroking the inside of my mouth with velvet strokes of his tongue. Savoring me. Other times, desire shoots through me, flushing my skin, while heating my pussy. And I can feel the ghost of his tongue languishing and laving and feasting, touching and tasting my whole pussy.

"Babe," Kyree murmurs gruffly, his lips gliding over my skin, along my cheek, then over my lips. "I want you so bad."

He slowly slides his fingers in my pussy, and I mewl out pure, sensual pleasure. I am blazing in heat for him, for his touch, for his kisses, for his good fucking. And I welcome his searching fingers into my wet cunt.

Yes, the tiny voice of caution in my head is screaming I need to end this.

And I will.

"Oooh…" I moan, trembling with carnal want.

But not today, not right now.

Maybe tomorrow.

"Mmmm…"

I gasp and hiss and whimper as my pussy stretches and molds over his cock. I slowly roll my hips until I have him deep inside me, until his hard, thick dick is sloshing in and out of the wetness of my pussy.

Then, again…

"Mmmm…"

Maybe not!

Because the truth is, I love the way his dick throbs inside my pussy, love the way it throbs against my tongue; love the way he tastes and feels. Love the way my body quakes with pleasure every time he fucks into my wetness.

Kyree brushes a kiss over my lips. "Your pussy's so wet." I tighten around his fingers; drawing in a sharp breath, before releasing a guttural groan. "I want you to come all over my dick," he says, his deep longing for me evident in his carnal touch. He pulls his fingers out of me, sucks them into his mouth, then splays his hands under my breasts, cupping them; pads of his thumbs stroking the underside, making my nipples ache.

"Yes, baby, yes…mmmm…you can have this pussy any way you want."

With his long legs, he leans as far back as humanly possible in the backseat of his mother's SUV. "Sit on my dick," he urges softly, huskily.

My nipples tighten as I straddle his thighs, reach between our bodies, then position myself over his dick so that the head is barely inside my slit. This is not the first time I am giving him my pussy without a condom. I want him inside me raw. Want to feel him emptying his balls in me. The deep-seated aching inside me is too much to bear. I need to feel him inside me. Need to feel the curve of his hard, horny dick stroking my walls. Now.

As if reading my thoughts, Kyree grabs my hips and thrusts me down, impaling me onto him. I cry out as his body arches up and he buries himself deep inside me.

"Yes! Yes! Yes! Ohgod, yessss!"

"Aah, shit, baby…your pussy feel's good. Damn. Aaah, yeah…I can get lost in this shit all night. Mmm."

"I know it does, baby," I whisper into his ear. "Your dick feels so good inside of it."

I pick up the pace. Surrender to the sensations. And allow myself to get swept up in the heat.

"Yeah, that's it. Ride this dick." He slaps my ass, then cups each cheek in his hands, squeezing them together each time I come down onto his shaft. He digs his fingertips into my flesh. And I swallow him up from tip to shaft, clenching his dick with swift squeezes of my cunt. My velvety walls wrap around his dick like a heated blanket.

Kyree grunts. "Uh, yeah…daaamn…you got that grown woman's pussy, babe. Aaah, shit's so fuckin' good…"

I smile inwardly as my pussy devours his cock, slathering it with my pussy cream.

"Aah, yeah…give me that juicy pussy…"

His eyes are raging with lust. His fiery hands singe my flesh as he grabs for my breasts. I roll my hips and rise up till his dick almost slips out of me, then sink back down on it. The movements cause Kyree to buck up into me, his head bending and his wet, warm mouth closing around a lust-tightened nipple, then biting into it. Pleasure and pain meld, and my insides melt all over him.

"Yessssss, baby, yessss…ooooh, baby, yessss…"

Kyree groans. "I'm about to bust, baby." He thrusts up into me. His dick rapidly pistons in and out, sloshing out my warm juices. "Aaaah, yeah…uhhh…"

My inner walls shake. "Yes, come for me," I moan at his ear. "Give me all that good dick. Give. It. To. Me. Aaaah…come…mmm…"

"I feel you grabbing my dick…aaah…feels sooo good…aaah…"

Galloping helplessly, the interior of Kyree's mother's SUV fogged and pussy-scented; I am lost to him in pleasure, surrendering to the thrusts of his dick, to the pounding in my walls. I throw my head back. Scream. Clench his thick shaft. And come. Drenching him with cream.

"You ready for this nut?"

"Yes, yes, yes…"

"Give it to me. Mmm. Come inside my pussy." I continue rocking my hips down on his shaft, roll up it, then slam down hard onto it. The thought of him planting his heated seeds inside of me, pushes me over the edge, and has me reeling into another climax.

It's wrong. I know it is.

But the thrill of it all pushes me over the edge. I am coming again. Soaking him. He fucks me with all his might. "Aaah, aaah, aaaah, aaah. Here it comes, baby. Aaah, aaaah…" And seconds later, Kyree roars over and over as scorching come erupts inside of me, coating my walls.

With ragged breaths, we both shudder and kiss hungrily, clinging onto the each other as he empties the last drop of his seed into me.

Bodies spent. I am dazed as we continue kissing and softly riding the wave, thrusting through heat and come, stirring into our mixed orgasms.

I know it's gotten late. Real late. And I should be scrambling out of his arms, but here I am. Still straddled over his lap in his mother's truck, my cum-soaked folds still pulsing for more.

I kiss him one last time before saying, "I better go."

He stares into my eyes, holding me down onto him by the waist. "Nah. Not yet. Feel that?"

I swallow. "Yes," I rasp as his dick begins to swell inside of me again. "Oh, yes. I feel it."

His lips curl into a seductive grin. "Good. That's what you do to me." He pulls me into him by the neck, kisses me on the lips again. "I want some more of you. I *need* some more."

His desire-soaked mouth pressed against mine, tongues caressing, the kiss causes me to momentarily forget that I have a husband at home; that I am old enough to be this boy's mother. That he is my son's best friend.

Clit throbbing, I let out a soft moan, feeling his dick stir and come alive inside of me. And now those things that weigh heavy on my mind are no longer important as I say, "Then take all you need."

"You sure?"

Heartbeat pounding in my ears, I nod. "Yes. It's yours for the taking."

Kyree accepts my invitation. The palms of his hands rub over my ass, caressing and pulling my cheeks open until my pussy is spread wide as he moves himself up into me. His curved dick brushes over my uterus, while sweeping over my G-spot. And just that quick, I am shutting my eyes, biting into my lips, giving into rippling pleasure cascading over my trembling body.

"I wanna fuck you in the ass."

"Uhhh…oooh…"

"You gonna let me get in that ass, huh…?"

Fire blazes through my veins at the thought of feeling him stretching my ass open. He'll be my first; and, most likely, my only.

"Yes. Yes. Yes."

With each thrust, his curved dick grazes my most sensitive spot, hitting every angle of my pussy. Again and again, he nudges me closer to the edge of another orgasm. Oh, God, he feels so good.

"Mmmm..."

"Play with your clit," he whispers, his warm breath fanning over my face.

Chest rising and falling, I reach between my legs, and sweep shaky fingers over my clit. I gasp for air as pleasure swells and grows inside of me. Deeper, faster, wetter, hotter, he's pushing me over into a black abyss so deep...

Squeezing, pulsing, squeezing, pulsing, the tidal wave of arousal rushes over me so quickly that I can't breathe, can't think. I am lost inside a bubble of aching want and need, of lust-induced desperation. There's no denying it. Kyree has me turned out. And this wet pussy's gone wild for his young hard dick.

I squeeze my eyes.

Allow the swell of my own desires to take control. And surrender to the ecstasy.

All Three Holes

ONE

"Aaaah, shit, baby…oh yeah, oh yeah, oh yeah…Goddamn, this pussy's so good. I'm getting ready to bust, baby. Aaaaah, shit…oooooh, yeeeeeeah…!"

Lord God, why? I think, rolling my eyes up in my head.

The headboard slaps loud and frantic up against the wall as Roosevelt pounds away, his thick ten-inches deliciously stretching my pussy.

Too bad I won't get a chance to enjoy it for long.

Aside from the fact that Roosevelt is grunting and growling and has kindly announced his looming release, I can tell by the swell of his dick that he's nearing the end of his rope. I turn my head and glance over at the digital clock on the nightstand. Eight minutes in.

Oooh, this quick-nut motherfucker's dick feels so good in my pussy.

But I'm so goddamn disgusted.

Disgusted that I can't even enjoy the wet sounds of my pussy for much longer, the clickety-click-click noises that shamelessly turn me on, because Roosevelt will soon rob me of its hypnotic melody.

Goddamn him.

Big dick. Big loads. But, sadly, he's a waste of a good fuck.

Yes, my man's a Godforsaken minuteman, figuratively speaking that is. I mean. He doesn't actually come in two pumps and a hump. But most times it feels like it.

The longest he's been able to hold out has been twenty minutes. No. Wait. Twenty-three minutes and forty-seven seconds. I know, because I timed it.

Like I always do.

And, yet, he seems to think that because he has a big dick that this is acceptable. That somehow this—him pounding away for under twenty minutes—is him beating the pussy up.

No goddamn it.

Beating this pussy up is leaving me feeling sore and raw. It's fucking me until I am babbling and slurring and tears are springing from my eyes, and I am seeing stars. It's having my pussy weep and cry out. It's having me walking with a limp, feeling the pounding throb of a dick days after it's been pulled out.

Oh, my man might stroke it up and stir the juices, but he damn sure hasn't beaten shit up in years. And I don't know when was the last time I've tapped out, with him, anyway.

Hell, I do know. In the beginning of our relationship, when he used to fuck me like I stole something from him, when he'd gut this pussy and have me howling like a wounded wolf, begging him to stop. Back when he'd have me running from the dick.

Pussy sore from a long fucking, throat sore from crying out, Roosevelt used to serve me the dick like it was nobody's business.

But now?

Mmph.

Twenty minutes of reckless, disrespectful pounding and then it's over.

And I'm left with a soppy-wet pussy still clenching for more dick.

"Uhhh, oooooh, shit...aaah, Roosevelt, baby...this dick is so good..."

Well, shit. It is. That's one thing I can't lie about. The dick. Is. Goddamn. Good.

Sadly, only for a very short period of time…

"Lord, God…ooh shit, oooh, shit…uhh…please, baby, don't!"

He's about to gyp me of a good fuck. My pussy needs more. Goddamn him!

I swear I don't want to kick Roosevelt's back in. I love him. Lord knows I do. Shit. You'd have to love his ass in order to put up with this level of disrespect. Yes. You heard me right. Disrespect.

He disrespects my pussy every time he pushes the head of his dick inside me, inches himself in, stretching my pussy and getting it all wet and juicy, then nutting in a roaring growl long before I do.

Yes, he licks my clit and tongues my kitty fabulously. And trust me when I tell you. I love listening to him lick my pussy. The sounds of his warm velvety tongue lovingly lapping into my wetness are always so erotic. They send me over the edge, having me clawing at the sheets, coming hard, and begging for the dick.

And he gives it to me.

The dick.

Thick and ribbed with veins.

Because that's what my pussy craves, that's what my body aches for. Dick.

Big juicy dick, like Roosevelt's!

But, uh, all I can expect from him, on a good day/night, is a maximum of twenty-three-maybe twenty-five goddamn minutes of hard dick.

It's so disrespectful for him to do my pussy like this. Slight me the dick. Leave my pussy stretched open and greedy and needy for a good long, hard fucking.

Still, I love him. Yes, yes, yes, I do. Even though he typically can't handle the heat more than fifteen minutes, on most days.

He says it's only when I talk dirty. Only when I moan for him to *fuck me* that he loses focus and can't hold out.

So what am I supposed to do? Lay still and keep quiet like some muted stroke victim, just so he can fuck me a few extra minutes longer?

Oh, no, boo. I don't think so!

I'm a shit talker.

I'm a shaker and mover.

I'm a hip roller and a pelvis thruster.

I'm an on-all-fours kind of woman who loves throwing my ass up on the dick, clapping my ass cheeks, while having my hair pulled and my head yanked back as I talk a bunch of shit. I love throwing my legs up over a set of broad shoulders, looking my lover in his eyes, clenching my pussy around the dick, or having my nipples licked by a wet tongue and grazed with a set of teeth, while I'm being choked and fucked.

So, there is no damn way I'm able to simply lay here and let Roosevelt pound my wet pussy with his big, hard dick and I not cry out and tell him to…*fuck me.*

But, because I love him so, I allow him to hold onto the lie. The lie that that's the reason he prematurely coats my insides with his thick cream every time he gets up inside my wet heat.

I know I got that good-good. And most of the men in my past have also struggled to hold on to their man juice, like Roosevelt, when I spread open my pretty kitty lips and welcome them into paradise. And don't let me get up on my knees and give it to them from the back, using my walls to suck them into my pussy, milking them, while this ass claps around their dicks.

Mmmph.

So I get it.

This pussy is certifiable.

Still…that doesn't mean I have to like these fast fucks Roosevelt dishes out.

And it doesn't mean that I'm satisfied with the outcome—a quick nut, because I'm not. I am tired of being let down. Tired of having to wait for him to recharge before he can go another round. What am I supposed to do while he's taking his power nap, snoring and drooling, like some well-fed pooch, while my cunt is left wet and agitated?

Play in it?

Mmph.

I want to be fucked long and hard, whenever, wherever.

I want Roosevelt to exercise goddamn nut control!

And this feeling of being sexually unfulfilled is…

"Oooh, ooh, ahhh…that's it, baby. Ooh, yesss…" Roosevelt hits my spot, and a loud moan rips from the back of my throat.

It's goddamn sinful for a man—*my man*, to have all this big, thick dick and not be able to give me at least thirty minutes of pussy-pounding, toe-curling pleasure.

And to make matters worse, egotism keeps Roosevelt from using the vibrating cock ring I bought him two Christmases ago. Even after I told him the benefits of wearing one, this damn man still won't wear it.

His excuse?

His balls are too big.

All I could do is give him a blank goddamn stare.

And, that's not the rest of it. Roosevelt's pride forbids him from even trying any of the stay-hard maximum-strength climax control gels I've bought over the years to prolong his ejaculations.

Are you kidding me?

He says he doesn't need that shit.

Yeah, okay. More lies.

A few times I seriously considered applying some of that Benzocaine inside my kitty hole on the sly, but the thought of having my pussy numb made me reconsider. All I kept thinking was, "dead cunt weeping."

In my mind's eye, all I saw was my pussy lips drooping and drooling, like I do when I'm at the dentist getting my teeth worked on.

No, God, no!

A numb, wet pussy is *not* it for me.

Soooooo…I suffer in silence.

Roosevelt claims that before he got with me he could fuck all night. Uh, okay. I'm still waiting for him to make me a believer. But, okay. That's what he says. So I let him run with it. Truth is, I don't know what it was like with him in the sheets when he was fucking them skinny bitches. I only know what it's like now. And, after five years of being together, you'd think he'd finally master how to handle this fat pussy.

But, nope!

If I get on top and ride him, it's a wrap. If I give him the back shot…oh, it's definitely lights out. Forget it. Ten minutes in, and he's splattering the inside of my guts.

I'm starting to think that maybe these big bouncy titties, and these thick hips, and this big, juicy ass, and this wet pussy are too much for him.

No, wait…I *know* they are.

Lolita Singleton is too hot to handle, boo. Okay?

Shit. I know I'm a bad, full-figured bitch with a wet, juicy pussy.

Hell, I'd fuck the shit out of me, if I could.

And probably nut fast, too, I muse.

But I'd at least want to try to extend my performance. Shit. Roosevelt isn't even forty yet and he's suffering from premature ejaculation, by my own definition, of course. Maybe it isn't that premature, but it's still an inconvenience. And puts a hardship on my throbbing cunt.

I told Roosevelt he should start doing some pelvic exercises to get this situation under control.

"Like what?" he asked suspiciously.

"Kegel exercises," I calmly stated.

He just laughed.

I gave him another one of my blank stares, thinking, "Nigga, there's nothing funny about you half-fucking me, leaving my pussy growling with hunger!"

Hell, I even bought a book on Tantric techniques. Told him it would help deepen our connection. And help maximize our pleasure. Code for: help keep your dick in my pussy longer. But Roosevelt, bless his heart, just wasn't able to connect the dots. So, as usual, I let it go. I know I have a good man. So, of course, I'd never make him feel any less of a man. I'd never want him to feel inadequate. All I could do, all I ever do, is gently encourage him to give it some thought, for us.

I let him know Kegel exercises aren't only for women; that men can benefit from them too, that many need to, like him.

But, being the stubborn man he is, he doesn't see his quick spraying of his man milk as a sexual problem, the way I do. So without, making him feel emasculated, I keep encouraging, keep nudging, keep hoping…that one day, soon, he gets it.

I'm still waiting…

Roosevelt grunts, pulling me out of my reverie. His dick goes in deep, then swiftly glides up and out of me, grazing my clitoris as he does. He plunges back in.

I swallow a scream.

My eyes roll back in my head.

Please don't come quick…

"Slow down, baby…*please*…ooh…"

He bites into my neck, causing me to cry out. "Yes, God, yessss!"

He grunts against my flesh. "God can't help you now, baby. Motherfuckin' good pussy…aaah, shit!"

He grabs my face and smashes his lips against mine. Tongue and teeth and succulent lips entice me. Seduce me. His dick hits my spot again, and I groan into his mouth.

Yes, the dick is good. Ooh, God, yes. I won't ever lie on how good it is. The sweet burn that stretches all through my canal, sweeping over my cervix.

But, but, oh, God…

I give in to his urging need. Give in to the rapid thrusts of his dick. "Give it to me, daddy," I say, grabbing his ass and digging my nails into his flesh.

"So fucking wet," he murmurs.

I grunt in spite of myself. His delicious strokes overheat my cunt. "Mmm-hmm. Yes, wet for you. Fuck me. Fuck this pussy…"

"Here it comes, baby. It's coming, coming…shitgoddamn…"

"No, no, wait…please, baby…not yet…"

"It's too late, baby. Pussy too, aah, good…"

Roosevelt's dick swells thicker. "Can't hold out…"

"Aaah, aaah, aaah…"

Lord, God, I beg of you…

In spite of my dismay that Roosevelt's about to fill my cunt with his heated seeds, my pussy clings to his dick, gripping his shaft. Oh yes, oh yes, oh yes, it feels so good. But I'm not ready for it to end. Not yet. No, no, no.

He pulls out, then slams back in, deep. One hard thrust after another. And another. And another. He's fucking me hard and fast.

"Please, baby…slow down," I beg, my body trembling under the weight of his thrusts. "Not yet. Please, please…ooh, ooh, not yet, baby…God, no…uhhh…"

My moans, my quaking pussy, defy what's in my thudding heart, what's stirring in my swooning head. The aching need for more than what Roosevelt is capable of giving...

All I want, all I ever want.

Carnal touch.

Mouth, tongue, dick.

Wet licks.

Deep strokes.

Long-lasting dick.

Roosevelt's body shudders.

My pussy floods with warmth and thick cream.

And all I can think is, this is a goddamn tragedy!

TWO

"Ooooh, you scandalous *bitch*," my sister Mecca says, leaning in, propping her elbows up on the table. "How the heck are you going to sneak off to a romantic island and *not* take your man?"

Over lunch, I shared with Mecca that I've planned a trip to St. Lucia next week. A trip I booked spur of the moment, after getting an email alert for last-minute deals flying out of LaGuardia Airport to Caribbean destinations.

I chose St. Lucia.

Chose to live on the edge a little.

Alone.

And what happens in St. Lucia stays in St. Lucia.

I shrug, reaching for my glass of wine. "Easy. I booked the flight. Then told Roosevelt I was going away with a few of my sorors for the weekend."

"And he was okay with that?"

"Of course he was."

She tosses her weave, swiping her bang from out of her eye. "Well, why didn't I get an invite, heifer?"

"Because I don't want your happily married ass becoming an accomplice to anything I may or may not do while I'm soaking in the sunshine, and the sights."

"An *accomplice?*" She laughs. "Oh, please. To what?"

"To whatever the universe and the gods have in store for me. You do remember what happened to Stella, don't you?"

She smacks her lips together. "Uh-huh. And you see what happened to that old, thirsty bitch."

I laugh. "Well, I ain't old. And I ain't thirsty."

"Well, bitch, what groove are you trying to get back then? Wait." She gives me a hard stare, raising her brow. "Is there trouble in paradise? Things with you and Roosevelt are good, right?"

"Yes, yes…of course. Things are great with us."

In dramatic form, she collapses back in her seat, placing a hand over her heart. "Whew. That's good to know. My heart couldn't handle the two of you being on the outs. The way Roosevelt looks at you, with so much love." She shakes her head. "Mmph."

"Girl, you know I know. That man loves me endlessly."

"Uh-huh, I know he does, which is why I'm still struggling to understand *why* you are going to St. Lucia. *Alone*. Not unless…?"

I raise a brow. "Not unless what?"

She shakes her head. "No. Never mind."

I smirk. "No, say it."

She tilts her head, narrowing her eyes. "Oooh, wait one goddamn minute. Say it ain't so, slut? You're whisking off to St. Lucia to be with a sidepiece, aren't you?"

I laugh. "No, girl, no. There is no sidepiece. Trust."

And that's the God honest truth. In the six years I've been with Roosevelt, I've never fucked anyone other than him more than once. It's always a one-night stand. No names given. No numbers exchanged. And I've only cheated on him twice, well, okay…three times. But the last time didn't really count. All he did was eat my pussy and licked my ass until my eyes crossed.

There was no penetration, and I didn't suck him, although I wanted to lick him from his shaft to the tip. Yes, God! I wanted my mouth stuffed with his dick, badly. But, he wasn't interested in being sucked, just devouring my cunt and my ass with his luscious lips and slick tongue.

"Lies," Mecca hisses.

I hold my hand up. "I swear to you, girl; hand to God. There's no sidepiece, no jump-off, nothing."

She tilts her head. "Uh-huh. Speaking of sidepieces, have you ever…?"

I give her an incredulous look. *"What,* cheated on Roosevelt?"

"Yeah. And don't lie."

As close as Mecca and I are, there are still some things that are not up for discussion, my occasional indiscretions being one of them. As much as I trust my sister, sharing with her how angry my pussy gets, at how disgruntled it is, with Roosevelt's lack of nut control, is a no-no. Those kind of personal details are not something you share with anyone, especially about your man. A one-night stand, yes. You gossip about that, if you must. But anything pertaining to sex with a significant other is off limits.

Sister or not, discussing what my man does or doesn't do in the sheets is not up for review, or critique. I learned a long time ago, what's not good for one bitch is always good for two others.

And fast-nut or not, Roosevelt's big-dicked ass might come quicker than I'd like, but he's my goddamn quick nut. And I'll be damned if I open the door to let another bitch waltz in to get a taste, or a ride up on that.

I look Mecca dead in her face and say, "Never. Have *you?*"

She frowns. "What, *cheated* on Ricky? Girl, no, I don't play them kinda bed games. As a matter of fact, change that to *hell no.* As much as Ricky does for me, I wish the hell I would. There's not a dick big enough to ever get me to spread open my legs to fuck over what I have at home." She shakes her head. "Oh, no, boo-boo.

That man's the love of my life. There's not another out here who can ever hold a candle to him."

I smile knowingly.

Aside from being damn good to her, Ricky's the only man she's ever been with. They were high school sweethearts, then college lovers, and now…married with three kids.

The perfect love story.

She places her wineglass to her lips, and takes a quick sip. "I can't believe you'd ask me some mess like that. Girl, please."

I shrug. "Well, you asked me, so I thought I'd return the favor."

She sucks her teeth. "Bitch, but I'm not the one trolling off to an island…*alone*; remember?"

I wave a dismissive hand. "Girl, stop. All it is is a quick getaway for a little rest and relaxation. That's it."

She eyes me. Twists her lips. "Mm-hmm. Okay, Stella. And out of all the places to go for a little R and R, you just happen to choose a Caribbean island instead of a quaint little Bed and Breakfast somewhere up in the mountains here, in Jersey?"

I grin. "What can I say, I wanted some Caribbean heat."

"Yeah, okay. Heat my ass. You want trouble, bitch."

I laugh. "Lies! Girl, you're talking like I'm going down there to fornicate or something."

She twists her lips. "Mm-hmm. Whatever. Toss around big words if you want. Let's see what happens when you find your ass tossed up on one of those big island dicks. Then what?"

"Then nothing," I say, flicking imaginary lint from my blouse. "I'm not going down there to be tossed up on any island dick, so get your mind out of the gutter."

Well, that's partially true. I mean, subconsciously, yes, I was still agitated with Roosevelt for not serving me up another hard round of dick right on the spot when I booked my flight.

And, yes, the thought of a sweaty romp in the sheets with some Zulu warrior had crossed my mind. But I entertained the idea only for a second. Okay, okay…for a few minutes. Not more than that.

But, flying out there for the sole purpose of getting fucked was, *is*, not my intention.

Or, subconsciously, is it?

No, no, of course not. I've already admitted I've cheated on Roosevelt a few times. So, what's to stop me from doing it again?

Nothing.

But that's not my intention.

"Okay, I'll take that," Mecca says, swiping her bangs over her forehead. "But, I'm going to ask you this one more time, then I'm moving on. You're going *alone?*"

I smile, easing my lips to the mouth of my glass, then taking a slow, deliberate sip; purposefully making her wait for my response. Although I am three years her senior, Mecca seems to think she's the eldest. And I don't mind letting her wear that crown. It fits her well.

I set my glass down. Finally give her the answer she's waiting for. "Yesssss, Mecca. I already told you. I'm going alone."

She rolls her eyes. "Okay. Refresh my memory, again. You're going waaaay out to St. Lucia, *alone*, to do *what* exactly?"

I laugh. "So much for moving on. Geesh. I already told you. To relax. To soak in the sun, and tan."

"Uh, huh. And get *fucked*. Don't do me, boo. What bitch you know flying to a Caribbean island alone, where there are a bunch of horny, big-dick islanders eager to please, unless she's got some hard dick already over there on speed dial, or she's in search for some?"

I give her a dismissive wave. "You're watching too much late-night television. For the umpteenth time, there's *no* other hard dick besides Roosevelt's."

She smacks her lips. "Okay, if you say so. Annnnnd, tell me again, for the third time before I really move on this time. Why is it you're going alone?"

I can't help but laugh at her ass. She can't help herself. Nosey-ass. "Girl, stop. You know I've been saying I needed a getaway for months now."

She sucks her teeth. "Uh, yeah, with your man, or *me*. Not whisking off to some spicy island alone, where God knows what could happen to you."

"I'm not *whisking off*, as you say, anywhere. I'm taking a well-needed getaway. Period. Hell. I deserve it. The way things have been at work the last several months, it's a surprise I haven't become a pill-popping junkie and alcoholic, messing with those petty bitches."

Mecca grunts. "Mmmph. I don't know how you do it, girl, putting up with them messy bitches. I told you what to do. Slide your hand up in one of them bitch's scalps, and yank her damn tracks out. That'll stop them bitches from fucking with you. Rip a bitch's edges out and that'll shut her up and sit her ass down real quick."

I laugh. "Uh-uh. Girl, I can't with you. And have me standing in a police lineup. Not. I'm not even about to fuck up my pension behind some catty-ass women who don't know how to work in a so-called professional environment."

Mecca rolls her eyes. "That's what the county gets for hiring them back-to-work bitches. Them hoes done got a little county job and some benefits, and now they think they're stars."

I continue laughing. "A damn mess."

"Uh-huh. Now back to your messy ass," she says. "Why didn't you tell Roosevelt what your plans were instead of *lying* to him?"

This bitch...

"Because I didn't want him to go," I say defensively, tilting my head. "That's why. And he would have wanted to go if I told him."

I take a sip from my wineglass.

She bats her lashes. "Uh, yeah. You think? Of course he'd want to go. It's a Caribbean island for *lovers*. And single hoes."

I cough, almost choking on my drink. "Ooh, you dead wrong for that."

She chuckles. "But you know I'm right."

"Whatever. Bottom line, I wanted to go it alone. And I am. Besides, it works out perfect since Roosevelt's flying out to Atlanta to meet up with a few of his frat brothers for the weekend."

She raises her brow. "Oh, so the both of you are gonna be off tricking, I see."

I laugh. "It's Morehouse's homecoming. You know he goes every year."

"Yeah, but your hot-ass isn't sneaking off to some romantic island every year for some salacious rendezvous, either."

I throw my head back, and laugh. "Girl, you're crazy. There's no rendezvous. And there's nothing salacious about wanting to travel to an island, alone."

She rolls her eyes. "Whatever. Smells like trouble to me."

I smile coyly. "I'm not looking for trouble."

She twists her lips. "Mm-hmm. Trouble might be looking for *you*."

I grin, wiggling my eyebrows. "Which is exactly why I didn't want you to go. What you don't know, or see, can't implicate you."

She grabs her napkin from off her lap and tosses it at me. "Bitch, don't."

I laugh. "Mecca, girl, you know I'm only teasing. I love Roosevelt," I say honestly. "I'd never do anything purposefully to hurt him, or us." *Well, not if I can get away with it, anyway. What he doesn't know can't hurt him.* "Besides, I know how much you adore him. Even if trouble did find me there, your ass would probably tell on me."

She flicks a dismissive wave at me. "Girl, not on your life. Yes, I do adore Roosevelt. But you're my sister. I'd curse you the hell out for being a trifling-ass ho, before I'd ever snitch on you, boo. That's what sisters do."

I smile. "Awww, I love you, too."

"True." She reaches over and grabs my hand. "I know you do. But, seriously, Lita," she says, calling me by my nickname as she lifts her glass to her lips. "I think you snatched up one of the good ones, girl."

"I know I did," I say thoughtfully, raising my glass as well. "He's my everything."

Our glasses clink.

"Then whatever you do," Mecca says, eyeing me. "Don't fuck him over."

THREE

"So, you got everything, baby?" Roosevelt says, grabbing my suitcase and carry-on as I step out of our bathroom; wearing a short denim skirt and a white off-the-shoulder blouse that crisscrosses in the front with a pair of orange pumps.

"Yes," I say, standing in front of the full-length mirror, then screwing on the backs to my diamond studs.

I can feel Roosevelt's eyes on me as I fasten my earrings in.

I pretend not to see him as he stands there, watching, as I reach for my orange lipstick, then glide a coat over my lips, followed by a coat of lip gloss to make 'em pop, and look real juicy.

Smiling, I watch Roosevelt, eyeing me. His gaze slides up my toned calves, up the back of my smooth, shiny thighs, then lock on my ass. I stare back at him in the mirror as he takes in the way my skirt hugs my hips.

I slowly turn to face him. Hand on hip, head tilted, grinning. "You see something you like?"

He licks his lips.

"Aww, fuck that." He drops my bags. "You looking too fucking sexy, with ya fine-ass, baby. I need to get in that pussy one more time before we leave."

He stalks over toward me; his dick already stretching down his left thigh.

"Oh, no," I say, shaking my head, laughter in my throat. "You're not about to have me smearing my lipstick, or missing my flight."

Lies, bitch, lies! You know damn well giving him some pussy, won't take long. I glance at the time. I have three hours before departure. *You can give him another taste, and still have more than enough time to check-in, go through security, and grab a double chocolate Frappuccino from Starbucks.*

He reaches for me, and I quickly sidestep, smiling. "Nope. No pussy. Now go take my bags downstairs."

He sucks his teeth, unbuckling his belt. "Yeah, you'se a fucking lie." He unzips his zipper. "My dick is hard." He pulls his jeans down over his hips, then his boxers. "We fucking, baby. So you might as well grab the dresser and bend over, or get up on them knees 'cause there ain't no way you leaving up out of here to fly across the ocean to cackle with your girls on some tropical island for three days, *and* think I'm not getting up in that ass."

His long, thick dick is curved upward, and so rigid that it barely moves as he stalks toward me with a single-minded determination. To fuck.

I laugh, dancing around the room to keep a distance between us. "I'm serious, baby. No. I'm already showered."

"So. I'm not tryna hear that. Shower again. Fuck it. I'll lick you clean."

I swallow. "Ooh, see now you're playing dirty," I say, shaking my head. Roosevelt knows how much I love watching him tongue my pussy clean after he's shot a hot load inside it.

He hasn't tongued his cream out of me in a long while. And now this six-two, chocolate motherfucker is standing here in his size thirteen boots, talking about licking my pussy clean. Oh, this motherfucker is up to something. And I'll bet these six hundred-dollar pumps that it's something no goddamn good!

I tilt my head. Narrow my eyes. Throw a hand up on my hip. "Who you going to Atlanta with?"

He frowns. "What?"

"You heard me? Who the fuck are you going to Atlanta with?"

"Yo, are you fucking kidding me right now? I'm tryna get some pussy, and you asking me some shit like that. You know who I'm going with. The same muhfuckas I go with every year. Who the fuck you going on this retreat with?"

I buck my eyes. "Oh, don't turn this on me, nigga. You haven't licked my pussy out in months; now all of a sudden you wanna clean your nut out. Sounds to me like you got some bitch on hold and your guilt is getting to you."

He scowls. "Yo, get off that dumb shit. There's no one on hold, but you. Now are you giving me some pussy or what?"

I suck my teeth. "I'm telling you now, Roosevelt. Go out there and fuck some other bitch if you want, and I'm gonna go upside your goddamn head."

He laughs. "Yeah, keep talking shit. How 'bout to go upside this dick. The only person I'm giving this to is *you*." He fists his cock, stroking it. "See this hard dick…?"

I glance down at his moving hand. The crown of his dick is trickling with wet, sticky nectar.

"It's all you, baby. Now take them motherfucking clothes off."

Just that quick I forget that I'm trying to be pissed and fight to keep from licking my lips. I keep staring him down. Roosevelt knows I won't deny him pussy. And him standing here naked isn't helping none, neither is the Acqua di Parma cologne he is wearing.

Still, in his heated attempt at seducing me, I don't budge. "I gave you some pussy earlier."

"*And?* He frowns. "Your point? My dick is hard now. And I want some more. What, you saving it for some other motherfucker?"

I roll my eyes. Shift my weight from one foot to the other. "Nigga, please. Take me to the airport, please."

"Yeah, aiight. You not leaving up outta here until we've finished fucking. So stop playing. You wasting time."

My pussy clenches as he prowls closer. I take a step back, then another.

"We're not going anywhere until you take care of this dick." He flicks his wrist up, glances at his watch. "The clock's ticking. Hurry up. You're gonna miss your flight."

See. This is the Roosevelt I fell in love with—the pussy-hungry Roosevelt with the rock-hard dick who's always ready to fuck on the spot.

But, right now, as tempting as the offer is, I will not be side-tracked. Well, I don't want to be. Oh, no. No, no, no. The only thing on my mind is getting to the airport, then getting on flight 1491 headed to my weekend rendezvous.

But Roosevelt doesn't care. His hard dick, and getting release, is all he is concerned with. So to keep him happy and speed this along, I acquiesce. Tell him I'll give him some head, a quick suck to soothe his balls.

The thought of Roosevelt's hard dick hitting the back of my throat makes my mouth water, and my cunt juice. It's been a long time since I've actually sucked a nut out of him. Believe it or not, he doesn't particularly care for having his dick sucked, but he lets me because he knows it's what I love doing.

Sucking him.

Licking him.

Gulping him down.

I swallow in anticipation.

Roosevelt's eyes darken with desire, as he fists his dick again. "Fuck that. You can suck this dick. But that's not what I want. I want pussy."

He closes the space between us. And before I can step away and resist him, he is up on me, his hands everywhere. His fingers cleverly sliding up my skirt, easing over the lace of my panties.

I'm wet.

I'm always wet.

Roosevelt knows this.

He knows it doesn't take much for my pussy to moisten.

But, today, I'm not sure if my cunt is wet because I'm sneaking off to an island by myself, with the possibility of scandalous fucking going on while I'm there. Or if it's because seeing Roosevelt standing here, balls hanging low, dickhead glistening with precum, his hands roaming my body that has my pussy ready to explode.

"You always playing games," he says hoarsely, his voice thick with lust. "Pussy all wet for daddy."

"I'm not playing games," I say, feeling my cunt coiling in heat. I smirk. "Maybe I want you to beg for it."

"Oh, that's what you want? Me to beg for what's already mine?"

He reaches under my panties with his thumbs. Pulls at my lips. Goads a moan from me. "Yes. Beg for it."

He pinches my clit over the silk fabric, and my body shakes, almost sending me into an orgasmic fit.

"Fuck that. I ain't begging for shit," he rasps. "Not today. Turn around and let me get up in this shit from the back."

"No," I say low and soft, almost pleading as I reach for his heavy dick. He doesn't stop me. "Let me taste this." I drop to my knees, looking up at him. "I want this big, juicy dick in my throat." I stick my tongue out. Flick it over his dickhead. Heat swells in his eyes as my tongue swipes over his slit, gathering the strand of precum from its tip.

A part of me wants to speed-suck him so that he'll spill his seeds and slump over real quick. Then there's the dick-sucking whore in me who wants to savor his dick slow and sweet. But since time is of the essence, I settle on sucking him into my mouth, swift and furiously. I cup his balls and give his dick a good washing.

He grunts in pleasure, placing his hands up on his hips. I suck him deep, pulling back every so often to run my gloss-painted lips up and down the side of his shaft, streaking it with lipstick. I lick up and down it, then suck it back into my mouth, suctioning out more precum.

"You want me to fuck that pretty mouth, huh, baby?"

I grunt in answer.

His dick slides in and out, stretching my lips open, its head hitting the back of my throat, plugging my airway. Spit splashes out of my mouth.

"Nice wet mouth. Yeah, shit."

Roosevelt rocks his hips in a sensuous rhythm. *"Aaah, shiiiit!"* he groans, rolling his hips sharply, filling my mouth and throat with dick.

I'm trembling with arousal, my lust-drenched cunt, soaking my panties. My mind reels back and forth from fantasies of being fucked by some hunky island dick to the big, thick dick already in my mouth.

God, I love this man. I swear I do. But my pussy is still so god-damn angry with him. He always does this shit to me. Gets me all worked up, stirs my pussy up real good, teases me with rippling strokes, takes me right to the edge, then leaves me goddamn hanging.

He does this to me. Forces me to sneak off and let other men do dirty things to my pussy. I know I wouldn't creep if he dicked me longer, gave me longer strokes, if he had more control of his nut.

I blame him for this.

My cheating.

Having me love this big, beautiful dick, but hating it at the same time.

Goddamn him!

Goddamn me!

"Aaah, shit. Goddamn, this mouth feels good. But I'm tryna fuck. Let me get in that pussy."

I grunt. Grab his balls. And keep sucking. My only mission is to get him to nut, to coat my throat and tongue with his milk, then get me the hell to the airport. Pronto.

But, of course, this motherfucking man has other plans. Ones that include hiking up my skirt, yanking my panties to the side, messing up my hair, and gutting my pussy from the front, the back, and any other way he damn well pleases.

He pulls me up from off my knees, and spins me around, man-handles me the way he used to, when we used to fuck morning, noon, and night.

Roosevelt's dominance is a delicious treat, but I still can't help wondering what's gotten into him. Why now?

Why all the sudden aggression?

And hungry need?

If I didn't know any better, I'd think he thought I had intentions of letting someone else gut this pussy. But I've never given him any reason to think such, so I quickly shake that ridiculous notion from my head. I know I treat my man right. And makes sure he's handled right. Every night. I'm not like some of them silly bitches out there. I take care of my man. Pussy and a hot meal every night when he steps through the door are two things my man's never denied.

I don't give a damn how pissed I am. He gets fed and fucked. Then, when the urge hits, when the need becomes too overwhelming, I go out and do me.

"Bend that motherfucking sexy ass over, baby," Roosevelt says, smacking my ass, making it shake. "Let me plunge this dick into that fat-ass pussy."

Before I can plant the palm of my hands down on the dresser good to brace myself, my skirt is already up over my hips, and Roosevelt is yanking my panties to the side, pressing the tip of his dick up against the mouth of my pussy.

He pulls open my cheeks, lunges forward and sinks his dick in in one deep thrust. I cry out. Cuss him under my breath for taking my pussy, for being so big. For making me feel so goddamn guilty for wanting more.

I start moaning like a wild animal. "Fuck me, goddammit! Yes, yes, yes. Big-dick bastard! Oooh, give me that big dick, baby. Ooh, ooh, ooh…"

Roosevelt slams into me, his dick stretching and grazing and knocking the bottom of my pussy.

My knees buckle. My arms stretch out and grip the edges of the dresser, slamming my ass back onto him. "Harder, baby, harder… Lord, God, yes…yes, yes…!"

I drag my nails over the dresser. Arch into the heat.

Roosevelt grunts. "You giving my pussy out to some other motherfucker, huh?"

Bam, bam, bam…

He pounds away.

"Lord, God, no, no no…uh, ooh…yes…"

Smack!

His hand cracks across my ass again, harder. *"Yes,* what? You riding some other nigga's dick?"

Bam, bam, bam…

I break out in a sweat as fire roars through me. Roosevelt is fucking into wet flames. He's fucking me as if he knows my dirty secret.

Yes, God, yes. Fuck the sin out of me!

Oooh, the dick is soooo motherfucking good.

With each rapid thrust, Roosevelt pulls the length of his dick all the way out, then slams back in, causing hot air to seep out. My pussy starts making wet sucking sounds.

"Yes, baby, make my pussy fart, baby…yes, yes, yes…"

Roosevelt grunts. "You letting some other motherfucker hit this shit…?"

Whack!

"*Nooooo*," I moan. "No, baby, no. This pussy's all yours. Can't no nigga fuck me like you. Oh, God, yes, baby, yes…goddamn you," I cry out, catching my reflection in the mirror. "My hair looks like shit. Uh…ooh…ah, ah, ah, mmm…you make me sick!"

The palm of his hand cracks across my ass over and over, causing the heat in my pussy to spread.

"Shut the fuck up with that dumb shit. You know you love this dick…"

He slaps my ass again, causing sparks to shoot through me.

"Uh, uh, mmm…yes, I love it. Oooh, shitgoddamnfuck…I love it, I love it, I love it!"

He slaps my ass again, his dick sawing in and out of me, his thrusts knocking me forward, causing the dresser mirror to sway back and forth.

I stare at his reflection in the mirror. Forehead creased. Nose flaring. Bottom lip swelling, his eyes rolling in the back of his head, he's nearing the point of no return.

"No, no, noooo. Don't you fucking come, yet! *Please*. Oh, God, no! Don't—"

"Fuck!" he growls, his dick slicing into warm, wet pleasure. "I told you I'ma bust this nut inside you, then clean you out. Aaah, shit…"

Hearing those words send me spiraling out of control. I come with a primal growl. My uterus shaking, my body shuddering, as

Roosevelt empties himself inside me, coating my walls as wave after wave of pleasure surges over me.

But I want more.

My pussy is still clutching for more.

I keep winding my hips as Roosevelt's dick eases out of me. I attempt to move, but he pushes me forward. "I'm not done," he whispers, pulling open my nut-filled pussy. "I'm ready for my snack."

My cunt clenches as his nut slides out of my slit. His tongue sinks inside and I moan. "Mmmmmmm, yes, baby…lick out your creamy treat."

There's no denying, his tongue strokes are divine. I clap my ass cheeks around his face, allowing him to feast on his, and my, love juices. He covers my pussy with his mouth, tongue inside, then mutters against my creamy cunt to push his nut into my mouth.

A mini-orgasm ripples through me. And, then I come inside his mouth. But before I can catch my breath, Roosevelt is lifting me up off my feet, tossing me up over his shoulder and stalking over toward the bed.

He throws me down on it.

There's a dark hunger in his eyes I haven't seen in a long time. And now I almost start to feel guilty, again, for flying out to St. Lucia without him. Almost.

"Baby, no. My flight…"

"Fuck your flight," he says, positioning himself between my thighs. "Feeding your man comes first."

I am shocked. And turned on. Goddam him!

"Spread them motherfucking legs," he says.

I slowly open my legs. And give him what he wants. Hoping like hell I don't miss my flight. But, as Roosevelt's tongue spirals over my clit, all thoughts of St. Lucia momentarily leave my mind as he wrings another orgasm out of me.

I hold my breath as he licks me with a broad flat stroke. Up and down, he swoops over my pussy with his wet tongue.

And just when I think I can't handle anymore, Roosevelt eases up from between my legs, then in one swift motion, he is on his back and I am being turned around to straddle his face, my simmering juices pooling from my cunt, sliding down my inner thighs. Roosevelt fists his dick. Tells me to sit on his face.

His fingers spread my wet lips.

Then comes his wicked tongue again.

Lord, God, yes!

Roosevelt rapidly fucks me with his tongue, growling into my cunt as his dick explodes, shooting thick ropes of hot, creamy semen into my mouth. My cunt grabs at his tongue as he spears into it.

I drink, gulp, and swallow. I keep swallowing, swallowing; gulping, gulping, gulping.

Every last drop…

FOUR

"YE-EHHHH!"

"Yehhhhhh-Ey!"

Eyes closed.

Lips pursed.

Hair swinging.

Titties jiggling.

Nipples peaked.

Hips swaying.

Ass bouncing.

Hands up over my head, white gold, diamond-crusted bangles clanking, I'm feeling sexy and free.

Fela Kuti's "Teacher Don't Teach Me Nonsense" blares through the speakers, giving me life.

Yes, God.

I hop, skip, shimmy my shoulders. Throw my head back. The music, its melodic beat, is hypnotic, causing my hips to sway, my pelvis to thrust. I feel myself getting caught up in it, like it's moving me from the inside out.

The island of St. Lucia is breathtaking. The people are warm and welcoming. The weather is gorgeous. And the nightlife is full of energy, giving me life.

Although I am still reeling from the shock of being daring enough to hop on a plane and travel across the Atlantic Ocean to vacation alone, I let go of my inhibitions and allow myself to get lost in the moment.

Red-glossed lips, mink-lashed, I am dancing the night away out on the party deck of one of St. Lucia's hotspots. *Serving* them—the locals and tourists, that is—in my skimpy, hip-grabbing white halter-top jumpsuit—underneath, I'm wearing a tiny thong—with a pair of red six-inch Manolo Blahniks.

I know I'm a bad bitch.

My sun-kissed skin is shimmering under the moon.

My hair is laid right.

Yes, Lord. You can't tell me shit.

Flawless.

This big, juicy ass is clapping for the gods.

I toss my head back. Throw my arms up in the air. Glance up at the twinkling stars. Close my eyes. Then slowly open them again, gazing out into the growing crowd.

All eyes are on me as I dish up a full-view of ass, hips, and tits.

A few men whistle and catcall.

Tonight, even if I'm not fucking—*yet*, I am giving them the illusion that I am.

That I am the island whore.

The harlot.

The jezebel.

The dancing thot.

In my mind's eye, all I see are a bunch of naked, hard-bodied men, a slew of hard horny dick.

All for the taking.

Fingers popping, pussy on fire, I'm dancing as if I am a woman with a purpose, to have a good goddamn time. I shake my ass as if I'm a single woman, as if I hadn't been fucked by my man just hours before my flight departed.

I wind down to the floor, then pop my ass cheeks. Bitches had better grab ahold of their men and hold 'em tight. There's a weekend slut on the loose.

"YE-EHHHH!"

"Yehhhhhh-Ey!"

I sway back and forth, lunge forward, shake and roll my hips. Not caring if my breasts spill out. Then I quickly get swept up in the fast, rhythmic beat of "Flatten Riddim" as it vibrates through my body.

I start high-kicking and spinning.

By the time the deejay eases into "Your Loss," a song by a reggae artist I've never heard of, Figaro, the dance floor is crowded, and I've worked up a sweat and a deep thirst for something wet…and refreshing.

"Damn, baby, I love the way you move," a baritone voice floats over the music in back of me. I turn to see who its owner is, looking up and gazing into the eyes of the closet thing to perfection I've seen in a long time.

Lord, God, he's fine.

He's holding a bottle of Piton in his hand.

For a second, I stand here mesmerized, taking in his smooth milk chocolate skin and his Trevor eyes that look like two black onyx stones delicately set in big round orbs, before finally opening my mouth to speak.

"Oh, you haven't seen anything yet," I say sassily. It's a loaded statement, one he quickly picks up on.

He takes a swig of his beer, then licks a set of full lips that causes my clit to pulse.

"Is that so?" he says, waves of desire sizzling off him as his seductive gaze wanders over my body. "Well, I can't wait to see what else that body can do."

A loaded statement filled with invitation.

"If only you knew, boo." I giggle to myself. He follows me back to the bar, telling the bartender to get me whatever I want. I ease up on a barstool and order a rum punch.

Grabbing a few napkins from off the bar, I dab my forehead, then along the back of my neck.

"Looks like you were out there having a real good time."

I smile. "Life's too short not to."

He smiles. "It was fun watching you. You kinda had us all in a trance."

I swivel my chair in his direction, crossing my legs. "Then I've done what I came to do."

He furrows his brow. "Oh, yeah? What was that?"

The bartender slides me my drink. I take a quick sip of the refreshing drink, then set it up on the bar. "To give people something to think about."

He laughs. "Oh, trust me, love. You definitely gave us fellas more than enough to think about. And fantasize about. You definitely knew what you were doing to us."

Now it's my turn to laugh.

The music abruptly stops. A speaker blows out. And the crowd groans in agitation. The deejay in his thick West Indian accent apologizes. Tells everyone to bear with him. People are milling around the deck, talking and laughing and eyeing their prey for the night, while waiting for the music to start again.

Mister Milk Chocolate.

A light breeze rolls off the ocean and blows in, cooling me.

Two drinks later, and it no longer matters that the music is still not back on. I've learned that Mister Milk Chocolate's real name is Evan. He's thirty-eight. A Scorpio. Originally from Brooklyn, New York, but—for the last ten years—has lived in New Haven, Connecticut.

He and some of his frat brothers are here visiting St. Lucia for another one of his frat brother's wedding. He ties the knot tomorrow afternoon. Then he flies back to the States on Sunday. The same day as I am.

I glance at his left hand, ring finger. There is no sign of a ring, or tan line. Not that it matters, or means anything.

Hell, I'm involved. But tonight, I'm out shaking my ass, moving like I'm happily single.

"So what fraternity do you belong to, if you don't mind me asking?"

He flashes a lazy grin. Tells me it's all about that Crimson and Cream.

I laugh. "I should have known. You're too damn fine to be anything else."

He laughs with me. "Many are called…"

"I know, I know," I say, cutting him off. "Few are chosen."

"You got it, love. What you know about that?"

"Oh, I know all about them canes," I say flirtatiously.

"Yeah, but I bet you don't know about the one I'm holding," he says back.

Ping. Incoming text.

I purse my lips. "Uh-huh. Hold that thought." I fish through my clutch for my phone, pulling it out.

When I see *Miss you baby. Hope ur having a good time* from Roosevelt, I almost feel guilty for sitting here with this chocolate Adonis, toying with fantasies of having—what I imagine to be big and thick, judging by the bulge in his white linen shorts—his jumbo-size dick in my wet mouth.

I gaze up at my bar companion. "Excuse me for one sec," I say just as the music starts to play again. I don't give a damn where I'm at, what I'm doing, or who I am doing it with, the one thing I make sure I always do is answer my man's texts and his calls. I don't care if I have a mouthful of dick. I stop mid-suck and respond to my man.

And that's how you keep his mind from wandering, conjuring up crazy shit, like you're probably out cheating on him, even if you are.

The one thing I will never do is, fuck up my home life. Oh, no, boo-boo.

I hold my Samsung up and angle it just so, taking a selfie, then quickly text, *Miss you too, boo. Yes. I'm having a fab time! Wish u were here. Jessica and the girls say hi.* Lies. But I know it's the right thing to say. That I wish he were here.

I chuckle to myself, making a mental note to give my soror Jessica a heads-up when I get back to the States, just in case Roosevelt decides to let curiosity get the best of him and asks her how our little *retreat* was.

The last thing I need is for her looking like a deer caught in headlights, and me scrambling not to get caught in a lie. I haven't told many. But I've dished out my share. Fortunately, I've kept my tracks covered and my lies straight, thus far.

No time for getting sloppy now.

I attach the picture of myself, head tilted, smiling.

Then hit SEND.

Mr. Milk Chocolate grins.

"So, who's that? Your lover?"

I nod. "Yes."

"I should have known a beautiful woman like you would have a man. Where is he? Back at your hotel?"

"No. Atlanta. I traveled light, this time."

He gives me a quizzical look. "And he *trusts* you on a beautiful tropical island, alone?"

Feeling the heat from my drink kicking in, I slowly run the tip of my tongue over my bottom lip. "Of course he does. Why wouldn't he? I've never given him any reason *not* to trust me." *Yeah, bitch, because your slick-ass hasn't gotten caught yet.* "Besides, he doesn't know I've traveled alone."

He laughs, shaking his head. "Wait. Let me get this straight. You're here in all of your sexiness, and your man doesn't even know that you're here?"

I toss my hair. "Oh, he knows I'm here. He just doesn't know I'm here by myself." I take a sip of my drink. "And what he doesn't know won't hurt him."

He grins, flashing a dimpled cheek, left side. Mischief flashes in his eyes. "You don't say?"

I'll admit, as I'm looking at him, my pussy pulses. Heat slowly throbs through my whole body. If opportunity presents itself, I will fuck him. I am sure of it. The moistness gathering in the pit of my cunt assures me of this.

I glance down at the bulge in his shorts again, and imagine myself down on my knees; looking up at him slantways, sucking his dick down into my throat, feeling the tingle of its tip every time my throat muscles contract around it.

I see him coming hard, his dick melting in my mouth, and me sucking him greedily. His dick sucked clean as a fucking whistle.

I swallow.

"So who does your man think you're traveling with?"

I take another slow sip of my drink, rinsing down my sordid thoughts. Then run my fingers through my hair. "He thinks I'm on an all-girls' retreat."

I smile coyly.

"Damn, sounds like somebody needs a spanking for being real naughty," he says, a dark smile crossing his lips.

Lord, God...

"There's nothing naughty about sneaking off for the weekend, alone."

He grins. "And your man allows you these so-called"—he makes quotation marks with his fingers—"all-girls' retreats without question?"

"Yes. Without question." I boldly toss my hair. Then glide my tongue over my lips again. "He knows I'm *always* coming home to him."

His smoldering eyes skim over my body. He gulps down his drink, then leans in, moves his mouth to my ear. "Then forgive me for saying, baby, he's a damn fool. There's no way I'd let all this sweet ass travel anywhere without me."

All this sweet ass?

Jesus, take the wheel!

A blush warms my face as I inhale, and catch a hint of musk off his skin, a mixture of woodsy masculinity and something splashed out of an expensive bottle. But that's nothing compared to the heat suddenly flaring between my thighs.

His boldness is intoxicating. And there's something about it that is pulling me in, has me feeling something new, something exciting and fierce.

My pussy clenches.

He glides a finger up and down my thigh as he speaks. "You're a sexy, beautiful woman, baby. Thick all over." He pulls in his bottom lip. "I bet you're real juicy, too."

Feeling empowered, I toss my hair, and say, "Wouldn't you like to know?"

He grins. "Yeah, I would." His large hand rests on the small of my back. "I can tell that thing is good. Real good. I want a taste."

Shivers dart through me.

I can feel my cunt juice slowly seeping into the seam of my jumper.

Lord, God…goddamn him!

"I bet you're already hot and wet and ready for me. Aren't you?"

He's right. I am. I am so hot, so goddamn ready.

I swallow.

If this fine motherfucker doesn't get away from me before my pussy explodes, I'm likely to fuck him right here for all to see.

"Can I ask you something?"

I swallow. "Uh, sure," I stammer.

He licks his lips. "Are you wearing panties?"

"A thong."

He smiles. "Nice. What color?"

"White."

Lord, God, there goes that tongue, again, licking over those succulent lips. He leans in, moves his mouth closer to my ear. "And what if I told you I wanted you to stuff it in my mouth, while I fucked you senseless?"

Those words send swirls of heat reeling through me.

I inhale. Catch the scent of him again, and my mouth waters. His fading cologne is overpowered by a sensual musk that suddenly makes me dangerously lightheaded at the thought of tasting him.

Licking him.

My tongue dancing up and down his skin.

Feeling every inch of him pressed into my mouth.

My heartbeat quickens.

I am melting inside.

The sight and smell of this man renders me speechless.

His gaze on me has my body on fire, but my mouth suddenly goes dry.

Goddamn him!

Thoughts of Roosevelt invade my conscience, and guilt gnaws at me. But then I look at the fine motherfucker standing in front of me and think of the endless possibilities the night might offer.

One being a well-fucked, well-pounded, very pleased pussy.

I reach for my drink. Toss it back. Allow the heat to swirl in my belly. Lips wet, throat moistened, finally regaining my composure, slowly I say, "Then I'd say, let's go fuck, daddy."

FIVE

As soon as the elevator doors shut, he has me pressed hard against the polished wall, his mouth covering mine. I gasp, breathless from his long, deep kiss.

"We were watching you all night, shaking that ass."

I pant. Catch my breath. "Did you enjoy the show?"

"Fuck yeah. Had my dick hard all night." With his lips to my throat, and his hands squeezing my voluptuous ass, he whispers, "Damn you thick as hell."

I moan. "Mmm. You like all that?"

"Hell yeah. Love it. I don't usually kiss random women. But you sexy as fuck."

I press my pussy into his thigh. "Well, I don't typically fuck random men on the first night. I usually spread my legs on the second, or third night."

He grins. Grinds himself into me. "Lucky me. You feel that?"

I reach between us. Feel his dick. Grab it. It's everything I thought it would be, thick and long. "Yes. Mmm. I hope you can handle me," I say breathlessly as he shoves a hand between my legs and cups my pussy.

"Oh, I can handle you," he murmurs. "There's enough dick to handle you all night."

"That's what they all I say," I tease boldly. "I don't want no minute-man, baby. Not tonight. My pussy needs to be fucked right, long and hard and deep. Can you handle that? If not, find me someone who can."

He throws his head back and laughs. "You talk a good one, love. But you ain't no real freak."

"Ooh, that sounds like a dare."

"Nah. It's an assessment."

"Then you had better reassess. I'm more freak than you'll know."

He smirks. "You ain't ready, love. But, soon as I get ya ass to the room, we about to find out."

"I don't want me no minute-man," I repeat in a singsong voice.

"Trust me. You about to find out I ain't no minute-man."

His gaze meets mine as he cups my cheek and eases my head back so that there is no mistaking the heat in his eyes.

"I like it nasty," I say, squeezing his dick. It feels long and thick. How I love 'em.

"Yeah, okay. That's what your mouth says."

"I can show you, better than I can tell you," I mutter as he smiles down at me. His smile is painfully sexy.

"We'll see," is all he says before he slides a hand into my halter-top and eases down and takes one of my breasts in his hot mouth, suckling my nipple until I feel wild with want.

He tells me tonight he's going to be my deepest, darkest fantasy. That he's going to give me what my body needs. Everything it craves. Everything my man doesn't give me at home. Lots of tongue, lots of dick…and a hard, deep fuck.

The minute he has me inside his hotel room and the door closes behind us, he is all over me again. And I am clawing at his shirt, buttons flying off as I rip it open, exposing his smooth chest.

He groans. "Shit. I can't wait to taste you. I want my tongue shoved so far up in your sweet cunt that you can feel it licking your cervix."

A shiver races up my spine. "Mmm," I purr. "Lick all in my wet pussy."

"Yeah, baby."

Baby.

The way it rolls off his tongue, slow and easy and sweet like melted chocolate, makes we want to suck him into my mouth.

Evan's gaze flickers over my face, causing the heat between my thighs to spread over my cunt, settling on my clit. My heartbeat throbs. Aches. Pulses right smack in the center of my legs. It takes everything in me to not push the emergency stop button, drop to my knees, and suck his dick, right here, right now.

One corner of his sexy lips curls as if he knows what he's doing to me.

Seducing me. Luring me.

I'm trolling for trouble.

He knows it.

I know it.

But, at this very moment, I don't give a damn.

Lucky for him, or maybe *me*...the elevator stops.

And the doors slide open.

"Ooooh, yes, baby, yessss! Right there...!"

Evan's tongue trails slow, wet circles in the center of my thigh, then a fingertip trails up my other leg, up along my shin, up over my knee and around to my inner thigh, slowly inching its way closer to my slick cunt.

Any thoughts of my man back home, any lingering guilt I might have felt, have long gone. At this moment, Roosevelt doesn't exist. And there's no room for guilt.

Only pleasure. Only heat. Only lust.

Repentance can come in the morning.

Right now the only thing that matters is this orgasm that's boiling up inside of me. He hasn't even touched my pussy yet, and I am already on edge of a climax.

Lord, God...

This is sinful.

By the time Evan reaches the sodden spot in the center of my panties, I am breathing hard, panting. Almost gasping.

"I can smell your pussy," he murmurs. "Soaked in your juices. Spread your legs wider. Let me breathe you in."

"Let me breathe you in."

Oh, how I want him to. Breathe me in. Sniff out my soul. Then lick away my transgressions.

Yes, yes, yes, breathe me in.

The sensuality in those three words, *breathe you in*, has my body fluttering like a moth to a flame. Attracted to the heat. Tempted by desire.

Lord, God...

His touch, his tongue, will lead to my downfall.

A wave of heat crashes through me as I spread my legs wider and he presses his nose into my center, then inhales. Deeply. Intently.

"Mmm, so sweet, so musky," he says, his words muffled wetly. He rubs his nose up and down along the center, smearing his nose in my cum-soaked, cum-scented panties.

"Aah. Mmm..." He breathes in, again, as if what's between my legs is the sweetest oxygen he's ever breathed in.

He gasps into my cunt as if he's fighting for more. More air. More high. More arousal.

He breathes in again. Tells me how he loves the smell of wet pussy. He inhales again. Licking over the fabric again, and again.

My pussy becomes his inhalant. Intoxicating him.

Breathe.

Smell.

Taste.

Evan breathes, smells, and tastes my pussy. Licks it. Loves it. Lavishes it.

My hands flutter over my belly, trail over my breasts. Trembling fingers circle my areolas, then find their way to my aching nipples, rigid with need.

His tongue flutters over my flaring lips, peeking from the outer edges of my thong, causing me to thrust my pelvis and rock against his face.

He licks over the thin strip covering my slit, slowly sucking it into his mouth, wringing out, and extracting, the sticky cunt sap that has stained my panties.

Ohmygod, this motherfucker's really trying to eat my panties off.

He licks and licks and licks, his tongue grazing over my lips every so often. He opens his mouth—over wet fabric, over my throbbing clit, and sucks them both into his mouth.

Finally, he pulls my thong to the side and moans into my pussy, licking an orgasm out of me.

There's a knock on the door. Three quick raps, then three more.

"Shit," Evan murmurs over my clit.

I moan.

He licks a few more times.

There goes the knocking again.

"Fuck," he mutters.

I blink. Ease up on my forearms. "Who's that? Did you order room service?"

His face emerges from between my thighs, sticky with my juices. "Yeah, something like that."

I give him a puzzled look. Try to figure out when he placed an order. I can't recall him using the phone. Maybe he had called down while I was in the bathroom.

Yeah, that had to be it.

"What did you order?"

A wicked grin spreads over his face as he eases up from between my legs. Dick rock-hard, my mouth waters. "That knock at the door, love, is your fantasy."

I give him a confused look, hoisting myself up on my forearms. "My fantasy?"

"Yeah."

Curiosity and anxiety sweep through me all at once. I sift through my brain, trying to recall if I'd mentioned any of my fantasies. I hadn't.

Or had I?

"Wait. Which fantasy?"

He flashes another one of those sexy grins. "Aah, don't you worry, love. Tonight, it's all about you. Making all your wishes come true. It'll be a night you never forget. I promise. You'll thank me later." He leans in and kisses me on the forehead. "I'll be right back."

I watch as he walks across the room, naked, taking in the spectacular view. Broad shoulders. Narrow waist. Firm ass. Muscled thighs.

My hand slides over my body, taking in the swell of my breasts, the clenching in my belly, the wetness in cunt. My right hand toys with my left breast while my left hand eases over my clit. But then I stop. Ease up on my forearms. Listen.

I don't hear any movement out front. No voices. And now my fears kick in. What if this is a setup? What if that fine-ass nigga plans on fucking me to death, then discarding my body, dumping it into the ocean?

It'd serve your sneaky, whore-ass right for being down here in the first damn place.

*Bitch, stop! If he were going to kill your drunk-ass, don't you think
he'd do it somewhere other than in his hotel room?*

"Well, to hell with waiting to find out," I say, swinging my legs
over the bed. "I'm getting the fuck—"

My mouth drops open as Evan reappears with two other sexy
motherfuckers walking in behind him. They're both tall. Dark-
skinned. Bald.

Identical twins.

My heart races.

Evan grins, fisting his dick as he approaches the bed. "You say
you're a freak, right?"

I swallow. Gaze from Evan to the twins and back. Then slowly
nod. Take in the masculine hunks before me.

"Yes."

"Then it's show time, love," he says. "Me and my boys here," he
points on either side of him, "Trevor and Travis are going to fuck
you good."

I blink. "Wait, wait. I didn't sign up for a tag-team." *Although it's
always been a fantasy of mine.*

"You said you wanted to be freaked all night, right?"

"Y-y-yes, but I meant…"

"Nah, love. No 'buts.' I know what you meant. You meant you
love dick. And you need that sweet-hole handled right. There won't
be much talking, baby," he warns. "Just lots of fucking. You ever
been fucked in all three holes?"

I swallow.

Yes, God…

But not like this.

I spring to my feet as the two Dark Knights, Trevor and Travis,
tear off their clothes, tossing them around the room.

"Oh, don't run now, love." Evan reaches for me. Pulls me into his arms. Strokes my back with his hand. His dick presses into my stomach, streaking it with pre-cum. "Show me and my boys how much of a freak you are."

His voice is low and hypnotic.

He leans in and covers his mouth over mine, his kiss wet and ravenous, his tongue stroking deep and fast as his hand slides into my hair, holding me by the roots as he greedily sucks on my lips, my tongue. He cups my left breast in his hand, kneading it, his thumb and forefinger lightly pinching and tugging my aching nipple.

I moan, instantly turned on and needy, forgetting only moments ago I was ready to flee the scene.

He groans, releasing me from his kiss, leaving me drowning in a newfound need, anticipating the pleasure he—*and* his guests— might bring.

"Let me and my boys fuck you, love."

I swallow again, hard.

Then blink.

Big, curved dicks spring from boxer briefs.

And all I can think, as they prowl toward me with lust-filled eyes and devilish grins, is, *My God…what have I gotten myself into?*

SIX

Lord, God…

They are fucking the shit out of me.

I am on all fours. And they take turns fucking my pussy. Rough. Strong hands grabbing my waist, balls slapping into my ass, face buried into the pillow, I am being fucked deliriously.

I bite into the pillow.

One after the other, they stretch me open. Fuck into parts of my pussy I never knew existed. They fuck sweat and spit and screams out of me.

Long, hard, and deep.

"Please," I beg hoarsely. "Ah, God…ah, ah, ah…ooh, ooooh, oooooh…"

Eyes watery, vision blurred, I blink. Blink again. Try to glance over my shoulder to see who is in back of me thrusting hard, sinking in deep, and wrenching a cry from me as an orgasm rips through me.

In, out, in…*thump, thump, thump!*

In, out, in…*thump, thump, thump!*

Switch.

Dick is pulled out, leaving my pussy vacant only for a moment, before someone else lunges in, sinking deep, then slamming in and out.

Grabbing my hips.

In, out, in…thump, thump, thump!

"Lord, God…yessss!"

"Oooh, shit, this bitch got some good pussy," the voice says.

"Ah, ah, ah, aaaaah…"

My cunt clenches, grips his dick, milks it.

"Ooh, so g-good. Mmm. Mmm. The dick is so good…"

"Yeah, that's right, sexy-ass bitch…mmm…throw that wet pussy up on this dick…"

I moan. Thrust back at him, my ass flapping around his dick. I don't know who is who. All I know is, each dick feels better than the next. Each thrust; every stroke has my pussy juicier than the one before it.

I don't know how much time has passed. But I don't know how much more of this, this fucking, I can take before I completely lose my mind. The nonstop pounding has been more than I could have ever imagined.

Bitch, next time be careful what you ask for.

Evan climbs up on the bed, positions himself in front of me. He grabs my head. Tells me to suck my cunt juice off his condom-wrapped dick.

I do.

Wrap my lips around his dick and suck him lovingly into my mouth, tasting myself, cupping his balls and cleaning him with my tongue. He stops me long enough to remove the condom, tossing it over the side of the bed, before thrusting his dick back into my wet, waiting mouth.

"Ah, yeah, love…suck that dick." He grabs the back of my head, bounces it back and forth on his dick. Wet gurgling sounds burst from the back of my throat. "Yeah, gag on that shit, baby."

My pussy is empty again.

Then, then…oooh, yes! It's filled again.

Lord, God, yes!

They've changed positions again, brothers taking turns, sharing the goodness.

My ass is pulled open. Spit splatters into my crack. Then I hear something open. Something cool and wet is being squirted over my hole. Lube.

I murmur into Evan's dick, arching my back.

A set of hands smooth over my ass.

Whap!

My ass is smacked.

The twin in back of me pounds into my pussy.

Whap!

Whap!

Whap!

I yelp.

Evan leans in, reaches for my breasts and cups them, tweaking and pulling and lightly twisting my nipples.

I cry out.

I can't think straight.

I am more aroused than ever in my life.

The steady slap of our fucking, the wet clicking of my pussy, the gurgling and slow humming in the back of my throat, all sweet melodies.

I come over and over, mewling, clawing at the sheets.

Lord, God, what is happening to me?

A hand caresses over the stings, then pulls open my cheeks.

A finger glides over my hole, teasing it, working the lube inside of it until my puckered opening relaxes.

I gasp as a finger slips in. A middle finger, I think.

"Oooh…"

His finger circles in and out of my ass, causing my pussy to quake. "Uh, uh, uh, uh, uh…ooh, ooh…ah, ah, ah…"

"Goddamn, this pussy wet," the twin, who's thrusting in and out, says.

A second finger eases into my ass, knuckle deep.

"Yeah, get that ass ready," Evan mutters, face-fucking me.

Get this ass ready?

For what?

I groan louder. "Uhh, uhh, uhhh…oooh…!"

Fingers pump in and out of me.

"Yeah, man, stretch that shit open," Travis says. Or maybe it's Trevor. I don't know. I can't tell them apart. I try to lift my head, try to catch my breath.

"Nah, where you going?" Evan grabs my head. "Get your mouth back on that dick. Take that shit like a freak."

"Yeah, fuck that bitch," one of the twins chimes in, the one fucking my ass with his fingers. I try to place whose voice belongs to whom, but my mind is a muddled mess.

"That bitch's pussy's good as fuck."

"Hell yeah, this shit's good."

I moan. "Aaah, uhh…oooh…!"

A third finger is being stretched into my ass.

I'm slipping in and out of consciousness.

The burning pleasure is too overwhelming.

I cry out.

Lord, God…!

When I blink open my eyes, I am still being pounded.

Still being fucked.

Still being probed.

And my mouth is still stuffed with dick.

But it isn't Evan's.

It's one of the twins.

Up on his knees, his legs spread wide, his balls dangling over his brother's head.

They've changed positions.

But when?

I must have slipped into a sexual coma because I am straddled over the other chocolate twin, riding his hard dick, heat swelling inside my pussy as his thrusts match my own. I don't recall changing positions.

My mind is swirling trying to assess the time. My eyes sweep around the room. There's a sliver of light coming through a slit in the drapes, the only indication that it's daybreak, that a new day is dawning as I am being fucked mercilessly.

I need to know who is doing what to me; for my own peace of mind, for my own sanity, the not knowing, the second-guessing, is driving me crazy, making my pussy hotter, wetter.

Still…I need to know.

The twin with his dick in my mouth grins, then tells me he's Travis.

Oh. That helps.

I grunt. Pull back from his dick, then lick over the head like it's a melting fudge sundae. He groans as the bed dips in back of me. It's Evan moving in behind me, his hands sliding over my back.

I tense, then quickly relax as he presses his mouth to the curve of my neck, then at the back of my earlobe. He licks me there. "You still think you're a freak, love?"

I grunt my answer. Rock my hips all the way down Trevor's dick.

I hear Mecca's voice in my head. *"Oooh, you scandalous bitch…"*

Travis feathers a hand over my jaw, turning me back toward his bobbing cock; its eye wet with arousal.

My lips part as he eases inward, holding my head in place with one hand.

"Yeah, get that dick all up in them pretty lips. Suck that shit," he says as he pushes farther in.

"You ready to get fucked in all three holes, love?" Evan asks, his voice thick and heavy like the cock already slicing into my cunt, and the one in my mouth. My entire body is already on fire. And hearing the question becomes gasoline to my already blazing inferno.

I feel like I'm having an out-of-body experience.

This whole scene is…insanely delicious.

"Yes, yes," I groan over a mouthful of Travis's dick, his scent filling my nose as his taste fills my mouth. My head bobs, my lips and tongue gliding over his shaft as he strokes inside my mouth.

Evan kisses the small of my back. Then lets his tongue slide up my spine, eliciting a shiver to my toes.

"Look at all this big, bouncy ass," he says, trailing his tongue inside my crack.

I moan. "Uhh, oooh…"

And when he smacks my ass, the sensation wrenches a groan from the back of my throat that vibrates over Travis's dick.

His quiet moan encourages me to keep sucking him deeper, to keep groaning, harder, faster.

"Goddamn," he growls when my tongue swirls around the head of his dick. Evan tells me to lean forward. Pulls open my ass. Then buries his tongue inside as Trevor grips my hips, and bathes himself in my liquid heat, thrusting upward as I suck his brother.

Lord, God, yes!

The Devil is a lie!

My breathing quickens, then catches in the back of my throat when I feel the tip of Evan's dick pushing its way inside my ass. "Relax, baby. Let me get up in this."

He pulls his dick out. Applies more lube, fingering it inside of me. Then presses his dick back in place.

I hold my breath, my body stilling.

"It'll hurt at first, love. But I promise once I get it all in, it'll feel good, baby."

I swallow.

I'll be the first to admit, I've had numerous threesomes in college. And I'm definitely not new to anal sex, although it's not something Roosevelt gets into.

But being fucked in all three holes at the same time?

Now this is a first.

An experience I'm not sure I am ready for. At least that's what I'm saying inside my head, but my body is screaming the opposite. My flesh is boiling with rippling sensations.

Trevor slowly rolls his hips, stirring inside my pussy, giving Evan time to ease his way into my asshole, and take it.

This level of nakedness, of vulnerability, leaves me exposed and aching, and weak with desire. My ass, my pussy, my mouth, bared open to all three of them.

I try to focus on the two dicks already inside me—my mouth, my pussy, both juicy and full—but the idea of having a third one stuffed, simultaneously, inside a hole that hasn't been used since before my relationship with Roosevelt causes all types of feelings to well up in me.

Anxiety.

Curiosity.

Excitement.

Anticipation.

Unexpected heat.

All overwhelming.

My eyes widen and I whimper when Evan presses in. I groan like a wild animal as the head of his dick bursts through the outer ring of my hole, slowly sinking into my ass. He pulls out. Drizzles more lube inside me, then pushes his head back in.

Against Travis's dick, I surprise myself when I cry, "More! Give me more!"

"Aah, yeah," Trevor mutters. "Little freak bitch wants that ass fucked, B." He thrusts up in me. "Give her the dick, yo."

"Oh, I got this," Evan says, slapping my ass. "This sweet ass is all mine." Trevor curls his fingers underneath my ass, lifting me slightly up off his dick.

Evan's crown kisses my hole again, and my whole body starts to jolt with vibrations as his head goes in deeper. He draws his hips back, then rolls them forward, plunging his dick in deeper. Inch by inch by inch. He takes my ass. Rocks himself into me as my pussy clamps around Trevor's dick.

Fiery passion sweeps through my body. Exquisite pain followed by the most paralyzing pleasure pierces through me, numbing me from the waist down as Evan spinal taps me, and Trevor guts my cunt.

Soon they both find a rhythm, taking turns thrusting and retreating, fucking into my body. I am joined with them. Impaled by them.

"Oh, God, yes," I say in a strained voice. The fire roaring inside of me is unexplainable. Incomprehensible. It's like dancing around the edge of an erupting volcano.

Never would I have thought this feeling, this overwhelming stretch and burn, could feel...uh, uh, uh, oooh...could be...mmm, yes...aah...so, so, rapturous.

Shit, shit, shit.

Mmm.

I never knew.

Never thought.

Being fucked in all three holes—three dicks inside of every part of me, working me over, controlling my pleasure—could be so deliciously dirty, yet sensual.

Evan moans. "Ah, shit yeah, baby." His hands slide around between Trevor and me, caressing and cupping my breasts, tweaking at my nipples, pulling and pinching them.

Heat shoots through my ass as Evan's dick stretches inside me. It hurts. Oh, God, how it hurts. But God, it feels so damn good.

I'm slowly being pushed over the edge.

Blazing white heat sears along my spine as Trevor's hands trail along my sides until he reaches my breasts, replacing Evan's hands with his, cupping and caressing them, plucking at my nipples until they are painfully aroused, rigid with want.

I pull Travis's dick from my throat. Gulp in air. Try to catch my breath.

"Ah, God, *yes.*"

"Get back on that dick," he groans, pushing my head back toward his bobbing, spit-slick dick.

I do as I'm told, my mouth pooling with juices as I open wide and take him between my lips again. I lean forward, moaning, my breasts now raking across his brother's chest. Trevor's hands are back at my waist, his grip tight as I ride him.

"C'mon, open that mouth wider," Travis urges, pumping into my face. "Let me feel that throat." I extend my tongue. Gag. Allow him entry to the back of my throat.

I close my eyes and savor the feel of having all three holes stuffed at the same time. My pussy, my ass, my mouth all squish-squish, working in harmony.

Click, click, click.

The wet sounds, the gurgling, the grunting, all become a sensual lullaby.

I am so wet, so very wet.

So deeply aroused.

Travis grabs me by the head and chokes me with his dick. I gasp.

Spit and drool splash out of my mouth. Tears spring from my eyes.

Evan grunts. "Aaah, shit, I'm coming, I'm coming...aah, fuck!"

My mouth still stuffed with dick, I moan as Evan quickly pulls himself out of my ass, leaving my wet hole stretched and stinging.

He shoots his warm custard, soaking my back and my ass as he sandwiches his dick in between my ass cheeks and slides his shaft up and down along my crack. His body shudders.

"Aaah, yeah," he groans, smearing his dick over my quivering flesh.

I arch upward. And just when I think he's done, when I think he will now have mercy on my weeping soul and throbbing ass, he says, "Nah, love. Where the fuck you goin'? I ain't done with this ass, yet."

He pulls open my ass and plunges back in.

Racing toward another orgasm, I cry, "Yes, fuck my ass! Ooh, yes! Yes, God, yes!"

Trevor groans, thrusting upward, matching the rhythmic thrusts of Evan, his dick grazing my spot.

I lift up and rock into the heat.

"Yeah, baby, ride this dick."

The room starts to spin. And blur.

Someone pinches the tips of my nipples, their fingernails grazing them ever so lightly. Right now, I don't know whose hands are where anymore. Could be Evan's, or maybe Trevor's.

I cry out. Gobble down more of Travis as he cups my face and feeds me his cock.

"Aaaah." I babble and moan, rocking my hips. "Ooh."

Lord, God, yes...

I wiggle and buck as much as being stuffed with three hard dicks will allow. Inch by inch, Evan eases in, then out, then in, matching the in and out motion of Trevor's dick, fucking my hole as if it's a second pussy.

This is so fucking incredible.

I know I should be ashamed of myself.

Whoring on an island. Alone. Fucking three total strangers.

Scandalous bitch…

Cheating-ass whore…

I've gone unbelievable wet.

Raw need is being matched with raw cock. The only condom worn is the one on Trevor's dick.

I know I am playing a dangerous game.

One filled with dirty heat.

My mouth, my pussy, my ass, all drenched in hotness and fierce want.

Soaking Trevor's dick, his balls, and the sheets beneath him.

Soaking Travis's dick as his balls brush against my chin.

Soaking Evan's dick as his balls slap the back of my pussy.

Hair flying, body violently jutting to and fro, someone pinches my clit. And that's all it takes to send me plummeting over the edge.

The primal grunts, the low groans, the hiss of air steaming around the room, the sharp scent of ass and pussy and deep-fucking hover over us.

I shriek in pleasure, falling into molten bliss; powerful orgasms tearing through me as Evan pounds into my trembling ass, exploding inside of me, flooding my hole with hot cum.

Flames sweep around me as a gurgling scream rips from somewhere deep in the pit of my soul and I come, hard, over Trevor's dick—squeezing him, just as his brother growls out, thrusting into my face, throwing his head back and spurting his thick semen into the back of my mouth.

I am flooded with passion.

Flooded with nut.

I swallow as much of Travis's salty cream as I can, allowing the rest to pool out of my mouth, dripping down my chin and onto my breasts. I keep sucking him until his balls empty and he goes limp and his dick plops out of my mouth.

Evan utters another groan, then presses a kiss to the back of my neck, then eases himself out of my ass.

Before my body can accept the emptiness, Trevor wraps his arms around me and rolls me over so I am beneath him. He stretches a leg up over his shoulder, wrapping my other leg around his waist and pumps fast and hard, the shaft of his dick grazing my clit as Evan does the unthinkable.

He takes my dangling foot, and sucks my toes into his mouth.

Lord, God, Jesus…

Oh, yes, oh, yes, oh sweet Jesus, yes, yes, yes.

I gnash my teeth, claw at the sheets.

Everything inside of me explodes.

I melt.

"Fuck me," I beg as my nails dig into his muscled ass.

"Fuck me," I repeat as my toes spread out into Evan's mouth.

"Fuck me," I cry out as Trevor's strokes brush over my spot.

"Fuck me," I beg some more, my eyes rolling upward, catching Travis stroking out another orgasm of his own.

My empty, aching ass clutches air, my cunt clamps around Trevor's dick and together he and his brother unleash their liquid heat, Trevor dumping his into the condom, and Travis releasing his all over my face.

"Goddamn. Whew. Shit," Travis says, climbing off the bed.

Evan removes my toes from his mouth, then licks the ball of my foot one last time before letting my foot go.

My body shakes.

Trevor rises up on his arms, then slowly slips out of my quaking cunt, leaving me weak and burning in the aftermath.

Heavy-lidded, I watch, lazily, as the twin hunks wobble across the room and stuff their sticky dicks back into their underwear, then slip into their clothes, quietly leaving the way they slipped in; probably with waiting wives or girlfriends back home, wherever they're from.

Evan walks them to the door.

I smile to myself.

Well-fucked.

Pussy and ass on fire.

Throat raw.

Lord, God, yes...

Them big hard dicks gave me my life back.

I roll over on my side, slide a hand between my thighs, relishing in the lingering sting inside the pit of my ass.

I can't wait to sightsee today. And enjoy what this magnificent island has to offer.

Then come tomorrow, I'll be flying back home to my life with Roosevelt—who will be none the wiser, leaving behind stained sheets and dirty deeds.

My scandalous romp tucked away in my secret memory bank.

But for now—my limp, warm body still trembling, I'm going to close my eyes and bask in the glowing heat of having been fucked in all three holes.

Evan climbs back into bed, spooning himself behind me. "That ass was good," he says, pressing his dick into my pillow-soft cheeks.

I moan, grind my ass into him. "Glad you liked it."

He wraps an arm around. "Yeah, I loved it. You handled my boys and me real right. Hope ya man never finds out what kinda woman he has. I'd fuck around and lose my mind if I were him."

I let his words float around me for a moment. Ponder on his possible meaning behind them. It can only be taken one way.

He hopes Roosevelt never finds out just how filthy I am.

That I am a cheater.

Before I can open my mouth, he says, "You've earned your freak flag, baby. Now I'm about to get up in this pussy. It's time for round two."

I blink.

Oh no, oh no! This nigga has got to be kidding me! Didn't he already bust two nuts?

I hear the sound of a wrapper tearing in back of me, and then Evan is lifting my leg up and sliding his dick back into my ravished pussy.

I am too exhausted to stop him.

Lord, God, Jesus...

Slivers of sunlight are slicing through the drapes, and all I wanna do is sleep.

A moan oozes from my lips as he strokes inside my wetness.

Lord, God...

I know I said I wanted to be fucked all night. But this, this... oooh, Lord, God...this kind of fucking is unnatural.

Be careful what you ask for.

Mmm, his dick is hard as steel.

What is this nigga on, Viagra and coke?

I'll need to plan my escape.

My whole day is going to be fucked up. I planned on starting the day early and touring St. Lucia; maybe visiting Sulphur Springs to take in the world's only drive-in volcano, or perhaps checking out the Pitons, those two colossal mountains towering up from the sea. Uhh...oooh...then I planned on taking a plunge into the azure Caribbean Sea, before lying out on the white sandy beach and soaking in the sun.

But now...mmph...ooh...mmm...

Looks like all I'll be doing today is crawling into a tub and soaking my raw ass and swollen pussy, hoping like hell everything snaps back before my flight hits the tarmac.

I know my man. He's going to want some pussy the minute he sees me. But this greedy motherfucker right here is trying to fuck the life out of me.

Another moan rips through me.

Lord, God...no!

Phone Bone

"Mmm…ooooh…my body's clenching with desire…"

"Yeah, baby…tell daddy what you wanna do to this hard, thick dick."

"Mmm. I wanna suck all over it. Lick it. Kiss it. Make sweet love to it."

"Aaah, yeah," I moan, squeezing my dick at the base. "Tell me how you gonna make sweet love to this dick, baby."

She moans low. "With a whole lot of spit. Mmm. I love giving wet, sloppy head. I'm gonna make love to it with my lips, my tongue, my mouth, and hands. Swirl my tongue all around that big, thick, juicy dickhead. Then glide my lips up and down your throbbing shaft. Mmmm…oooh, your dick is so big, so good. I wanna clean your wife's pussy juice off it…"

Oh shit.

My dick instantly gets harder and thicker as my hand rapidly glides up and down my shaft. "Word? Aaah, shit…so you like licking pussy?"

"No. I love *licking* dick soaked *in* pussy. It's soooo good…mmm. Oooh…I love the taste of a big, juicy cock smothered in pussy. Fuck your wife. Let her come all over your dick so I can suck it clean. Mmm…aaaah…tell me how big that dick is, daddy."

"It's big. Real big, baby. Thick, dark chocolate with lots of veins and a big dickhead."

"Mmm…Oooh…aaah, I love big dick. Love black dick smothered in sweet black pussy…"

"Yeah, baby. Got her nut all over my big dick. Is that what you want?"

"Mmmm, yes, yes…I'll suck that dick so clean, baby. Mmm. I'll be your personal, slutty cock washer…"

"Hell yeah," I say, stroking my dick. "Clean that shit. Wash this big dick with your tongue."

"Yes, yes, oh yesss…I'm a dick-sucking bitch. Call me motor mouth, baby. I'll just keep sucking and sucking and sucking, gulping and gulping every inch of that big hard dick."

"Yeah, aiight, Motor Mouth…aaah, shit, yeah. Lick around these balls, too."

"Oooh, yes." She makes wet slurping sounds in my ear. "My tongue is flicking all around your balls. Mmm. Feel my tongue?"

"Yeah. Aaah, shit yeah. Suck 'em in your mouth."

She wants me to describe my balls to her. I tell her they're big, round and smooth, the size of two extra-large chocolate eggs. She moans again. Tells me how she's sucking them into her mouth while she's stroking my dick. My dick is leaking a bunch of precum. I'm so fucking turned on right now.

I wanna fuck.

And bust this nut.

"Mmm, yes, yes, yes…ooh…I'm so wet," the anonymous voice on the other end of the phone says. Her voice dips to a seductive whisper. "Listen." She puts the phone between her legs and lets me hear her fingers click in and out of her wetness. I close my eyes and listen. Mm, fuck. I love that sound, the sound of wet pussy. That's one of the sexiest sounds ever. Well, aside from the sounds having my dick sucked. There's nothing else like it. Wet pussy.

"You hear how wet I am?" she finally says.

I open my eyes and lick my lips. "Yeah, baby. Tell me how wet you are?"

"Waterfall wet. I'm soaking the sheet beneath me. My warm juices are flowing down into the crack of my ass. You wanna taste?"

She starts sucking her fingers into her mouth, tasting herself, moaning. I close my eyes and picture her licking her cum-glazed fingers, sucking them, rolling her tongue over each finger. And the sound of her swishing her fingers around in her mouth causes my dick to jerk, then bounce up and down. I grab it. Stroke it. Then let it go. It jerks and bounces again. She has me hard as fuck. I slide my hand over the head, then swipe my thumb over my piss slit, smearing my precum over my dickhead.

"Mmm, I can't wait to feel you sink your big, hard cock between my warm, wet pussy lips."

"Aaah, shit, yeah, baby. Put this dick all up in between them pussy lips. Stir your juices all over my head, then rub it over your clit. Tease your clit with my dick."

"Mmm, yes. My clit is so swollen, so full of lust."

I hear a wet, smacking sound.

I swallow.

She's smacking her pussy.

Then starts moaning. "Mmm, mmm, mmmmmm...you hear that...? That's my wet pussy. It's so juicy for you."

"Yeah, baby. Smack it harder."

Whap!

"Harder."

Whap!

She moans.

"Harder."

Whap! Whap! Whap!

She cries out.

"You want me to fuck it?" I ask, squeezing the head of my dick. Precum seeps out. I swipe the pad of my thumb over it, then start jacking my dick in deep, fast strokes.

"No, no," she says breathlessly. "Not yet."

"Tell me what you want."

"I want you to kiss it. It's all red and swollen. And hot. It's so, so, hot, baby. I want you to kiss the sting away."

I give it a kiss. Then another. Then another.

"Mmm. Your lips feel so soft. So good." I ask her where she wants them now. She tells me kissing her clit. I make more kissing sounds.

"I'm kissing you clit, then nipping it with my lips, before licking it."

"Ooh, yes. Ooh, yes. Mmm. Now I'm rolling over on my stomach and hunching up on my knees. Now you're kissing me, again—kissing all over the humps of my ass cheeks. Mmm. I love feeling your soft lips all over my ass, baby. You like kissing my ass?"

I moan. "Yeah. I love kissing that fat-ass."

I don't know if her ass is fat or not. It could be iron-board flat for all I know. But in my head, that's what she has: a fat, bouncy ass. I pucker my lips and start making more kissing sounds.

"Mmm. Yes. Kiss it. Kiss it. Now catch my juices with your tongue and lick in my crack. Oooh…I wanna feel your long, sweet tongue in my crack. Mmmm. Lick in my ass, baby…"

I rapidly stroke my dick, stretching out my long legs, opening and closing my toes. I'm on the verge of busting this nut. I feel it filling up in my balls.

I groan. Feel myself on the edge of a nut. "I'm reaching between your legs, playing with your clit."

She moans loudly. "Mmm. Pull open my pussy, and put your tongue in it."

"Yeah, baby." I flick my tongue in and out of my mouth, making licking sounds. "Aaah, yeah, that pussy tastes good. Wet, juicy pussy."

"Ooh yes, yes, yes…lick it, lick it. Uhh, uhhh, uhhhh…"

"Yeah, come all over my tongue, baby. Look at that pretty pink pussy. Aaah, uhh…tastes so motherfucking—"

"Yes! Yes! Yes! I'm com—"

"Hello? You still there?"

Silence.

"Hello?"

Hard dick in hand, while hanging on the precipice of popping a big, thick nut, I frown.

The motherfucking line is dead.

"Fuck," I mutter as my nut spurts out of my dick, splashing on my stomach and over my hand. I keep stroking until another nut spurts out. I grab my dickhead and squeeze out the last bit of my nut, before grabbing a towel and cleaning myself up.

"Shit." I lift up in my seat and pull my sweats and underwear up over my hips. I stretch out in my chair, removing my bluetooth, then leaning my head back on the headrest.

Damn that was a good nut.

I guess you're wondering what's my deal. So I'll tell you straight up. I'm a thirty-five-year-old man in a loveless marriage. Stuck in an unhappy situation with the mother of my daughter. Nah. Actually, it's a fucked-up one. I hate this bitch. Excuse me for calling her out of her name. But that's what she is. Well, that's what she's become. A bitch. Not that I've ever called her that to her face. She's still the mother of my daughter, even if I don't have any respect for her. Still, on many occasions—when she starts with her shit, I've come real close to it, calling her a *bitch*. And I think it. All. The. Time.

Every waking moment that I'm around her, I feel it.

She's a fucking spiteful-ass *bitch!*

I never thought I'd ever call a woman the *B*-word. Never had. Until recently. Until this mood-swinging, bipolar bitch showed me who she really is.

Fucking miserable!

A lazy-can't-hold-a-job paranoid piece of ass!

We've been together, unfortunately, for nine years, and the longest she's held on to a job is like, two, maybe three, months. Then she either quits or gets fired. But she's never the problem. Everyone else is.

It's always the blame game with her.

Poor Stephanie. Everyone's always picking on Stephanie. Bullshit. It's her shitty-ass disposition that keeps her from holding down a job, and no one wanting to fuck with her. Yeah, on paper she looks good, and she can sell herself in the interview, but then she gets the job and they start to see what type of broad she is.

Always late.

Always defensive.

Always calling out sick.

Always making excuses.

So they write her up. She curses them out. Then they show her to the door.

Shit, her own family stopped fucking with her because of her attitude. Her sister *and* her mother, both have a restraining order against her. They literally want nothing to do with her ass.

Man, if that doesn't scream craziness, I don't know what does. I should have known then that there was something wrong with her. Nah, nah, if I'm really being honest, I should have known she had a screw loose when I saw her with a hammer chasing down some cat she used to mess with in broad daylight.

Dude was literally running through parking lots and around parked cars trying to get away from her, yelling for someone to "come get this crazy bitch."

And the cops didn't do shit.

But, nah, I still fucked with her. Let myself get caught up into thinking that she'd never come at me like that. Thinking my dick game—and the fact that I'm a good fucking man—would keep her satisfied.

But then I met the real Stephanie.

And now I know.

The bitch needs meds and a straitjacket.

No matter what you do, no matter how hard you try, you can't make a miserable bitch happy. Sadly, I've had to learn that shit the hard way.

Nine years too late!

I swear to you. If I could turn back the hands of time, I wouldn't be in this shit. I would have fucked her, just to see if the pussy was as good as the word on the streets said it was, then kept it moving. Then again, I would have kept my hard dick in my draws, and run in the other direction. And I damn sure would have never married her.

But here I am.

Trapped.

And these last few years have been nothing but h-e-double-l.

Her sister and mother were smart as hell to cut her off, especially after I learned she'd pulled a knife out on her sister and threatened to slice her face, all because she didn't like her sister telling her she was useless.

Well, shit. It's the truth. She is fucking useless.

And I married her ass!

And it's been a fucking nightmare trying to get rid of her. She's like a fucking roach. You kill one, and five more appear.

All I can do is shake my head. And let her play victim all by herself.

In the beginning, I used to feel sorry for Stephanie when I didn't know better, that is. But now I don't feel shit. No. Scratch that. I do feel something. Disgust. This broad doesn't do shit. Won't cook. Won't clean. Won't even go out and get a fucking job. Or keep one. Some days, I don't think she even washes her ass. Not that I've smelled her. She just always looks like a funky-ass mess to me.

Yet, she's always so quick to call me stupid for only having a GED, then throw up in my face, to remind me, that she has a master's degree; that she's college educated. Like I give a fuck about her bullshit-ass degree.

Whoopty-*fucking*-doo!

I stare at her long and hard every time she starts talking that dumb shit, thinking, *Yeah, bitch, whatever. So what, you went to college and got yourself a few degrees, you're not doing shit with 'em. So that shit doesn't mean shit if all they're doing is collecting dust, or somewhere buried under a dresser drawer full of ugly-ass cotton panties and raggedy-ass bras.*

Just because she can string a bunch of big words together doesn't mean shit. Yeah, I dropped out of school, and got a GED instead. But I'm the one with a job. I'm the one with a pension. I'm the one with a few dollars stashed. I'm the one with good credit. And Stephanie's ass can't get shit. So who's really the stupid one here?

This educated bitch is.

The only thing she *will* do is, keep her feet and nails done and make sure our daughter's hair is combed and she's dressed and ready for school. Other than that, she doesn't do shit. Well, except sit on her ass and be all up on Facebook and Instagram, practically all fucking day, while watching shit she's taped on DVR, burning up unnecessary electricity. And if she's not doing that, then she's got her face pressed into the pages of some nasty fuck-book.

I don't know why the fuck she's reading that nasty shit for 'cause it's not like she's ever tried to do any of that shit she's reading with me. Hell, maybe if she would have done more sucking and fucking and less shit popping, we might have still had a shot at making shit work.

But not now.

And thanks to her always being parked in the same spot day in, and day out, we have a lopsided sofa and a cushion with her ass print stamped in it.

I used to snap on her. But then she'd start with the crocodile tears, or the "I'm depressed" bullshit. Other times if I pushed too far, she'd start yelling and name-calling, then start with the "Motherfucker, get off my back before I stab you" craziness.

A few times she's actually jumped up in my face with a knife and my daughter got caught up in the middle of our drama, trying to keep us from tearing each other up. And once, about three years ago, she called the police on me *and* lied telling them I tried to choke her. I told the police, "I'm not gonna lie. I've thought about choking her ass plenty of times. But I've never put my hands on her." But they still arrested me after she was the one who put her hands on me.

Amaya was hysterical. And this bitch had the nerve to be smirking.

That did it for me.

I don't want Amaya seeing that shit. And I damn sure don't want her thinking, or *feeling*, like she has to play referee because her crazy-ass mother can't keep her hands to herself. I'm not putting my daughter through that.

Hell no.

I said I'm here for Amaya. And that's that.

So now I let the bitch do her. Sit on her ass all day, then lay up in bed late at night eating boxes of Entenmann's cookies, bags of Doritos, then washing the shit down with wine most nights, vodka on other nights. Weed on the weekends.

Always that good shit.

Hell, I smoke, too, just to deal with the stress of living under the same roof with this crazy bitch. A blunt a night, that's all I need to keep the edge off. Oh, and one before I step through the door and have to look in her face.

Hell yeah. I gotta be high to deal with her. Being around her is stressful as fuck. Her mouth. Man, listen. Her mouth is so fucking reckless. Sometimes I really wanna put my fist through it and knock out all her fucking teeth. That's how bad it gets. Well, it had been. The last three weeks or so, things have been kinda calm. She's not bitching as much. And she's even asked me to sleep in the bed with her.

Not.

But I've given her some of this dick and fucked her to sleep, just to keep the peace. Still, wet pussy doesn't mean shit if it's attached to a fucked-up, crazy-ass bitch.

Now, she's scrambling trying to figure out what she can do to make up for all the shit she's put me through. Not. A. Goddamn. Thing.

I guess she sees I really don't give a fuck. That she's a nonfactor. I get up in the morning, do what I gotta do, drop my daughter off at school, then head to work.

Most nights I'm home from work by six, only because I need to make sure Amaya's homework is done and that she isn't being fed McDonald's or some other fast-food bullshit. So I cook. Do the dishes. Get Amaya ready for bed. Then come into my man cave and lock myself in.

Now all of sudden it's fucking with her that I make her ass invisible. But when I was sweating her, practically begging her to not give up on us, she gave me her ass to kiss. Now she wants to try to make things work. So she's being *nice*.

Bitch, bounce.

It's too fucking late. Her disrespect has done too much damage. Now I've emotionally checked out. All I am now is a physical body in this crib, and an unhappy participant in this shithole of a marriage.

Hold up.

I know what you're thinking: Why am I still here? Why don't I leave if I'm so miserable?

Stephanie's even told me to get out. Then the one time I did attempt to leave, she blocked the door and started fighting me for leaving, accusing me of wanting to go off "to fuck some other bitch."

I laughed in her face and that only pissed her off more. She spat in my face. And the only thing that stopped me from breaking her jaw was Amaya. She begged us to stop. And I did.

Stephanie, on the other hand, wanted to keep shit going. She always does. But now when she comes at me with that dumb shit, I give her a blank look. Fuck that. Me leave? Is she fucking kidding me? Why should I? Why doesn't she go? The lease is in my name. And I'm the one paying all the bills around here. So I'm not going any-motherfucking-where.

Well, not until this lease is up.

Still, as far as I'm concerned, this is my shit. So I'm gonna ride this storm out until I can get rid of her, for good.

Hell, I've tried putting her out, twice. But she turned around and called the cops on me. Told them, crying, that I was putting her out and she had nowhere else to go, that I was throwing her and our daughter out on the streets. The cops stood there and looked at me like I was the biggest asshole. Then they had the audacity to tell me I couldn't put her out because her name is on the lease, too. The worst thing I ever did, was putting her name on this lease.

Now I can't get rid of her ass.

She's even threatened to take my daughter from me, again. And she knows I'm not having that. The last time she ran off with my Amaya, she stayed gone for almost six months. That fucked me up.

I couldn't eat, or sleep. Or even think straight.

Stephanie knows Amaya is my whole world. And her packing her shit and taking my daughter with her almost had me wanting to beat her ass.

Even though she moved like forty-five minutes away—and I got to see Amaya on the weekends, it felt like she'd kidnapped her and ran off to another country. Coming home and seeing my daughter's closet and dresser drawers cleaned out had my head all fucked up.

I've been in my daughter's life since the day she was conceived. I cut her umbilical cord. I held her in my arms before her own mother did. I got up in the middle of the night and fed her when Stephanie was too exhausted to nurse her. So, no, I'm not leaving. Not without my daughter. Period.

So, yeah, it's no secret. She knows that the only reason I'm still with her is because of Amaya. That's her only leverage. Our daughter. And she knows she has me by the balls. She knows if we didn't have Amaya, I would have bounced seven years ago.

That's when the shit started getting crazy with us. Or maybe it was always crazy, but in the beginning, it was all good, at least that's what I want to believe. So I didn't pay most of her bullshit any mind because she had a little waist, fat ass, looked good in the face. And she was putting it down in the sheets.

So by the time I started noticing it, it was too late. She was pregnant with Amaya and I wasn't going anywhere. Period.

So I married her.

Big fucking mistake.

Seems like once she got that ring, and had Amaya, she got real loose. She started getting careless with her mouth, cursing me out in the streets and around my daughter. She started thinking it was okay to jump up in my face. And, like now, back then I put up with the shit because I wanted to be in my daughter's life, by any means necessary.

And, I will be.

So I'm fucking stuck, for now.

And I suffer in silence.

And, while Stephanie's drinking and eating herself into piggy heaven, getting all fat and sloppy, I do what I gotta do to be a full-time father to my daughter. I make sure Amaya has what she needs. I make sure shit around here gets done, because that's what I'm supposed to do. I take out the trash, and clean the crib, and do my daughter's and my laundry, and handle the groceries and everything else, leaving Stephanie to her own demise.

So in a word, I'm married to an educated, lazy-ass, loud-mouthed bitch, who is all too comfortable with her tore-up weave and her fake lashes, flopping around the house in funky-ass sweats and over-sized shirts and those ugly-ass Chinese slippers with the rhinestones.

Now. You tell me. Who the hell wants to come home to that shit every night?

Not me.

Like I mentioned, I don't even sleep in the same bed with her. One, she hogs the bed. And, two, she snores like one. Sleep apnea or not, the bitch looks like Hannibal with that breathing apparatus strapped to her face at night.

And yet, she wonders why I don't wanna fuck her. Not that we don't fuck. Just not on the regular. And only when jerking out this nut isn't enough.

Yeah, I can't stand her ass. But, fuck. I'm still a man with needs. And I still have a dick that gets hard, and horny.

And she's still a piece of ass, who's laying up in here not paying one motherfucking bill. So, uh, yeah, the least she can do is roll over and get up on all fours whenever I'm feeling generous enough to grace her with a few hard strokes.

So when I give her this hard dick—after I've gotten myself aroused thinking about fucking someone else—it's a pity fuck. A hard, dirty pounding—from the back; always from the back—out of anger and desperation and fucking disgust.

It's fucked up to say this, but I can't fuck her unless I'm thinking of someone else. I close my eyes, imagine I'm somewhere—anywhere else but here, with *her*—then beat her shit up wishing it were her face. Smacking her ass, hard and rough, is the only time I aggressively put my hands on her.

Every time I fuck her, I try to beat her ovaries up. Try to gut out her uterus. Sometimes, I even grab her in a chokehold while I'm hitting that shit from the back, wishing I could snap her fucking neck. That's how bad it is. That's how deep my hate for her runs. But then I think about Amaya and keep from snatching her breath.

And the irony is, she loves it. Begs for it.

Her pussy gets real wet when I yank her by the hair and try to snatch her scalp off. Or when I manhandle her.

"Yes, nigga, ooh, fuck me! Beat that shit up! Aah! Aah! Aah! Yassss! Yasss! I know you hate me, nigga. But you love this pussy..."

Yeah, okay, if she only knew.

True. I used to love the pussy. Used to.

All that pussy is to me, now, is a wet hole. A convenience. A cum-dump. And it being at my disposal when I'm high and horny enough to wanna put my dick in it is all I care about.

Here's another crazy thing. After I beat that shit down, she's good for a few days, up whistling and smiling and trying to be nice, wanting to fix us.

But, like I said, it's too late. There's nothing to fix. We're gonna keep doing what we do.

Nothing.

So now when she gets in her feelings, I leave her ass sitting in them, biding my time. And, if she starts popping shit, I let her argue by her damn self, which usually only sets her off more. Then she gets it in her little, crazy-ass head that there's someone else.

"Motherfucker, are you cheating on me?!"

"Hell no, I'm not cheating. I should be. But I'm not."

"Well, you're fucking something because you're damn sure not fucking me!"

"Listen, go 'head with that. I'm not doing this with you with Maya in the other room."

"Nigga, I don't give a fuck about Maya being in the other room! Maybe she needs to hear how fucked up you are."

"Listen. Watch your fucking mouth, aiight?"

"Or what, nigga? I asked you a fucking question. Who you out there fucking?"

"No one. Damn. Now get the fuck off my back."

"Nigga, I ain't on your back, yet! I know you fucking some dirty bitch. But if I find out who the bitch is, I'ma fuck her up. Try me!"

"Think what you want. I can get pussy anytime I want. But I don't. So to answer your question, dumbass, I'm not fucking you because of you, not because of some other broad."

"Nigga, fuck you and that little-ass dick! You ain't gotta fuck me, bitch! That little-ass dick ain't about shit anyway."

"Yeah, aiight. Then why you sweating it if it ain't about shit, huh?"

"Motherfucker, get the fuck out of my face!"

And, of course, Amaya heard that shit, too.

I frown, shaking the thought of our last argument two weeks ago out of my head. Yeah, I'm miserable in this marriage. But I'm still married. So until she leaves, or I can get up this money to file for a divorce—and get custody of our daughter—cheating is out, no matter how bad I want some stress-free pussy.

Shit, if I could afford one of those "happy-ending" massages, I'd let some slanted-eyed babe work the nut out of me.

But I'm not even chancing that. Just my luck, she'd fuck around and catch me getting this dick handled. Then try to fuck me over more than she already has. So, nah, I'll get this nut off solo—well, with the help of porn and phone sex, for now. Otherwise, I'm not giving her any ammunition to use against me when it's time to take her ass to court. But, trust me. If I was the kind of man to step out and fuck other women, I would. It's not like I'm not being tempted. Pussy is always being thrown at me.

It's like the more I say no, the more it's being tossed at me. Still, as hard as it is, I resist. But fuck. Do you know how badly I want some new pussy? Some head? I'd love to have my dick sucked right now. And these balls licked, slow and wet. Would love to give this dick to someone who appreciated a good man and some good goddamn dick.

But I don't need the added drama.

Not right now.

So I'll pass.

I just want this bitch gone.

I want her to go on with her pathetic life, and leave Amaya and me alone. Let her ass be the weekend parent. It's not like she's doing much of the parenting any-damn-way. But, for now, I take the high road. Bite my tongue. And keep pretending.

I glance at the time on my iPad. 7:30 p.m.

I scowl, wondering where the fuck Stephanie is with my daughter. But I'm not about to text her to find out. *On second thought*, I think, grabbing my cell. *Where's Maya?* I text.

A few seconds later, my phone *pings*. It's her. I'm surprised she's hit me back so quickly. Usually it takes her twenty, sometimes thirty, minutes before she decides to get back at me, if not at all, unless *she* wants something.

@ TeeTee's. she's gnna stay the night. teetee's takn the kids 2 storybook land 2morrow. i 4got 2 tell u

You forgot? Yeah, right. Whatever!

She ain't forget shit!

I don't respond back.

TeeTee is my sister. So it's not that I have a problem with Amaya staying over. It's the fact that Stephanie stays doing shit without consulting me, *first*, to see what I think. But I know her passive-aggressive ass. She did that she being funny. I know Amaya told her that I was planning to take her up to Pennsylvania Dutch Country tomorrow because I overheard her telling her in the kitchen the other night.

"Who else's going?"

"Nobody. Just me and Daddy."

"Mmph. Dutch Country, my ass. Why is he taking you there?"

"Because I like it there. And I asked him to."

"Mmph. All I know is, I better not find out he's bringing some Quaker bitch around you, or I'ma get real ugly on his ass."

"Mommy, don't talk like that. Why are you always so mean to Daddy?"

"What? Oh, so you're taking up for his ass, huh?"

"No. I'm not taking up for him. I just don't like when you say mean things about him."

"Girl, take your little fresh-ass to bed before I smack you in your mouth."

It took everything in me not to storm in and shut it down. But I let her have her moment. Although Stephanie's never put her hands on Amaya, she's come at her real crazy with her mouth. And Amaya is smart enough to know what time it is. She knows her mother's a loose cannon.

Now I gotta be up in this motherfucker with her ass..

Ping. Another text message. *Now what the fuck does she want?*

I'm omw home. U want sumthn while I'm out?

I frown. Stephanie hasn't asked me if I've wanted something while she's out in years. Now all of sudden she's asking?

Yeah, for your ass to stay gone!

Nah. I'm good, I text back.

I open my desk drawer and pull out my stash, deciding to roll a blunt and chill out.

Usually "I'm on my way home" means I'll be home in about two hours. And that's fine with me.

I pack my cigar with weed, then light it.

Thirty minutes later, I'm real mellow, feeling nice as hell. And, Stephanie's still not home like I knew she wouldn't be. If I'm lucky, maybe she'll stay out all night.

I decide to hit up a few of my boys trying to see who wants to get up and maybe hit up a titty-bar. But, to my dismay, they all on house arrest tonight. Wifeys got 'em all on lock.

I shake my head. It's Friday night, and I don't have shit to get into tonight. At least if Amaya was home, I could rent a movie and order pizza or play one of her favorite board games with her.

This is some pathetic bullshit.

I light another blunt, taking a few deep pulls.

"Hey, you want some shrimp fried rice?" Stephanie says all nice and sweet, knocking on the door and walking in at the same time. I didn't even hear her come in the crib. I cringe. Fuck. I'm in the third bedroom, the one I've taken over, and turned into my man cave.

I keep from sucking my teeth at the unwanted intrusion.

This bitch…

"Nah, I'm good," I say, not looking up at her, scrolling through my Facebook newsfeed, hoping she gets the hint.

That I'm not beat for chitchat.

"You wanna watch this Zane movie with me. It just came out on DVD."

Now this makes me look up at her. Look at her. Standing here with her broad-shouldered-linebacker-looking ass. She used to have a sexy-ass body, thick in all the right places. Now she's all stomach and back fat, just sloppy with it. And I'm supposed to wanna be with something looking like this. Fuck outta here.

I blink. She's gotten her hair done. She's cut that raggedy weave out and has her hair cut in a short style and has it highlighted. And, I won't front. It looks nice on her. She even has on lipstick. A burgundy color, I think. I have to be straight up. She might have let her body go, but she's still pretty in the face. Still, I keep from frowning at her offer. Why the hell would I want to sit through some shit with a bunch of sex scenes in it with her?

I give her a blank stare, trying like hell to keep from saying what I'm really thinking. Then to sweeten the deal, she adds, "I bought two bottles of Moscato, and a bag of weed, if you want some."

Drinks. Smoke. Sex flick. Oh, she thinks she's slick. But I'm not even about to fall for the trap. Tomorrow, she'll be right back on her extra shit.

Man, relax. Just keep shit light.

She's standing here, running a hand over her hair, waiting. She wants me to acknowledge her new look.

"Nah, I'm good on the drinks and flick," I say. "But I might light up with you."

And maybe give you some dick if I get horny enough.

"Oh, okay. I'm gonna take a shower, first."

I give her a head nod. "Aiight."

"You want the door closed?"

"Yeah."

I wait for the door to shut, then reach for my cell, sliding my bluetooth back over my ear. I redial 1-900-SexHeat. A chat line for cats like me not looking to actually go out and cheat, but are looking for a quick way to get off without a bunch of bullshit.

I rub my dick over my sweats, feeling it harden at the thought of another round of some hot, dirty phone sex.

I hear the shower running upstairs. *Yeah, wash that ass*, I think as I light another blunt. *And clip them pussy hairs.* I inhale the smoke deep into my lungs, holding it in as I punch through all the recorded greetings from hundreds of thousands of horny women wanting to talk to unhappy, sexually frustrated men like me, perhaps even like them.

Some might consider it cheating. I don't. It's only cheating if I go out and fuck. All this is is heavy breathing, low moaning, and whispering. I call it a great escape.

Fantasy.

An illusion.

Role-playing.

A seductive break from reality, that's it. There's no intent on fucking any of my phone bone encounters. Hell, most of the women I speak to live hundreds of miles away. So it's safe. No temptation to seek any of them out. It's simply something to take my mind off the bullshit here, while getting a good nut.

There's nothing wrong with that, right?

Right.

It's innocent, clean, healthy fun.

A stress reliever.

Damn, just thinking about some fantasy sex got me wanting to bust another load bad as fuck. It's something I do twice, maybe three times a week. Phone bone.

Keeping it straight up. Smoking a blunt relaxes me. But busting a nut over the phone helps keep me sane. And puts me to sleep. And, yeah, watching porn helps. But there's nothing like hearing the moans and groans of an anonymous woman. I can mentally fuck whomever I want, whenever I want. However I want.

Dirty and raw.

So, nah, it's not cheating. It isn't about seeking a love connection. It isn't looking to replace what's missing at home, either. Like I said, I have access to pussy, anytime I want it, but at what cost?

More drama?

More headache?

Not interested.

Phone sex, for me, is strictly about release, talking dirty, masturbating, busting this nut, then disconnecting. There's no emotional connection. No other expectations except getting me off, or each other off, on command.

I don't care what her race is, or whether or not she looks like a sea cow or Mother Goose on the other end of the phone. All that matters to me is how sexy her voice sounds, how well she moans, and how creative her imagination is.

Like now…

I press the prompt, selecting the voice that catches my attention. Then rise from my chair. Pull my sweats down over my hips, then pull my fat dick out of my boxers. I don't have the biggest dick. It's only seven, seven-and-a-half. But it's thick as fuck and it stretches a pussy up real nice. And I have some nice, big balls loaded with nut. My dick is what it is, but I imagine it to be more. Shit, sometimes while watching porn, I've found myself measuring my shit, comparing my size to some of them hung porn stars, wishing I had a bigger dick. Not that I'm not happy with my size. Like I said, it's thick as fuck. And my shit gets the job done, well. Still, sometimes I wish I had been blessed with a few inches more.

But during my phone sex encounters, my shit is always nine, ten, eleven, sometimes twelve, inches.

Tonight, I'm ten inches of hard dick.

"Tell me what you want, baby," the voice on the other end of the line says softly.

I reach for my warming lube. Squirt some in my hand. Then grip my dick at the base and slowly slide my hand up and down and around over the head, then back down my shaft.

"I want some wet pussy, baby."

"Mmm, yes. Tell me more."

"I wanna lay back and watch you suck and deep throat my dick 'til it gets rock hard, then climb on top and ride it slow and deep."

"Ooh, yes. My juices are already trickling out of me. But before I slide my wet pussy down on your dick, I'm going to suck it. You like your dick sucked?"

I groan. "Fuck yeah. I love that shit."

"I'm sliding my body down yours, kissing all over your chest, licking over your nipples…"

I slide a hand up under my T-shirt and pinch my right nipple until it pebbles. I'm big on nipple play. For some reason, mine are wired to my dick.

"Mmm," she moans. "The head of your dick is already wet for me…"

"Aaah, shit yeah," I groan. "You got my shit so hard, baby. I'm horny as fuck."

"Oooh, yes. I love hard, horny dick. I love feeling it brush over my tongue, then hit the back of my throat. Mmm. My throat is so tight and wet for your hard, horny cock, baby."

I groan, deepening my strokes, my hand gliding up and down my shaft.

"I'm kissing the head of your dick—like this—" She makes kissing sounds. "And like this—while playing with your balls."

I listen out for the shower upstairs. It's still running. *Good.* Stephanie's usually already up in her room, in bed, or not home when I'm getting it in on the phone. But knowing she's upstairs, and the possibility of her walking in on me, catching me with my dick in my hand excites me more than I already am.

Fucking another broad in our, well, Stephanie's, bed—not that I would ever do it—and she walking in on us is a fantasy of mine.

"Yeah, baby…what else you gonna do to this dick before I fuck you with it?"

"I'm going to wetly lap up the length of your dick, then lick over that head, then suck you into my mouth—*mmmm*—savoring your sweet, salty precum. Mmm…oooh, it's so good. I love how you taste."

"Yeah, suck on this dick. Suck this nut out." I rapidly stroke myself, feeling my nut rising to the surface. I quickly change strokes, milking my dick nice and slow.

"Ooh yes…mmm…I love the smell of your musky heat as I suck your balls into my mouth one at a time."

"Aah, yeah. I love these balls sucked. Get 'em nice and wet, baby. Let me feel that spit sliding down into my ass."

She moans. "My panties are soaked. I want you to rip them off of me with your teeth, then shove your tongue deep in it."

"Yeah, you like that pussy licked?"

"Mmm, yes. I want you to bite my clit."

"Yeah, pinch that shit. Make believe it's my teeth, biting on that fat clit."

"Ohgod, yes, yes, yes…"

"Can I tie you up, then paddle your ass?"

"Yes, yes, yes, yessss!"

"Let me fuck you in that ass…"

"Wait, no. Not yet, baby. Please. Let me feel it in my pussy first. I'm ready to climb up on top of you and feel your hot cock inside of me. Oooh, I'm grinding my wet pussy on your thigh. Can you feel how wet I am?"

"Yeah, baby. Aaah, yeah…you're so wet. I'm gonna finger your ass while you're riding my dick getting it ready to be fucked. Mmm, aaah, yeah…ride that dick, baby. I want you to ride it until I spray my big hot load of cum all over your sweet walls. You want this hot nut in your pussy, huh, baby…?"

"Mmm, yessss," she purrs into my ear, "flood my pussy…"

"Then I want you to sit on my face and let me eat my cream out of you while you suck the rest of my nut and your cunt juices off my dick."

"Oooh, yessss, daddy. Oooh, I love a nasty man. How big is your dick?"

"Ten thick inches, baby."

"Ooh, yes, I love big dick," she murmurs. "I'm getting so wet thinking about having that big, hard horse dick fucking my pussy. You want this wet pussy?"

I groan. My dick is thick and hard and aching right now. "Yeah, I want it. I deserve it." My dick throbs in my hand as she tells me she wants me to tickle her pussy lips with my tongue.

"Yeah, I need that baby. My tongue all over them puffy lips."

She giggles and that makes my dick throb even harder. "Ooh, that tickles. Mmm. Yes. Tickle my pussy. Mmm. Oooh, yes…you're worthy of some good, wet pussy on your dick and face and all over your tongue, boo. Mmm. You deserve to feel and taste how wet and juicy my pussy gets…"

"Hell yeah. I deserve that shit, baby."

"Are you married? I love married cock."

"Yeah, I'm married."

"Mmm. Your wife doesn't fuck you?"

My dick pulses at the thought of Stephanie walking in and catching me on the phone getting off with another woman. "Nah. *I* ain't fucking *her*."

Not on a regular.

"Mmmm. Why? Why aren't you giving your wife that big dick?"

I grunt, tightening my grip on my dick. "She doesn't deserve this shit, baby. But you do. She isn't worthy of this good dick. Tell me what that pussy looks like?"

"Um, ooh, too bad for her. That's just more dick for me. My pussy's the color of brown sugar…"

I lick my lips. "Damn. I bet it tastes sweet like brown sugar, too."

"Mmm, yes. Real sweet. And sticky, too, like molasses."

"Damn." I fist my dick, rapidly stroking it.

"And it's a pretty wet pink in the middle."

I cup my balls. Squeeze them. "Goddamn, baby." I flap my tongue, making slurping sounds. "Feel my tongue all up in that sweet pussy?"

"Yes. Mmm. Oooh. Yes. Lick that pretty pink pussy. Oooh…"

"Yeah…yeah, baby. Aah, shit. Let me lick your ovaries. Tongue all around your uterus. You gonna let me stick this dick in your ass, huh, baby…?"

"Ooh, yes, yes, yes…tongue it, first. Get it nice and wet for that big fat cock. Then slide your fingers in it."

"Yeah, fuck. You want my fingers deep in your ass while I'm sucking on your clit, huh, baby…?"

"Yes, yes, yes, yes…ooh, go knuckles deep. Mmmm…my pussy's so fucking wet for you. Oooh, I love hard dick, baby. Love sucking dick. Love lots of fucking. Mmm. I love my ass stretched and fucked real deep, baby. You wanna feel me coming all over your dick?"

"Yeah, baby, come all over it. Get that wet pussy up on this dick…"

"I'm straddling you now. Mmm. I'm reaching between us, grabbing your hard cock. Oooh, it's so hot in my hand. Mmm…I'm rubbing it over the mouth of my pussy. My pussy's clenching for it. Can you feel it…?"

"Yeah, baby. I feel that shit. Aaah. Give me that pussy."

"I'm sliding down on it. Ooooh, it's stretching me. Aaaah, uhh, ooooh…God, you're so fucking big…I'm all the way down on it. Mmm…ohgod…"

"Yeah, that shit feel good, baby. Are you my whore?"

"Yes, baby. I'm your whore. I'm your filthy, little cum whore. I'm fucking my pussy on your dick. You like this whore pussy?"

"Yeah, I love that shit. Fuck that wet cunt. Aaah, shit, baby…"

She moans. "I'm coming…"

"Aaaah, shit. I'm getting ready to bust this nut, baby. Where you want it?"

"In my pussy, in my throat, in my ass. I want it deep in me. Drown me in it. Drench me in it. Oooh, aaaah, yes…smother me with it, baby!"

I grunt. Then groan. My dick is so fucking hard. And ready to explode. I hear the surround-sound in the living room come to life. Smell the weed.

I stand up. Kick off my sweats and underwear draped around my ankles. Keep stroking my dick. Waiting. I'm ready to bust this nut. But I'm trying to hold out. Trying to wait for Stephanie to walk in. I wanna bust this nut on her face. Then throw her down over my desk and fuck the shit out of her.

This chick on the other end of the phone keeps talking, low and dirty, telling me how hard she's coming on my dick, how fast she's riding it. She's moaning and purring.

I step away from my desk. Open the door. Bite my bottom lip.

"Aaah, shit," I mutter, standing in the middle of the doorway, waiting, waiting, waiting.

Yeah, crazy ass, come catch me getting this nut...

"Here it comes," I whisper, dipping my knees, moving my hips, pumping my dick in and out of my hand.

"Mmmm. Yes, yes, yes...come for me, baby..."

I tell my phone freak to keep talking that nasty shit as I'm walking out into the living room.

Stephanie looks over at me. Her eyes grow wide. "Ohmygod! What the fuck?"

"Come get this nut," I groan, standing in front of her, blocking her view of the television.

Stephanie's mouth drops open in shock. She hasn't seen this side of me in years. Maybe it's the haircut. Maybe it's the weed. Maybe it's having an anonymous woman in my ear, moaning and begging for this dick, this nut, while Stephanie's sitting here, watching me. Surprised. And, suddenly, turned on.

"Mmm, ooh..." the chick on the other end moans in my ear. "Yes, yes, yes...feed my pussy that hot nut, baby..."

"Here it comes," I say to her, staring at Stephanie. "Come get this fucking nut."

"Yes, yes, yes...oooh, yes. Give it to me. Give it to me. Uh, uh, uh...mmm...you feel so good in my pussy..."

Stephanie licks her lips. Hops up from the sofa (I've never seen her chunky-ass move so fast) and drops down on her knees, grabbing me by the hips and sucking my dick into her mouth. She digs her nails into me and sucks me hard and fast.

I let out a loud grunt and shoot my load, pumping my hips and flooding her mouth, with the soft whimpering of my anonymous whore floating in my ears.

Legs Wide

Open

B old and brazen, my slick lips spread and my wet pussy stretches over the extra-thick width of Charles' seven-inch dick. It's late. Well after eight in the evening. And here I am hoisted up on my desk. Legs spread wide. Head tossed back. Nipples puckered tight. Getting fucked down.

"Yes! Yes! Yes!" I mewl, digging my nails into his ass, pulling him in deeper. "Fuck me, baby! I love it when you fuck me! Mmm, yes. Fuck me. Fuck me. Fuck me goooooood. Oooh, yes…"

Charles fucks me like I stole something from him, sawing into my pussy with rapid speed. "Yeah. Fuck. Give me that sweet-ass pussy, baby. I love fucking this dick into you." Charles holds my legs up over my head, holding the heels of my shoes like they're handle-bars, and he's riding his coveted Hubless Harley—the one I've ridden on the back of, twice so far. "Muthafuckin' good-ass pussy."

"Mmmm…mmmm…yes…"

He moans. I moan. We moan together.

And then…and then…ohgodohgod, he wraps my left leg around his waist, keeping my right leg up, and begins plunging into me. He slams in hard and deep and fast. My body shakes as I absorb his thrusts. I feel my face flush. I bite down on my lip, feeling heat swell inside of me. Charles finds my spot and rapidly strokes into it.

"Fuck. Shit. You're so fucking wet for me," he murmurs. "You always are."

I look him in his eyes, getting lost in his gaze, in his every stroke. "Yes. Ah, God, yes. You do this to me."

Pleasure grips and tightens around me.

"You love this dick?"

"Yes, yes…oooh…uhh…"

"You want me to keep fucking this pussy…?"

"Yes, yes, yes…"

Twisting his thick fingers through my hair, Charles tugs, then bends and covers my mouth with his, filling my mouth with his heated tongue.

God his dick feels so good inside me! It's like a chocolate-dipped, king-sized Snickers bar. And the more he fucks into my pussy, the more I want it. The more I crave it—his thick chocolate, his creamy nut.

Charles and I have been screwing each other for the last eight months. It isn't something either of us planned. It just happened. Okay, okay…I know affairs don't just happen. They manifest themselves out of insecurity. Out of some sense of twisted need for validation outside of home, outside of a relationship.

This, this…thing with Charles quickly progressed to him sliding his dick into me once to him sliding it into me once a week to three times a week to this…him fucking me every chance we get, sometimes twice in the same day—once during our lunch hour at some local motel, then later in the evening here at the office when everyone else has long gone.

We fuck and fuck and fuck.

And then…

I wobble home. Back to my boring life, my walls still throbbing, pussy fucked out the box.

"Whose pussy is this, huh?" Charles leans in, and bites my right nipple over the flimsy fabric of my blouse.

I shriek in ecstasy. Tell him shit I'm not sure is true. "Yours. Oh, dear God, yes. It's all yours, baby. Mmm." But in the heat of the moment it feels right. It feels…uh…it feels…mmmm…oooh…it feels like the closest thing to whatever truths I conjure up in my mind, contradictions and all.

That this thing between us—these fuck sessions, the late-night texts, the naughty IMs and email exchanges, the backseat romps—can all stop…if, if, oooh, if…I wanted them to. That this married, wet, horny, throbbing pussy belongs to this married fat, juicy dick-having man even when I know it shouldn't.

Yes, I'm married.

He's married.

And we're having a dirty office romance. And, yes, sometimes there's a glimmer of regret every time I step through the door of my gated home and have to look into my husband Craig's eyes. But it's always quickly replaced with justifications as to why I cheated on him in the first place. He doesn't turn me on, anymore. He's boring. He lost his drive. He never wants to do anything. Never wants to try new things. He's always complaining.

And the sex…

"Oh God!" I squeal, feeling my juices squish and slosh out of me as Charles' dick glides in and out of my weeping cunt, slick and cum-coated. The muffled thumping of his muscled thighs hitting up against the back of my toned legs and the clickety-click-click of my wet pussy is a sensual melody to my ears as he power-fucks his way in and out of my heated center.

Charles licks and nibbles the back of my right calf, then my left, as he fucks me on my desk. I turn my head, and catch a glimpse of the back of the crystal picture frame holding the photo of Craig and me. A photo we'd taken our last night in Hawaii, several months prior to my, mmm…oooh…God, yes…my, my, indiscretions.

It had been an unexpected trip. One I wanted no part of. Being an IT manager, Craig's company had decided to send him to a three-day conference. He saw it as a second chance. I saw it as an inconvenience. He said it'd be a chance for us to rekindle sparks that had long fizzled in our marriage.

But, for me, paradise was for lovers. Something Craig and I were not. Not anymore, that is. We were simply a boring married couple living a boring married life having boring occasional sex—in my opinion, of course. We were stuck in a rut, getting along, and moving along. And I did what I had to do to keep peace in our home, and in our marriage—for the sake of the kids.

Of course, Craig hadn't gotten the memo—that I was bored with him, that I was unhappy with him—since I'd never shared my sentiments with him. Well, not to that degree. As far as he was concerned, there was still hope for us. Unfortunately, I didn't share his enthusiasm.

Still, after several days of me making excuses as to why I couldn't go—and, then, several more days of being browbeaten by Craig about why I needed to go. About him needing to spend quality time with me, his wife—I reluctantly caved in, and agreed to go.

Surprisingly, once I allowed myself to relax and live in the moment, the trip turned out to be a lot of fun. And I came back feeling refreshed and with a half-hearted commitment to try to give my marriage another shot. If for nothing else, then for the children, especially since we both believed they deserved a home with both parents in their lives.

The trip hadn't changed my feelings toward Craig. If anything, it made it painfully clearer that I'd outgrown him, us. But I'd stay with him. And suffer in silence. Well, at least until the kids turned eighteen.

But...

Then this happens. My torrid affair with a man I can't seem to get enough of. The man I'm willing to risk dangling over the edge for. Charles. Ohgod! He's everything Craig is not. Charles is driven. Spontaneous. Open-minded. Inhibited. Daring. Adventurous. And unpredictable.

And the sex...oooh, yes...the sex is everything. Charles gives me life. He has me doing things I've never even done with my husband. And he makes it easier for me to endure going home, knowing that he'll be here with dick in hand, waiting to fuck me back to life.

I blink away any convoluted thoughts of Craig, and with a swipe of my hand, I knock the picture frame over as Charles changes his strokes. Slow, deep...fast, shallow...deep, deep, deeper, faster, faster...slower, slower, shallow, deep...deeper, faster...

"Ooh, oooh, oooh, aaaah...yes, yes, yes."

I wish I could say horrible things about Craig. God knows I do. But I can't. He's a good man, and a great father to our daughters. But I don't feel the same kind of love for him I once did. I care for him, deeply. But I've fallen out of love with him. There was a time when he was a great lover, too. Sex with Craig was everything, in the beginning. There was a time when all he had to do was look at me, or walk into the room, and I'd instantly become wet with desire.

But then...I don't know, after the twins were born, something changed. Gradually, I changed. I wanted more, sexually. Wanted to experience new things, sexually. Wanted to explore...sexuality, mine.

I married Craig not because of the size of his dick, but because of the size of his heart. I knew he'd make a good husband and great father. But there was never any open conversation about my changes, about what I now needed, wanted, without fear of feelings getting in the way. So I simply pushed on, ignored what I wanted, and pretended. I'm still pretending. And it's killing me.

Now when he touches me, I cringe inside. Not because he repulses me, but because I am disgusted with myself for not telling him this, for not wanting to let him go. Craig deserves better than what I can give him. He deserves to be loved in the same way he loves me. He deserves to be desired in the same way that he desires me. I know I should tell him this. But I can't hurt him. Taking our children from him would devastate him.

Still, even if I wanted to, I am not prepared to leave Craig. We've built a life together. A good one. One I am not ready to let give up. One I know he isn't willing to let go of, either. Besides, he doesn't deserve to be hurt. And I know that I can never be with Charles. He's not leaving his wife and three children for me. And I don't expect him to.

So…oooh…mmm…so…

I stay with what's comfortable and consistent—no matter how boring, no matter how unhappy I am in it because, regardless of my situation, it is in these moments when I am with Charles being fucked that I am my happiest. Primal need runs hot in my blood, like lava.

Boiling.

Roiling.

Coiling.

Oozing out of every pore in my body.

I am a woman on fire when I am with him; a wet inferno of desire, of hungry need. Slick heat boiling over into an endless stream of arousal. That's what I am. The flames rise at the base of my spine, higher and higher, until they are spreading through me, completely engulfing me.

"Yes, that's it!" I cry out. "Fuck me like I'm your dirty little office whore!"

"Yeah, that's right. Fucking grimy-ass whore!" He slams his dick in. "Goddamn slut!" He pulls his dick out. "Wet-ass pussy!" He slams back inside of me. "Sneaky, cheating-ass ho!"

"Yes, motherfucker, yes! Cheating-ass bastard! Fuck me like you hate me!"

Charles grasps my hips and pushes his dick in deeply. I wrap my legs around his waist and groan, tightening around him, giving him unfettered access to me. My pussy happily, greedily, welcomes each hungry thrust. My walls, the mouth of my cervix greets his thick cock with want and need. Each stroke brushes up against my clit, causing sparks of heated desire to pulse through my entire body.

"That's it, baby…open up for me…give me all of that wet pussy."

"Ooooh…aaah…uhhh…"

Charles fucks me like he loves me. Then fucks me like he hates me. Rough and dirty. He fucks me like he needs me. He fucks me like I am the best piece of ass his dick will ever feel. And it's always stress-free.

"You like this dick?"

"Yes. I love it!"

"Yeah, I know you do," he mutters against my lips before slipping his tongue into my mouth, taking every part of who I am with the stroke of his dick and the sweeping sensation of his tongue as it swirls around mine.

I am completely, utterly, turned upside down, inside out. He has me dangling on the edge of the sweetest, most powerful orgasm ever.

Liquid fire dances through my blood. I am overheating with lust.

Mewling, I feel myself swell and tighten. My fingernails claw at the top of my desk, before finding their way into the meaty humps of his muscular ass. I dig in as he fucks himself into the fire, pounding into a sea of wetness.

"Aaah, fuck," he groans against my mouth. He sucks my bottom lip into his mouth, then bites into its plump skin, causing my cunt to vibrate.

I moan, loudly.

Charles changes his rhythm, moving in and out of me, slow-fucking into overwhelming need, stroking, stroking, stroking....

With a cry, I pump my pelvis to greet his thrust. He thumps my pussy until my breath catches. He slow-fucks me until my breathing turns ragged, until I feel myself unraveling.

Gasping his name, I shut my eyes tight against the sudden surge of heat radiating through the center of my pussy. He kisses me again. Harder. Hot. Until I am breathing his air and he is breathing mine. I try to remember when kissing started between us. Try to remember when kissing him felt so...so...natural.

Or had it always felt right?

I cannot recall. And, at this moment, it doesn't matter.

None of this makes any sense. All it was ever supposed to be was a one-time fuck between us. Not this. Not us plotting and planning and waiting for the next time we can wear the other out.

Not us scheduling weekend getaways under the guise of being work-related conferences. None of this was supposed to happen.

But this is what it's evolved to, the both of us lying and scheming. I'm not sure what wicked tales he goes home and tells his wife, Melody, of fifteen years. But I have become a masterful storyteller. I have become a master of deceit. All in the name of good hard dick, I have become an adulteress.

And, now, there is no turning back, even if I wanted to.

I am on the brink of...

"Ooh, ooh, ooh."

"I'm going to make you cream all over this dick," he whispers to me, his dick fighting against my clamping walls. I am on the verge of an orgasm.

"Do it. Yes. Make. Me. Come. All. Over. Your…fat…mmmm… dick."

Charles pulls me to the edge of my desk, lifting my hips and slamming into me hard, his cock becoming a piston of passion. His balls slap-box the back of my pussy.

The musky scent of sweet fucking fills my office. It intoxicates me. And all I can think to do is cry out as Charles pulls his dick out of me, quickly leaning in and burying his face between my sticky thighs, sucking my clit into his mouth. He sucks hard and fast.

"Oooh, yes, yes, yessssssss! Suck that pussy, baby."

His middle finger slides deep inside my pulsing core, taking me to higher sexual peaks. Nirvana. Mmm. Yes, Lord! Desire loops tight in my belly as his long tongue slides over my clit and his finger furiously strokes my G-spot.

"Oh God, oh God, oh God…yes, yes, yes, yes…"

Tingles shoot up my spine. My orgasm is swelling. Charles senses this and pulls his finger out, leaving my vibrating pussy vacant.

I thrust my pelvis. Wind my hips. Beg him.

"Please…"

"Please, what?" He mutters against my weeping sex, looking up at me. He sinks his tongue into my slick folds, and licks upward, lingering over my clit.

My head falls back.

"Oh God…yes…"

"Yes, what?"

"Give me the dick. Give me the dick. Mmm. Please."

His tongue swipes my clit again, then he is sucking it back into his mouth, licking it. Teasing me. Taunting me. Coaxing another orgasm out of me.

And then he is slamming his dick back in.

I shiver and moan, as need zings through my body.

He isn't as long as my husband Craig's dick—God, how god-damn messy it is comparing Charles to Craig while my skirt is hiked up over my hips and my panties pulled to the side—but… mmmph…what Charles lacks in length, he makes up for in girth. And right now he is pounding the shit out of me. Fucking me hard. Fucking me fast. A sweet burn rolls over wet waves of heat as my juices slosh out of me and roll down into the crack of my ass, coating my asshole and pooling onto my desk.

I gasp for air. Scream out. I am drowning in the pleasure. Awash in searing sensations overflowing with sin and lust and burning arousal.

"Ohgod, yes," I sob. "I-I—"

Charles thrusts himself into me with hard, pounding strokes, lifting my hips off the desk. His fingers dig into my hips, then my ass, cupping my cheeks. Inside me, I feel him swell surprisingly thicker. He's fucking me senseless, ravaging me witless.

The slick walls of my pussy are clenching around his relentless strokes, deep, so very deep. "Oooh, yesssss…"

My body shakes as I absorb his thrusts, and dark pleasure builds up so fierce inside of me that I want to growl and gnash my teeth at him, draw blood.

"Faster, faster. Yes, yes, yes. Harder. Oooh, oooh, oooh. I'm—"

Fire bursts inside me, causing me to scream into Charles' mouth as he fastens his mouth over mine, his hot tongue sweeping the inside of my mouth.

I squeeze my eyes shut, reveling in the feel of dick and heat and wetness. The orgasm that floods out of me knocks me breathless.

Charles tenses, his voice going hoarse as he shouts and fucks me, riding into his own budding climax. He quickly pulls out, stepping back and allowing me to take him into my mouth, sucking his thick, white cream deep into my mouth. I gulp him in, swallowing his hot seeds.

Mmmm…

Right down to the very last drop.

"Hey," I say, crossing into the master suite of my 2,400-square-foot home I share with Craig and our nine-year-old twin daughters, Mia and Tia. My heels sink into the plush mauve-colored carpet.

Craig is standing in the middle of the room drying himself off with a plush burgundy towel. Beads of water slowly cascade down his bare chest. I try not to glance down at his dick. Even soft it's long and plump and thick with veins.

I run a hand along the back of my neck, and swallow back bitter-sweet memories of how good it used to feel inside of me.

"Hey," he says back, wrapping the towel around his waist. "Long night. Again."

"Yeah." I step out of my heels, then scoop them up. "We'll probably be working late the rest of the month."

"Oh, yeah?" he says. "Why am I not surprised? Seems like, lately, that's all you do. Work late. You spend more time at the office than you do here."

Please. Not this again.

He's right, though. The last several weeks, I've been staying later and later at the office *working* as far as he knows. But, the truth is, as you already know, I'm spending every free moment I have time with my legs wide open, with Charles' tongue or his dick fucking the shit out of me.

I run a hand through my short pixie-cut. "I know. Things will slow down once this huge case is over."

Being a defense attorney and working at one of the largest, most prestigious criminal law offices in the state means getting some of the most difficult criminal cases, like this case I'm assigned to right now.

My clients are a fifty-seven-year-old and twenty-two-year-old, mother-son team. The mother shot and killed her husband of twenty-three years right after sex because he hadn't ejaculated enough sperm to her liking. An argument ensued. She was convinced he was out cheating on her again. And she'd had enough. He slapped her. So instead of calling the police on him, or better yet... leaving him, she waited until he was asleep, then shot him the groin and chest before shooting him in his head. Consequently, she feels justified because he'd had multiple affairs in the past and had already given her genital herpes two years earlier.

Sadly, her son helped her dispose of his father's body by removing his teeth and chopping off his fingertips with a hatchet, then dumping his body over a bridge. Now, while his mother is facing first-degree murder charges, he's facing conspiracy charges, body disposal, and tampering with evidence.

"Let's hope," he says, skepticism etched in his tone. "Did you eat, yet?"

I'm relieved he doesn't say more, and nod. *Yes. A mouthful of cock and cum.* "Yeah, I ordered a shrimp salad."

I silently pray he can't smell—not the shrimp, but the lingering juices of my well-fucked pussy. Although I brushed my teeth and freshened up in the women's lounge at the office, I still try to avoid Craig when he reaches for me, hoping he doesn't smell my dirty deeds all over my skin. That he can't smell Charles' nut on my lips. Or the lingering scent of my pussy stained on my fingertips as I played with myself while on my knees sucking Charles' dick.

"I'm exhausted," I quickly add, hoping he gets the subtle hint—that there'll be no pussy tonight, if I can help it. I give him a quick peck on the lips, something light to appease him...for now, hopefully.

No luck. He pulls me into his arms, pressing himself into me. I

fight to keep from tensing up. He licks his lips. Stares me in the
eyes. "Hopefully not *too* exhausted for your husband. I need some
loving. *Bad.*"

It isn't a request.

Shit. So much for subtleties! How the hell am I going to get out of fucking him tonight? I can't use the cramp lie, again. And I can't tell him it's that time of the month because he knows my cycle, eerily better than me.

I give him another kiss on the lips in order to pacify him. But
he tightens his grip around my waist and I can feel his dick slowly
coming alive as he grinds himself into me. His right hand slides
down to my ass. He cups it. Squeezes it.

"I'm serious. I want my dick inside you…tonight."

I swallow. "Craig, please." I am pinned by his gaze. He stares at
me, pupils dilated with want. And need. And hunger. His lids grow
heavy, his breathing less controlled. I feel his dick pulsing behind
his towel, the long, heavy length of it straining for release. There
was a time when my pussy would clench for it. "I need to unwind
a bit. Let me go shower, first."

As if burned by my response, his hand leaves my ass, and he
loosens his grip on me. I step out of his embrace, dodging another
kiss, and his demand.

But, just as I think I am free, he grabs my arm, pulling me back
into him. "You don't need to shower." He nuzzles my neck. "You
still smell sexy to me." His tongue trails along the back of my ear,
then along the column of my neck.

Ohgodohgodohgod…*no!*

I swallow the lump in the back of my throat. Suddenly I am feeling sick. Why does he have to be…so goddamn loving all the time?
Why can't he simply be a fucking asshole? A dirty, lying, cheating-
ass bastard like so many other men I know? Why does he have to
want me so, badly?

Why does he have to make me feel so, so…goddamn dirty?

Because you are!

A filthy bitch!

Your whoring-ass doesn't deserve a man like him.

But why can't I have the best of both worlds?

Craig doesn't have to ever know.

Bitch, listen to yourself! You can't because it isn't right!

Who am I hurting if he never finds out?

Yeah, okay. Good luck with that.

Eventually he'll find out.

And when he does…?

"You know I'd never do anything to hurt you, right?" I hear Craig say, slicing into the monologue going on inside my head.

I blink. Force myself to look up at him. Then take a deep breath to steady my nerves.

I wish I could justify my cheating as payback for Craig having stepped out on me, first. I want so badly to blame it on him. But I can't. Unlike most women, I haven't shared their pain of infidelity. I don't know what it's like catching my husband cheating on me, or lying to me.

Yet, here I am. Doing the exact same thing to him.

His gaze flicks over my face.

I inhale. Exhale. "I know." I shift my eyes from his stare. His big, thick hands go up to my breasts, fondling them over my blouse. And then his fingers are plucking my buttons open.

Halfway down, I grab his hands. "Let me go shower."

He shakes his head, pulling from my grasp. "No. Not tonight."

"But—"

"Not another word. Shower after."

Panic flames in my blood. *Oh dear God…he knows!*

I look up into his brown eyes, fringed by thick dark lashes. If I deny him tonight, I am certain this will turn into a fight. Evolve into a long night of tossing and turning, or me retreating to the guest bedroom.

"Craig, please…"

He drops his towel, revealing his nakedness, his dick springing to life. "I shouldn't have to keep begging for my wife."

He's right. He shouldn't have to. So I acquiesce. Giving in to his want, this time. It doesn't take long before he opens my blouse and slides it off my shoulders. My breath catches as the garment flutters to the floor. My bra unsnaps. It, too, drops to the floor as my breasts swing freely. And then Craig is dipping his head down to kiss and nibble at my shoulder.

He growls low in his throat. "I want you."

Bitch, give him some quick pussy and be done with it. It's the least your cheating-ass can do.

With that, he sweeps me up off my feet, slinging me over his broad shoulders. Manhandling me in a way he hasn't in years. He palms my ass as he makes his way over to our king-size bed.

I find myself frantically squeezing my pelvic muscles together; hoping, praying, my pussy has snapped back enough to conceal having had another man's dick fucking me not less than an hour ago. I am thankful that Craig's dick is much bigger than Charles'.

He won't notice.

He lays me on my back on our bed. Spreads open my legs. And tells me he's going to lick my pussy until I cream all over his tongue.

Ohgodno!

He presses his nose into my panties. Sniffs. Then licks my sex, the throb of my clit, over the thin layer of fabric. I am so relieved I put on a fresh pair of panties before leaving the office. He sucks and licks and nibbles at my clit, then licks my slit over the lace, wetting it with his tongue.

Craig glances up at me. Says, "I can't wait to feel your wet pussy all over my dick. It's been too long, baby." He licks over my panties again. His hazy gaze still on mine. "I can't wait to taste your juices, and hear you moan. You wanna moan for your man, baby…?" He licks again, his eyes remaining locked on mine as his tongue swirls, slyly and sensually, over my panties, soaking them.

I gasp, turning my head, unable to bear looking at him any longer. Seeing his desire for me burning in his eyes is too much. A moan surges out of me, in spite of myself. Reflexively, my hips rock as my pussy responds to his slow, teasing strokes.

Craig pulls my wet panties to the side. Stares at my pussy, studies it. Then runs the tip of his tongue over my lips. The thought that he might possibly be able to taste Charles—or smell him—inside me while tasting me frightens and arouses me.

His tongue, long, soft, wide, and wet, plunges in, completely buried inside, his nose smashed up against my mons. One hand reaches up and pinches my right nipple, while he eases a finger inside my cunt, wriggling it alongside his tongue as if he's searching for some buried secret.

Ohgod, no! Yes, yes, yes…mmmm…

He licks from the base of my slit, all the way up—slowly, to my clit, curling his tongue. His tongue flutters over every inch of my sex. One finger turns into two fingers, his mouth suctioned over my clit, his tongue swirling over it, stroking it as his fingers probe deeply inside of me.

Oooh, Charles, baby…yes, yes…lick that pussy…

Craig's fingertips sweep over my cervix, causing me to cry out. Ohgod! How dare he make me feel so good! How dare my body defy what's going on in my head!

My eyes flutter close, and when they slowly open, they're unfocused, rolling back.

I blink. Try to zoom in on the sight before me. My husband's face smeared in my juices, but—*God help me*—all I can see is Charles.

"You filthy whore," my BFF Sonji jeers, biting into a lobster croquette. "You're still fucking that fine-ass lawyer?"

Sonji and I are out having drinks at the Mojito Lounge in Elizabeth. And I've spent the last forty-minutes sharing what's being going on since the last time I saw her, about three weeks ago. She's the only person I trust with my secrets. Not only did we attend law school together at Columbia, she and I have been friends for close to twenty years. She was also my maid of honor at my wedding, and is the godmother to my daughters, so we share a very close bond.

"Ssh. Bitch, will you keep quiet," I hiss back. "And, yes. I'm still seeing him."

She wags a finger at me, raising a brow and licking crumbs from her lips. "Uh, correction, heifer. You're *fucking* him. *Seeing* him would mean you were *dating* him. And we both know that's not happening because you're married. And, if my memory serves me correctly, so is he, no?"

I roll my eyes. "Seeing, fucking…same difference. And, yes," I lower my voice, "he's married."

"Scandalous." She shakes her head. "The dick must be good."

"Girrrl, I can't lie." I close my eyes, clutching my chest.

She laughs. "Girl, sounds like that man has you strung out. I hope you know what you're doing."

With a dismissive wave of my hand, I say, "Please. I'm having fun. No strings. No stress. Just lots of sex."

She considers me for a second, then says, "And what about Craig?"

I shrug. "What about him?"

She tilts her head, twisting her lips. "Bitch, don't sit there and play coy with me. You know what I mean."

I sigh. "I'm not happy with him. But I don't think I'm ready to leave my marriage, either."

She raises a brow. "Well, how long do you expect to keep fucking Mister Good Dick?"

"For as long as I can," I say sheepishly.

"And when Craig finds out, then what?"

I shake my head, sighing. "I haven't thought that far out. Right now, I'm simply going with the flow." I meet her questioning gaze. "And, you mean, *if*, Craig finds out, which isn't going to happen because I'm not going to tell him. And I know Charles isn't about to come knocking on my door with a confession. So that leaves only one other person. You."

"Girl, bye. My lips are sealed. I love Craig and all. But my loyalties lie with you, boo. Still…" She pauses as she reaches for her third glass of Chardonnay. She takes a slow sip, eyeing me over the rim.

"Still, what?"

"This wine tastes good, though."

I laugh, balling up a napkin and tossing it at her. "Screw you, heifer."

"Mmph. No thanks. Someone else already has that position."

"I can't stand you."

She smiles. "Lies. But seriously, Kisha; you need to let Craig go if you're not happy with him. You know he doesn't deserve this."

I frown. "Why does it feel like you're on his side?"

"I'm not on his side. I'm not on anyone's side. All I'm saying is, you and I both know you have a good man. Do you know how many women would kill to be in your shoes right now? I'd hate to see you throw it all away for a piece of dick that isn't even yours."

"I know, I know. You're right." I shift in my seat. "But I'm not ready to let go. Not yet. That man has me doing things I haven't even done with Craig."

She smirks. "You're such a slut."

"Only at the office, boo. Only at the office."

We both crack up laughing.

"So when do I get to meet this sexy sidepiece?"

"Well, as a matter of fact," I say, a smile easing over my glossed lips. "What are you doing next Thursday evening? His wife is going out of town for a few days, so we're going to spend the night together in the city."

She blinks. Blinks again. *"What?"* she shrieks in disbelief. She repeats what I've said, then shakes her head. "Oh, heifer, now I *know* you are really out of control."

I smirk, placing my glass up to my lips and taking a sip. "I'm simply living on the edge a little."

She reaches over and grabs my hand. "Kisha, girl, I love you. But this shit you're doing is dead wrong. No judgment. Do you. But…" she squeezes my hand, "you do know there's the possibility that this won't end pretty?"

I gulp down the rest of my drink, then slowly say, "I know."

"Hey," I say, walking into the bedroom. It's been a week since Sonji's cryptic warning, but that hasn't kept me from being with Charles every chance I can. In fact, we've been going at it hot and heavy. Sexing all through our firm's building. My office, his office, in the conference room, the copier room, the file room, even at the receptionists' desk—wherever, we've been fucking, fucking, fucking.

Tonight, he ate my pussy in the backseat of his SUV, then I kindly returned the favor—stretching out my jaws and sucking him whole until he exploded his hot load down my throat—before sliding into my own vehicle, and heading home.

Craig is sitting up in bed, bare-chested, holding the TV's remote in his hand flipping through channels. "Where you been?" His slanted brown eyes never leave the forty-six-inch flat-screen mounted on the wall.

"At the office," I say calmly, slipping out of my heels, then sliding my skirt down over my hips.

He peels his eyes away from the television, just long enough to shoot me a look of disbelief that screams, *"You lying bitch!"*

He frowns. "This late? It's almost eleven o'clock."

"I know. I should have called you. With this big trial coming up, there are so many loose ends and still a lot to do to prepare. I honestly loss track of time."

He looks away. The muscles in his jaw tighten. "I called you three times. And left you two messages." Suddenly his voice is clipped and it's clear he isn't happy that I hadn't returned any of his calls.

"I didn't get them," I say, quickly moving about the room, removing my blouse, then my bra.

Truth is, I'd turned my phone off.

He tsks. "Well, I texted you. But I guess you didn't get that, either, huh?" Sarcasm drips from his tone.

Technically, no. "I didn't," I lie, crossing in front of the TV to get to our bathroom. I stop at the foot of the bed and look at him. "My phone died. And I forgot to bring my charger with me."

Craig tilts his head. I know he doesn't believe me. I walk over toward him, lean in and attempt to kiss him. But my lips only graze the side of his cheek when he jerks his head back.

He grits his teeth.

I sigh. "I'm going to take a quick shower."

His mouth twitches suspiciously. "Who is he?"

What the…?

I whirl around to stare at him. "Excuse me?"

He narrows his eyes. "I asked you who's the motherfucker you're cheating on me with?"

Deny, deny, deny…

"Ohmygod. Where is this coming from? I can't believe you'd think, let alone *ask*, some mess like that," I wail defensively. "There is no *motherfucker* I'm cheating on you with."

He grunts his response.

I plant a hand up on my hip. Give him a defiant stare. Feign insult. "I'm *not* cheating on you, Craig."

"Oh, really?" He stares at me, hard. His tone drips with accusation. "That's what you say. But your actions are starting to make you look real suspect."

I snort. "And what exactly does that mean?"

He frowns. "It means exactly what I said. You're standing there telling me you're not cheating…"

"I'm *not* cheating on you."

"Yeah, okay. But your actions have me thinking something totally different."

"And *what* exactly is it that you're *thinking?*" I ask, bracing myself for what's to come.

"You drop the girls off at school in the morning, then don't walk back up in here until close to eight, nine o'clock most nights. While I'm home playing Mister Mom to our daughters, you're out doing God knows what. So *you* tell me what it is I should be thinking."

"I'm working," I say indignantly. *And fucking!* "That's what the hell I'm doing. And you should be *thinking* that everything I do, I'm doing for *us*. Nothing else."

He laughs. "*For us?* Are you kidding me? Do I look that damn dumb to you, huh, Markisha?"

"I'm not calling you dumb. All I'm saying is, you're looking for a problem that isn't there. Stop letting your imagination get the best of you."

"Oh, so now I'm imagining all this, huh? I'm imagining some other man is fucking my wife, huh?"

"Yes. That's *exactly* what you're doing." I swallow back the pile of lies filling up in the back of my throat. "You know I have this big case. And it's taking up a lot of my time. We discussed this. You know sometimes I work long hours. It comes with the job."

He grunts. "And I'm cool with you working late *sometimes*. Not practically every damn night."

"It's not every night."

"Markisha, give me a break. Over the last few weeks you've been coming home late more often than not."

I didn't think your ass noticed.

"And *that* I have a problem with, especially when I can't get ahold of you."

"I told you my battery died."

He smirks. "Yeah, okay. How convenient."

I sigh inwardly. I can tell this is going to be one long, endless night of arguing. And I'm not for it. "Listen, I don't want to argue. I'm tired. It's been a long exhausting day. Can we not do this tonight, *please?*"

He huffs. "Yeah, whatever."

"No, it's not 'whatever.' You know we both agreed that you'd take on most of the household responsibilities with the girls until I made partner."

He sighs. "Yeah, okay. And I support your career. And I want you to make partner. But what I don't support is you forgetting that you're still a wife and a mother. What I didn't agree to is, you neglecting your responsibilities to your family. If you want to move like you're single, then do that. But you can't live here. I want a wife and a mother to my children. Not a roommate."

I blink. *Oh. No. The. Hell. He. Didn't!*

I slam a hand up on my hip. "I haven't *forgotten* anything. And I resent you for saying that."

"Well, guess what, Markisha? Get over it. I *resent* you putting more energy into your career than you do your goddamn family."

"That isn't fair. You know—"

"Yeah, I know. And neither is being neglected by my wife."

I swallow. "How have I neglected *you*, huh? What, because I'm not at your beck and call whenever you want sex? Is that what this is about, huh? You think I'm out cheating because I'm not fucking *you* every night?"

He glowers at me. "Yeah, that's exactly what I'm thinking, especially when I have to practically beg to make love to you, then you tell me you're too tired."

"I *am* tired." *Yeah, from getting my back knocked out.* "You know I work long hours, and—"

"Yeah, yeah," he says dismissively. "Whatever you say. All I know is, someone's been getting pussy and it hasn't been me."

I let out a nervous laugh. "Don't be ridiculous."

He raises a brow. "Oh, you think this shit's funny? I'm not being ridiculous. Tell me. When's the last time we've made love, huh?"

I blink. Swallow hard. Try to remember the last time I'd given Craig some pussy that wasn't out of pity or guilt, or obligation. I come up short.

"Yeah, just what I thought. You can't tell me 'cause you don't even know. Well, I know the last time I had my dick inside my own wife," he snaps. "Six damn weeks ago!"

I blink. "It hasn't been that long, Craig."

"Well, obviously I'm the only one in the room keeping count," he says snidely. "All I know is, I'm getting tired of playing with my own dick. And I'm exhausted from having the same conversation over and over, again. Take care of your man, Markisha."

His comment sounds like an ultimatum. I swallow back my guilt. "Or else what, Craig?"

Silence.

I stand in front of the television, blocking his view. Hands planted firmly at my hips. Head tilted. "I asked you a question, Craig. Or else *what?*"

He reaches over and turns off the lamp on his nightstand. Then aims the remote at the television and shuts it off, leaving me standing here flabbergasted with the answer to his question hovering in the darkness.

The following afternoon, I'm at the Marriott with no regard for anything Craig implied the night before. Butt-naked on my knees; face down, ass up.

Charles is in back of me, my ass spread open, his dick slicing into the back of my pussy until I feel dizzy with pleasure.

"Ohgodohgodohgodohgod," I chant, rocking my hips to meet his thrusts. "Yes, yes, yes, yesssss…"

I know fucking Charles clouds my judgment. That I struggle to separate *feelings* from *sex*. Still, I keep fucking him knowing that what we share isn't love. That it'd never be.

But the truth is, I. Don't. Care. Charles touches me, fills me, in ways Craig doesn't. Every time he fucks me, he fills places that have gone empty and aching over the last several years. What we share isn't meaningless sex.

Not to me.

But it isn't love, either.

Or is it?

No, no, of course not!

Lust. That's all it is.

And…

Obsession.

Yes, that's the only reason I'd be on an extended lunch, in this hotel room—naked, letting another man fuck my pussy to shreds.

God help me!

I grunt. "Mmmph…oooh, yes…"

Charles moves faster, harder. His balls slap up into me. "God-damn, this motherfucking pussy's so good!"

Slap!

His hand comes down across my ass.

I groan.

Slap!

Again. My ass quivers beneath his hand. The sting and burn causes my flesh to tingle.

"Yes, baby," I crane my neck, looking back at him. "Ooh, yes. Slap that ass! Make it hurt, big daddy!"

Slap!

"Yeah, you like that shit, huh, bitch?"

Mercy.

"Ooh, yes!"

He yanks me by the back of my hair, ramming his dick in me.

"Uh! Ooh! Yes, motherfucker, yes! Do it again!"

Slap!

I bite down on my bottom lip and grunt as he gives me long, hard plunges that jostle my body. My breasts bounce as he pounds into me. I rock my hips for more of him.

"Ooh, yes, yes, yes…fuck me. Mmmm…Fuck meeee…"

Charles thrusts—"I'ma gut this sweet pussy out"—and slaps

my ass again. My pussy clenches his thickened shaft. His hips smack against my ass. His dick touches a part of me that hasn't been touched before as his fingers dig into my waist, then slip down to my hips, gripping as he rapidly pounds deeply into my body, stroking over that magical spot. I grow wetter around his dick. Suck him in. Each stroke flings me perilously closer to climax.

"Yeah, that's right, baby. Milk me. I feel you squeezing that dick." He leans forward and growls in my ear, then nips my earlobe as he reaches under me and finds my aching clit, sticky and swollen. He pinches it. And growls some more.

My tongue lolls out of my mouth. My eyes roll up in my head. Fire shoots through my entire body.

"Ooh, get it, get it…yes, yes, yes…mmm…mmm…uh, uh, uh…"

It's all too much. The fucking. I squeeze my rolling eyes shut. I can feel all of the blood in my body filling my clit, swelling my cunt. The surge builds and builds and builds and comes from someplace deep as his dick fucks me at a perfect rhythm.

I am coming harder than I've ever come.

"Ohgod, yessss! Fuck. fuck. Fuck. Oooooh…"

"You like that? You feel that, this hard dick swelling up inside you…?" he says, between feverish thrusts.

"Yes, yes, yes," I mewl, feeling every thick, pulsing inch of him. Dizzy with bliss, pleasure ignites through every part of my body as I reach one climax after another.

Over and over and over.

"Ohmygodohmygodohmygod," is all I chant, my body writhing beneath Charles.

I give him my pussy. Let it become his possession.

He fucks me with all his might—

And then…oooh, oooh…

Hot scorching cum fills the thin sheath between us.

Charles bucks his hips, continues stroking into me until his dick shrinks and finally slips out of me, leaving me vacant as he flops over onto the bed, collapsing beside him.

I fan myself. "Ohmygod, I need a cigarette. And I don't even smoke." I stretch and moan, turning to him. "That was so damn good."

He gives me a cocky grin, rolling over on his side and kissing me lightly on the lips. "Yeah, I did put it on you."

I suck my teeth, punching him playfully in the arm. "Oh, please. What. Ever."

"Yeah, okay. You know you can't get enough of this good dick."

Smiling inside, I don't respond.

"No need to admit it," he says smugly. "Your body told me all I need to know."

Hot, sweaty, and still breathing heavy, he curls his arms around me and molds his body into mine, pulling me into him, hooking his leg over mines. Nothing else is said. He kisses the top of my head, then strokes through my damp hair until his breathing slows and we are both drifting off to sleep.

Two hours later, Charles and I stroll back into the building that houses the Strathmore, Strauss, Landers & Associates offices and ride the elevator up. I'm floating, and smiling on the inside. All I can think about is the delicious fucking that he delivered. And the sweet pounding of my heart as I climaxed. My pussy is still throbbing. Wanting more.

I cut my eye at him, imagining being bent over. Right here. Trapped. Him inside me. Fucking me deep.

He clears his throat, smirking. "You still need that cigarette?"

I roll my eyes. "Maybe. Or maybeeee," I say, licking my lips teasingly. "I need something thick. And hard."

We stare at each other with hungry eyes and knowing smiles for a long moment until he winks, then drags his gaze away, looking up at the camera.

Silence lapses between us as the elevator ascends. I shift my weight from one foot to the other, feeling my insides pulsing for more of him.

Charles straightens his tie, and sniffs. Then sniffs again.

"I can smell your wet pussy," he whispers out of the side of his mouth as the doors open. I giggle like a schoolgirl with her first crush, poking my tongue out at him stepping out of the elevator and running right into...

"Craig!" My cheeks heat with shock. He's the last person I expected to run into. *Here*, no less! Craig rarely comes to my office. As a matter of fact, he hasn't been to my office in almost a year.

Despite the blood draining from my face, I force a smile and feign excitement. "Ohmygod! This is a surprise." I fight to keep my voice from quavering. "W-what are you doing here?"

He kisses me on the cheek. "Surprised?" He smiles. "I thought I'd sneak out of work early and come take my wife out to lunch. But looks like I'm the one who got surprised when I got here and you were already gone."

He eyes Charles, and suddenly the air around me thickens, and starts choking me. I feel myself getting lightheaded as I draw in a deep, burning breath.

"Craig," I croak, stepping aside as someone steps into the elevator. I hear the doors close behind me. "You remember Charles, don't you? Charles, you remember Craig, right?"

"Hey, man," Charles says, grinning and extending his hand. "Good seeing you."

Craig grits his teeth, sizing him up, as the two exchange handshakes. "So you're the one who's been keeping her away from home."

"And I appreciate you letting me borrow her. Believe, man. She's always in good hands."

The innuendo hangs in the air like a thick blanket.

Ohmygod! What the hell is he doing?

Craig's eyes narrow suspiciously.

Shit, shit, shit!

God, please don't let this turn ugly.

It takes everything in me to keep from hitting the floor.

Craig assesses the situation looking from me to Charles, then back over at me. I can see the wheels in his head spinning.

I swallow hard. Out of the corner of my eye, I spy a few of the third-year associates as they look over in our direction. Great! Nosey-asses! The last thing I want is to be the center of gossip.

"I bet she is," Craig says tersely. "Working all those late nights together…"

He allows his statement to linger between us.

"Well, I'd better get going. I have a conference call at three." Charles looks from me to Craig. "Craig, my man, it was good seeing you again."

He extends his hand again. Craig looks at it as if he's deciding whether or not to leave him hanging. My heart starts pounding.

He knows.

And then Craig shakes it. "Likewise."

Charles sweeps his gaze to me, clearing his throat. "Markisha, I'll talk to you about that case later."

I nod.

Craig waits until Charles saunters off and is well out of earshot before saying, "I waited for almost two hours for you. Where were you?"

"At a meeting at the prosecutors' office," I lie.

He raises a brow. "Really? That's odd. Because when I called this morning, your receptionist told me your schedule was clear until three."

That messy bitch!

I keep my gaze trained on his. "It was. Until I got a call from the prosecutors' office."

He eyes me warily. "What time did you leave?"

"Ohmygod, what is this?" I hiss, clenching my teeth. "An inquisition?"

His jaw tightens. "No. It's me trying to understand where my wife was for the last two-and-a-half hours.

He glances at his watch. "I got here at twelve. And you were already gone." He glowers at me. "So where were you?"

He knows I'm lying.

"I told you. A meeting. Then we stopped for lunch."

He snorts. "I just bet you did. What did you *eat?*"

Dick.

I glance around the lobby. "Can we not do this here? Please. Let's go into my office."

His nostrils flare. I can tell he's seething inwardly as he presses the elevator button. "I'm going to pick up our daughters from school. I've waited around long enough."

I step in to give him a kiss, but he jerks his head back.

I grapple for words as the elevator opens and he steps inside, his hand pressing the button to take him to the building's main lobby.

"I'll see you when I get home. Okay?"

"I won't wait up," he says, his lips tight as the doors close and his face disappears from view.

"I think Craig knows."

I close Charles' door behind me, moving across the gray-colored carpet in his office. I'm smartly dressed in a brown pencil skirt and pink sleeveless blouse. My six-inch red bottoms make my back arch and my ass pop.

My nerves have been on edge ever since last night when Craig confronted me while I still had a mouthful of his nut in my mouth. Something I never expected from him. I almost choked. In all the years we've been together, he's never flat-out accused me of—*cheating.*

"Are you fucking him?"

"Am I fucking who?"

"Charles."

"Of course I'm not fucking him! Charles and I are colleagues. And we're working on this case together so we spend a lot of time together."

"Yeah, I just bet the two of you are. I can't put my finger on it, but I know there's something going on between the two of you. It's in my gut."

"Well, I don't care what your gut is telling you. I'm telling you, I'm not screwing him!"

"For your sake, Markisha, I hope not."

The tinge of guilt that elicits all but drowns out the voice in my head that says I should end this affair with Charles before things get messy. But I'm not ready to.

And, last night—even after I quickly showered, then slipped into bed and eased my hand into the slit of Craig's boxers, snaking his flaccid dick out and sucking it to life—I tried to rationalize in my head that there was nothing wrong with having the proverbial cake and eating it too.

He'd lain there, unenthused, unresponsive, unfazed, as I licked and sucked and slid my lips up and down the shaft of his dick. I remained undeterred by his detached disposition, feverishly sucking and gulping and licking and moaning until I'd eventually gotten the best of him and he grunted, groaned and began moving his hips.

That was my signal to keep laving him with my moist tongue. So I did.

Craig grunted.

And I sucked.

He grunted again.

And I sucked him deeper.

Licked him wetter. Sucked him harder. Massaged his balls. Then sucked them. Stroked him. Guilt brought me between his legs. Desperation forced me to give a porn star-worthy performance.

I sucked and gulped and swallowed Craig deep into my mouth and down my throat until his hand clamped around the back of my head, his hips joining the pulsing rhythm of my mouth and throat.

Craig growled. His grip around my head tightened. And then he was stabbing up into my mouth, mercilessly jabbing the back of my throat until a thick rope of heated seed flooded the back of my mouth.

I take a deep breath and cough as Charles looks up from the deposition transcript in his hand. There's a glint of amusement in his eyes as he looks at me. "You think your husband *knows* what?"

I take one of the two chrome-and-leather chairs in front of his desk and sit, crossing my legs. "About us."

He raises a brow, and grins at me. "Exactly what is it you *think* he knows…about *us?*"

I shift in my seat, uncrossing my legs. "You know exactly what I mean. I think he knows I'm cheating on him."

"With me?"

I shake my head. "No. I mean, maybe."

"Well, which is it?"

Suddenly, the muscles in the back of my neck tighten. "He doesn't know for sure. But he suspects it. He flat-out asked me last night if we were fucking."

"Okay," he says calmly. "And what did you tell him?"

I give him an incredulous look. "What do you think I told him? I told him no."

He smirks. "So you lied."

I tilt my head. "Wouldn't you?"

"You need to figure out how to keep your husband happy," he says, ignoring the question.

I roll my eyes, but nod knowingly.

"Listen. I'm not interested in getting caught up in any marital drama. No matter how good the pussy is."

I cringe. He says this as if I'm some disposable piece of ass.

Bitch, because you are!

"So, you're still sleeping with your wife?" Immediately after I say this, I want to slap myself for asking such an asinine question. Of course he's still fucking her! Why wouldn't he be? She's his wife, for God's sake.

I stiffen as jealousy I know I don't have a right to possess edges over me.

As if he's reading my thoughts, he says, "She's my wife. I fuck her to keep her happy. And you should be doing the same. Handle your business at home. There's no reason for you to be denying him pussy *unless* you *want* problems. Withholding pussy makes a man's mind wander. The last thing you want is, him becoming more suspicious than he already is."

"It's too late. He already is."

"Then you need to spend some time putting his mind to rest." He slides his gaze up the length of my legs. "We have a good thing going, baby. I'd hate for you to mess it up."

I sigh, uncrossing my legs, then crossing them at the ankles. "I'll handle it."

He lowers his voice. "Good. Because I'd hate not being inside you, feeling my dick sliding in and out of that wet pussy."

Thoughts racing, salacious and wild, I nearly swallow my tongue. Before I can open my mouth to speak, he adds, "I got one place in your life, Counselor. And that's between your legs."

My pussy clenches.

Damn him!

He licks his lips. "My dick's hard."

Ignoring how my pulse quickens, I shift in my seat. "I don't need to hear that right now."

He gives me an amused look. A slow lazy grin eases over his handsome face. "It's the truth, love. Tell me you don't want this dick inside of you."

I press my legs together, and bite my bottom lip to stifle a groan.

"You know I do," I admit in a shaky voice, my insides purring with want.

He nods. "And right now, I want you underneath my desk sucking my balls while I stroke this dick."

My mouth starts to water. I feel myself melting as my pussy slowly heats.

The man is a terribly delicious distraction. One I know I am unable to resist.

I take two sharp breaths. Try to keep myself planted in my seat. And swallow. My wicked craving to crawl under Charles' desk and oblige him is stronger than I imagined. And that frightens, and thrills, me.

Charles looks at the clock. "Listen. I have a briefing in ten minutes, then I have this motion to file before heading out to a meeting at the DA's office." He rises and rounds the desk, sauntering toward me. The imprint of his dick bulges in his pants, causing my mouth to water. He glances over his shoulder, then leans in and licks my neck. "Keep your tracks covered, love. So we can keep fucking."

There was nothing more Charles needed to say to me. I knew what I had to do. The message was loud and clear: If you want this dick, then handle your position at home. Which is why I haven't stayed late or given Charles any after-hours office pussy in the last few days. Still, I've made time to suck his dick before heading home—don't judge me. I still needed a taste—but that's it. Instead, I've been going home and fucking Craig's brains out, while thinking about Charles.

Seeing him at the office or in court looking scrumptious, then *not* having him inside my pussy for the last few days has been driving me insane.

All I keep hearing is, *"Keep your tracks covered, love. So we can keep fucking."*

So that's what I've been doing. Covering my tracks. Fucking Craig, begrudgingly.

Sadly, I've come to realize I want Charles' dick *and* my life with Craig. And I don't see why I can't have them both. I don't want to let go of my side dick. And I'm not ready to let go of my husband. I thought I might be. But I'm not. Maybe it's me settling. Maybe it's me simply being selfish. Maybe it's being a little bit of both. All I know is, I want my daughters to grow up in a home with both their parents, like I did. And I want to keep getting that good dick. So to ensure that happens, I'm willing to do whatever I have to, even if it means pretending to want sex with my husband.

"Stop."

I don't let Craig's words deter me. I nibble on his earlobe, then brush my mouth against the sensitive part of his neck. I smooth my palm down his bare chest and abdomen.

"I'm serious, Markisha," he says huskily. "You can't just use sex to smooth things over."

"I'm not," I whisper, blocking out visions of Charles. "I want you." I lick his neck. "I need you."

He grunts. "Since when?"

I don't answer. I climb up on top of him instead. Center my pussy over his crotch, then grind into him over his boxers until his dick responds to the friction, thickening and straining in his underwear. He gives into his own want. Raises his hips, slides down his underwear, and slips himself into me, getting lost inside the warmth of my pussy.

And for the rest of the week, I fuck my husband with reckless abandon while thoughts of my lover run rampant in my head.

Two a.m., my phone buzzes. I lift my head from my pillow, glancing over at Craig. He's snoring lightly, his back to me. I reach for my cell, then glance over at Craig again, before punching in my passcode. It's a text from Charles.

Slowly easing out of bed, I tiptoe into the bathroom, phone gripped tightly in my hand, then quietly shut the door behind me and lock it before walking over and sitting on the edge of the sunken tub.

I open the text message. *I want that pussy!*

I grin. Text back: *Y aren't u in bed?*

Can't sleep. Dick aching

Ooh. Poor baby. Wish I could suck u to sleep ☺

Damn. Me 2

I lick my lips at the memory of being up on my desk, my ass

marinating in a puddle of my own juices as he fucked me. Marsha Ambrosius' song "So Good" plays in my head as I dip my hand between my legs, surprised at how wet and hungry I am.

My cell buzzes again.

Where's ya hubby?

Asleep

My finger hooks inside my panties, grazing my slick lips, then slowly circles over my clit.

U give him sum pussy?

Unfortunately ☹

Good. U miss this dick?

Toes curling, an audible gasp rolls out of me as two fingers slink into my pussy, and my walls clench around them. I'm so wet and juicy. Horny beyond belief.

With one hand, I text back, *Yes!*

WYD?

Playing w/myself

Shit. Can u talk?

Yes

Call me

He doesn't have to ask twice. I spring to my feet, quickly double-check the door to make sure it's locked, then call him. He picks up on the first ring.

"Hey." His voice is low and husky and thick with desire.

I pinch my right nipple, then my left.

"I wanna put my dick in you."

I moan low as my hand dips back between my legs. "Mmm, yes…" An audible gasp escapes me as I slide my finger inside a rippling sea of heat. "My pussy's so wet." My fingers push in and out of my moist, sticky cunt. "Mmm. I wish you could see me playing in it. It's so hot."

He hisses in a breath. "Fuck. I'ma fuck the shit out of you."

"Mmmm. Yes. Fuck me." I close my eyes and imagine his hard dick. Imagine the feel, the taste, the thrusts. Imagine the way my walls clench around it, milking it, sucking it in. Imagine his hands roaming all over my body, caressing my breasts, spreading over my ass, pulling me open.

I remove my fingers from my juicy cunt. Pinch my clit, then sink my fingers back in. "Ooh. Yes. Fuck me hard."

"Yeah, that's it. Play with my wet pussy. Get it nice and ready for this fat dick."

"Yes. Yes. Ooh, I want you to put your tongue in my pussy. I want to feel your hot breath on my clit. Then in your mouth…"

"Yeah, baby. You have some sweet pussy."

I moan. Two fingers become three, fucking urgently into me. I rest a foot up on the ledge, opening myself more, welcoming the greedy thrusts of my fingers.

I am so overwhelmed with desire. I want Charles so badly. I want his dick. His tongue. His fingers.

In me.

All over me.

Again and again and again.

I moan. I writhe. My outer pussy lips stretch open. They are so slick, filling the air with my sweet musk.

"Come for me," Charles demands, his voice husky and low.

Losing myself in the wet sounds of my pussy and the guttural groans on the other end of the phone, I cry out in ecstasy; forgetting Craig is on the other side of the door sound asleep.

I arch my back. And come in a rushing wave of pleasure.

Two nights later, I'm down in our entertainment room telling Craig that I have to fly out of town at the end of the week to interview three potential witnesses in this upcoming murder trial I am assigned to. It's part fact, part fiction. I am going out of town, just not to interview witnesses.

Craig is watching a soccer game on the ninety-inch flat-screen. It's been weeks since I've been down here. I look around the room. Then back at Craig. He doesn't respond when I tell him this. Doesn't even look over at me.

I frown. "Did you hear me?"

Eyes glued to the TV, he grunts. "Yeah. I heard you. Who else is traveling with you?"

The least this bastard could do is look at me!

"Two other attorneys," I say casually.

He nods. "Mmm. Charles going?" Finally, he looks over at me, his eyes searching mine.

I don't blink. "No." The lie rolls off my tongue so freely that I almost believe it myself. "He'll be handling things on this end. Why?"

"Just asking." He goes back to watching television.

I scowl, crossing my arms over my chest. "Oh, come on. Don't give me that bull crap, Craig. Sounds like a fishing expedition to me."

He swings his head around, giving me a look of disbelief filled with suspicion that I almost cringe. "Should it be?"

I huff. "No, it shouldn't be. If there's something you want to know, Craig. Ask."

He tsks. "Right. And you'll give me the truth."

With a defiant look, I plant a hand on my hip. "Of course I will. I have no reason to lie to you, Craig. And I'm getting a little tired of you insinuating that I do. It's starting to make me wonder what it is *you've* been lying about."

He narrows his eyes at the challenge, seemingly unmoved by what I've tossed at him. "Have you?"

"Have I what? Lied to you?" I tilt my head. "Have you?"

No," he scoffs. "I have no reason to *lie* to you. And I've given you no reason to think otherwise. You, on the other hand…"

Yeah, bitch! Take that!

I scowl. "Are you serious? You have *no* reason to be concerned about Charles. There is *nothing* going on with us."

Dammit! Shit! That comes out without thought. Damn. Damn. Damn.

Craig narrows his eyes. "Who said anything about *Charles?* Or that I was concerned about *him?*"

My stomach lurches as I sputter out, "So you're concerned about *me?*"

"Your words, not mine."

I suck in a sharp breath. Then there's a moment of silence. "Craig. You need to get out of your head and stop letting your own guilty conscience get the best of you. Your paranoia is getting tiresome. And I refuse to stand here and let you accuse me of things I'm not doing."

"If you say so."

He says nothing more. Simply stares at me, brows raised.

Between gritted teeth, I say, "Fuck—you."

He nods. Turns his attention back to the game, placing his hands in back of his head. Then has the audacity to ask, "Am I getting some pussy tonight?"

Hell no!

With a vicious curse, I storm off, leaving a trail of anger behind me.

"So, you ready for three days of nonstop fucking," Charles murmurs as he tickles that sensitive spot between my thighs and pussy. In two more days we'll be leaving for a three-day rendezvous to Santa Monica. Something in the back of my head, though, tells me that I should be home, instead of here tonight. But the way Charles' hands feel on me has me casting off whatever feelings of foreboding I have looming over me.

I arch my back, and moan. "Mmm…yes, yes…oh, baby, yes. I can't wait." His fingers trail up and down my skin. The sensation causes my thigh muscles to tighten. I stretch them open as wide apart as I can.

He brushes his mouth over mine, and my lips part, inviting his tongue into my mouth. Like bees to honey, the sweet taste of his kiss lures me. He tastes so damn good. The kiss deepens, his heated tongue dancing around mine until I am dazed.

"Mmm. Wait, wait," I say, after finally tearing my quivering lips from his, and catching my breath. "Maybe we should call it a night. We—"

"Nah. Fuck that. Maybe we should fuck first, *then* call it a night. I'm not going home with this hard dick in my pants."

I purr as he slowly starts to unbutton my blouse, cupping my breasts through my lace bra.

Charles leans in my ear, flicks his tongue around my ear. "I can smell you. Wet and ready for me."

"Oooh, yes. You know I stay ready for you."

"Mmm. Exactly how I like it."

I reach for his hard, throbbing dick stuffed in his pants as he slips off my blouse and tosses it over in the corner. "And this," I say, squeezing and stroking his cock, "is exactly how I love my dick." I caress it over the fabric slow and sensually. "Thick. Hard. And ready."

"Yeah, it's all yours, baby." He leans his head in and traces his tongue along the line of my collarbone. I shiver. "What did you tell your whack-ass hubby?" Charles wants to know before his tongue grazes the tips of my nipples.

I pant. "I told him I'd be out of...mmm..." I let out a moan as my nipples harden in his mouth, "town...oooh...yesss...inter... uhh...viewing...aaah...witnesses."

I arch my back for more of him, his mouth, his tongue, his touch. Charles knows his way around my body better than my own husband. He pushes my breasts together in his large hands, switching between each one as he sucks them into his mouth, harder. Longer. Wetter.

I choke back a moan. "I'm addicted to you."

His hooded eyes flick over my face as he licks his lips. "I know you are. And I'm gonna feed that addiction, baby."

My pussy clenches with anticipation, clawing at his belt buckle. "I can't wait. Let me feel it."

He grabs my hand, smirking. "No. Not yet. You'll get it when I give it to you."

I moan. Ask him how he plans on giving it to me. He tells me bent over my desk, plunging into my pussy. And then, without another word, he is back to sucking my nipples into his mouth, mouth and tongue working in sync, softly suckling. He nips each one over my bra with his teeth, tugging and teasing, sending shockwaves through my body. Each time he releases a nipple, I twist to arch my other breast to him, into his wet, greedy mouth. He pinches both nipples. Hard.

"Yes, yes, yes...ooh, yes."

His lips and tongue travel lightly down my body, leaving wet trails of heated bliss over my skin, leaving my nipples aching and wet—and me already on the verge of a powerful climax.

When he reaches my navel, he pauses, blows into it, then circles it with flicks of his tongue, then kisses it before straightening his body and pulling me off my desk. He stops me from unfastening my skirt. He wants to do it. And I let him unzip it, then let him slide it over my hips. When it falls around my ankles, I kick it out of the way. Nothing is said. The hungry look in his eyes, tells it all. He wants to devour me. And he knows I want him to.

Everything is happening fast. No. Slow. Then fast. Files and documents are swiped off my desk, and then I am being hoisted back on it, leaning back, my legs wide open and Charles' face is between my thighs. Right where I want it to be, kissing and sucking my pussy over my drenched panties.

It doesn't take long before he is pulling my panties to the side, parting my swollen folds with his fingers, and eagerly lapping at my plump clit, then tonguing my dewy slit.

His eyes flicker up at me. "You like that," he rasps.

"Oh, God," I moan. "Yes."

Charles sucks me back into his mouth, soaking his tongue inside my juices. I cry out. And come. And then he is yanking me off my desk, spinning me around, yanking my panties down, then bending me over my desk, wedging himself between my legs.

"I'ma fuck the shit out you," he growls, undoing his belt, then dropping his pants and underwear.

I wiggle my ass, bracing myself with my hands spread out on my desk. His dick bobs between my ass cheeks. "Yeah, daddy. Fuck me," I say, glancing over my shoulder at him as he rips open a condom with his teeth, then rolls the thin sheath onto his rock-hard dick.

Then his strong hands are cupping my ass, kneading over tingling flesh. Parting, spreading; his dick probing at my opening until he sinks himself in, pausing himself while I stretch around his width. Mmm. Heat spreads through me.

"Uhh…oooh…aaah…yes…"

And then Charles is fucking into me, going as deep as his body and length will allow, his hips smacking against my ass.

"Aaah, shiit. Sexy ass. Fuck. Mmm. Nothing like fucking married pussy."

"Yeah, take my husband's pussy, baby. Take it. Mmmm…pound it, daddy. Oooh, pound it, pound it, pound it!"

"You wanna leave that nigga for this thick dick…?"

He begins pumping into me hard and as fast as I beg for it. "Yes… mmm…I mean…no…oooh…yes, yes, yessssss…"

"Is his dick bigger than mine?"

"Uhh, yes, yes…"

"Oh, that nigga gotta big dick, huh?"

"Yes, yes…God, yes! Oooh, yesssss…"

"But I bet he ain't hitting that shit like this, huh?"

He thrusts again. Hard. Each thrust is more powerful than the one before it. Each deliberate push takes my breath, and causes my pussy to cry out for mercy.

I grind my teeth together. Grunt and groan and moan and whimper.

"Is that motherfucker's dick better than mine?"

"N-no, no," I croak out breathlessly, panting and bracing myself up against the desk. "Yours is so much better, baby. Uhh…oooh… aaaah…"

"Yeah, I knew that corny-ass nigga wasn't hitting this shit right." He grunts, running his thick fingers through my short hair and clenching the skin at the back of my neck. "Tell that nigga to get his dick stroke up."

Slap!

My ass cheek pops. My flesh tingles. The room goes blurry around me as my orgasm builds and builds, spreading like a burning fire. Unpredictable. Sudden. Wild.

"Oh God, Charles, baby," I moan uncontrollably. "Fuck me."

"Yeah, that's right. Give me that nut, baby." He pounds harder and faster, grabbing my waist. "Come all over this dick."

I am being swept up in another climax.

"Ooh, oooh, oooh…yes, yes, yes…like that, like that…mmm, mmm, mmm…ohhh shit…oooh, baby, baby, yessss…I'm com—"

"I fucking knew it!" I hear the click, then a camera light flashes. My head snaps in the direction of the door. Heart pounding, face drenched in sweat, my eyes practically pop out of their sockets. I blink. No, no, no! My husband is standing in the middle of the doorway with his cell up at us.

I scream. "Aaah! Ohmygod! Craig!"

Blood drains from my face as he snaps another picture of me with my ass out for all to see. Sneering, he looks over at Charles as he quickly pulls himself out of me and yanks his pants up, stuffing his dick inside, condom and all.

Charles raises his hands. "Man, look—"

"Nigga, shut the fuck up! *Look* my ass! I've seen all I need to see. And now I got the proof I need. You can keep her! I'm through!"

My knees buckle. I've never known Craig to call anyone the N-word. Not even in jest.

Craig spins on his heel and is quickly out the door as I scramble to grab my skirt bunched up over in the corner. With my pussy dripping and my panties still wrapped around my ankles, I run out of my office, tripping and stumbling. But that doesn't slow me down. I yank my panties from around my feet, and sprint down the hall after him, breaking the heels on both of my stilettos in the process. "Baby, wait!"

He keeps walking toward the elevators. Each step angry, hurt.

"Craig, *please!*" I am trembling so hard I piss on myself. "It's not what you think. I know what you saw, but it didn't mean anything. I swear. It just happened. And then I couldn't stop it."

He spins around. "You *couldn't stop it?!*" His eyes are stretched open, and he's practically foaming out of both sides of his mouth. "You cheating-ass *bitch*...!"

Eyes wide in stunned horror, I freeze. *No, no, no. He didn't just call me*...bitch. In all the years, we've been married he's never called me out of my name. He's been pissed before, but never enough to be disrespectful toward me.

Fist balled, nose flaring, expression gone grave, Craig tells me he wants to beat the shit of me. He calls Charles every dirty motherfucker under the sun, then stops and shakes his head. "I knew you two were fucking!" Spit flies out of his mouth. He jabs at the air between us. "You ain't shit, Markisha! Fuck you! And fuck him!"

"I should fuck his bitch-ass up." He starts back toward my office. "Motherfucker, you like fucking other men's wives...?"

I run behind him, grabbing him by the arm. "Craig, no!"

He yanks his arm. "Get the fuck off me." He raises his hand to strike me, and I jump, fear covering my face. Craig closes his eyes, shaking his head. When he opens them, I think I see them watering. "Shit. What the fuck am I doing?" He takes a deep breath. "I should be shaking that motherfucker's hand, and thanking him. What the fuck am I pissed at him for? He didn't disregard our wedding vows. *You* did. *You* offered him up a piece of horny ass and he took it. *You* did this. Not him. So I have no beef with that man. My beef is with you, Markisha. YOU! Not him!"

I stalk back toward the bank of elevators.

I feel myself starting to suffocate. I gasp for air. "Craig, I didn't want to hurt you." Everything in me trembles as I gulp in air, taking a step back. "I swear to you. I didn't set out to cheat on you."

He swings around. His jaws tighten, then he snaps, "Is that *before* or *after* I walked in and caught you bent over your goddamn desk with your ass spread open, huh?"

I lower my eyes.

"Exactly what the fuck I thought. Answer me this, Markisha: was there ever a moment where you *thought*—in between all your muffled groans while spreading your legs and taking back shots— that you might lose your family? Or did you not give a fuck?"

I've never seen him so livid. So profoundly hurt.

And rightfully so.

I let my tears fall unchecked. "I-I—"

He sneers at me. "Save them fucking tears, Markisha. From where I'm standing, *you* gave up on us the second you spread open your legs and let another man *fuck* you!"

I cringe. The word *fuck*…it sounds so dirty when he says it. And it is.

"I don't believe this shit! *I* let you play me for a damn fool. I can't believe I was fool enough to let *you* make me *think* I was going crazy. That *you* fucking around on me was all in *my* goddamn head. You stood there and lied in my motherfucking face without blinking an eye. And I was too fucking blind to see it. Too damn stupid to believe you'd do this to me, even though my gut told me something wasn't right." He stares at me, hard.

I swallow. "Craig, we can work through this. I know we can."

His eyes go dark as he frowns, shaking his head. "*We* can't work through shit. Not now. Whatever problems you felt *we* were having shoulda been worked on before you fucking cheated on me." His jaw clenches.

"Craig, *please*. I can explain…"

"You can explain, *what?* How I caught your whoring-ass getting *fucked* from the back by some other motherfucker?! That you've

been lying to me this whole fucking time?! That you've been playing me for some goddamn fool?!"

He stares at my hand. Sees my panties. The evidence of my dirty
deeds is gripped tightly in my hand. Fire flashes in his pupils. "*Bitch*,
you can't explain SHIT to me! The proof is in your damn hand!"

Dick For Hire

"I know one thing. I hope you don't plan on lying around this house all day. There are three bins of dirty clothes that need to be washed."

"Aiight, yo. I got it."

"Mmph. Well, since you don't got a job. It's the least you can do."

"See. Here you go wit' that slick shit again."

"I ain't talking slick. I'm talking facts."

"Man, fuck outta here wit' that dumb shit. I ain't tryna hear that. You act like I ain't out here lookin' for work. You think I like sittin' up in this muhfucka e'eryday?"

"I think you like playing Xbox, that's what I think. And I don't know what you're looking for while I'm at work. But I know what I'm looking at when I run your pockets. Empty-ass pockets."

"Man, why e'erything always gotta be about money wit' you? You act like it's my fault muhfuckas ain't hirin' me."

"Well, maybe they would hire ya black ass if you stopped flopping around in Timbs 'n' hoodies, and got that haircut."

"Man, fuck outta here. I ain't cuttin' my dreads."

"Well, you ain't gonna be laying up around here, either. I don't give a damn how good the dick is. Or how fine you think you are. I'm not gonna keep sucking and fucking a nigga who ain't holding shit down. Sorry. But I'm not gonna keep supporting no grown-ass man."

"Yo, Nivia, word is bond. Watch ya fuckin' mouth, yo. Stop comin' at me like I'm some lazy, bum-ass nigga, yo. You really comin' at me crazy right now, like you been holdin' shit down all along by yourself."

"*Nigga, if you're sitting ya nasty ass up on my couch in ya drawz playing Xbox and eating cereal all damn day, burning up my electricity, while I'm out busting my ass, then if it acts like a bum-nigga, then it must be a bum-nigga.*"

"*Oh, word? Is that how you talkin' now? So all I am to you now is some bum-nigga, huh? I wasn't hearin' you talkin' all that dumb shit when I was out there hustlin' 'n' shit, coppin' you all them muthafuckin' Louis bags and red bottoms 'n' shit you got stuffed in them fuckin' closets. You wasn't poppin' shit when I dropped twenty-gees to get us this spot or put ya ungrateful ass up in that shiny, big-body whip you got parked out front.*"

"*Yeah, well, guess what? I wasn't popping shit because you were bringing money up in here.*"

"*Yo, what the fuck?! So what you want me to do? Go back to sellin' drugs? Is that it? I just did four muthafuckin' years, yo. And I'm still on parole. So what the fuck is you sayin', huh? I told you I was done wit' that life. I'm not goin' back to prison, yo. For you or anyone else. So if that's the kinda muhfucka you want, then go out 'n' get 'im. Because I ain't tryna be that muhfucka.*"

"*I didn't say go out and start selling drugs again, nigga. And I'm not looking for one who does, dumb-ass. I'm looking for you to get a job. And keep one. Or at least act like you're trying.*"

"*I am tryin'. Damn! What the fuck you want me to do, yo, huh? Put a gun up to a muhfucka's head 'n' make 'em hire me? These cracker-ass muhfuckas ain't tryna hire a felon. Period.*"

"*Nigga, you can get a job if you want to. I told you Wegmans is hiring. Did you go down there and put in the application like I told you to?*"

"*Yeah. I told you I did. And they still haven't called me back.*"

"*Well, until they do, the least you can do is have dinner cooked when I get home from work, and this house clean. I shouldn't have to work all day, then come home to a bunch of dishes in the sink. And not one god-*"

damn thing cooked. This shit is getting old. And I'm getting sick of it."

"Yeah, aiight, man. Whatever."

"Whatever, my ass, Levar!"

"Yo, fuck, man. I ain't tryna beef wit' yo. But you stay talkin' shit. You know that, right?"

"Well, maybe you shouldn't have gotten fired from Walmart. But you did. So if you don't want me talking shit, then you need to get up and find another damn job."

"Yo, what the fuck is your problem today? Didn't I just dick you down real good? So why is you poppin' shit?"

"Nigga, a hard dick ain't gonna keep these bills paid up in here. I don't give a fuck if you gotta sell apples and oranges on the side of the road, or sweep up horse shit. Hell, go out and sling dick if that's gonna keep these bills paid. All I care about is you working, period. It's bad enough I'm paying all the bills. But I shouldn't have to keep paying your child support, too."

"Man, whatever. Relax. I got this."

"Well, how 'bout you go relax them bills that keep piling up on the damn counter, and get. A. Motherfuckin'. Job."

ONE

"Yo, you got that bread?" I say the minute I step inside this muhfucka's crib 'n' the door shuts.

"Yes. A hundred, right?"

"Yeah. You wanted me to shit on you, right?"

"Yes."

This nasty muhfucka.

"Then I'ma need to see that paper, first," I say, eyeing him. He's about my height, six two. Brown hair. Brown eyes. His ad said he was thirty-eight, but he looks older. He's barefoot, wearin' a navy blue bathrobe.

I peep a wedding band on his finger.

Damn, this muhfucka's married. I wonder if he lets his wife shit on him. Nah, if so, he wouldn't be payin' muhfuckas to take a dump on him.

"Oh, sure. No worries," he says, turning to walk off. "I have your money. Follow me."

I follow him through his condo, scoping the place out as we make our way down a hallway. I can't front. The muhfucka's crib is right. He has all types of high-end shit up in here, and expensive-looking artwork and sculptures.

Yeah, this freak-ass muhfucka's caked up.

Yo, hold up. Before you start judgin' me, know this, I ain't gay, bi, or some down-low muhfucka. I'm just in a tight spot at the moment. So I'm doin' what I gotta do to keep a few dollars in my pocket.

And keep my girl off my back. So this shit I'm doin' is strictly business, point-blank, period.

And I don't consider nothin' I'm doin' as cheatin'.

It's me gettin' this paper, that's it.

Hell, I woulda never been browsin' the sex ads late last night if I wasn't feelin' pressed for money 'n' curiosity hadn't gotten the best of me. I heard there was a buncha horny muhfuckas on the Internet willing to be generous for all types of sex. So when I peeped this muhfucka's ad lookin' for someone to shit on him, it sounded—nasty as it is, like a quick way to make some fast cash.

So here I am.

About to drop my drawz 'n' shit on this freaky muhfucka.

Hell. I wouldn't even be at this muhfucka's crib about to take a shit on him if Nivia wasn't always poppin' shit about money. I'm not sayin' it's her fault that I'm here. I'm here by my own choice. All I'm sayin' is, that shit's annoyin' as hell. Don't no muhfucka wanna keep hearin' that shit from his girl. I already feel low as fuck as it is that I can't do for my family like I want, the way I used to. That shit fucks with me e'eryday. So I don't need my girl beatin' me in the head about it. That shit be makin' me wanna smack her fuckin' teeth out.

Don't get it fucked up. I love my girl. She's my heart. But, on some real shit, she's spoiled as fuck. And I know I made her that way. Still, yo, she stay naggin' the fuck outta me about this work shit. Like I don't know I need to find a fuckin' job. What the fuck she think I be doin' all day?

Don't answer that shit. You already know. She thinks I'm layin' up in the crib all day scratchin' my balls 'n' shit; doin' nothin'. Yeah, aiight. That's a buncha bullshit, yo.

Yeah, aiight. Maybe she's right. I could try'n keep the crib a lil' cleaner. And, aiight, yeah…I can at least have dinner cooked for her. But damn. I'm like, fall back. Shit's stressful enough. She acts like I don't know the light 'n' cable bills gotta get paid 'n' our two kids gotta eat.

Shit. I wouldn't be in this fucked-up situation—unemployed and all fucked up—now, if that stupid, flat-assed bitch with the big-ass titties hadn't come up in my line with a cartload of shit, poppin' shit 'cause I wasn't movin' the line fast enough for her ghetto ass. She lucky I had already smoked a blunt before I got up in that muhfucka or I woulda probably knocked her dumb, snaggletooth ass out.

But I checked her ass. And the bitch tried to turn up. Then came back with some cornball-ass nigga, like that was supposed to mean something.

So when he came at me, like he was tryna put that fist work in, I took off my apron 'n' knuckled up.

Yeah, we got to fightin' up in that muhfucka. But I didn't start the shit. I cracked the nigga's jaw 'n' finished it, then went back to checkin' out my customers.

Still, I got fired.

And, since I wasn't workin' there long enough to collect unemployment, I was assed out. Luckily I had a few dollars saved. But that shit only lasted for a minute. And the bills still keep coming in.

I've been out here looking for work like crazy for the last five months. But muhfuckas ain't hiring. Or maybe they just ain't hiring *me*.

"Okay, here you go," dude says, bringing me outta my thoughts. He hands me a crisp Benjamin.

"Aiight, cool," I say, stuffing the bill in my pocket. I glance at my watch. It's a little after ten in the morning. And I gotta be at my next destination two towns over between twelve, twelve-thirty. "So where we doin' this?"

"Right here. On my bed."

He points to a king-size, four-poster bed. Probably the same one he lays up in wit' his wife. But that shit ain't my worry. So let me take this dump 'n' get the fuck on.

In the center of the bed is a large white pad 'n' some white towels.

Dude takes off his robe, then crawls up on the bed, propping up on his forearms. He's wearing a skimpy pair of white satiny bikini briefs.

I pull off my hoodie. Then turn my back to him 'n' kick off my boots, before stepping outta my sweats 'n' drawz.

He groans. "Oh, God, you have a beautiful ass. I would love to have my face shove up in it."

My jaw muscles tighten. "Yo, dude, you gonna need to keep them ass comments to ya'self. I don't need to hear that shit."

Yo, focus, nigga. Get this paper 'n' get the fuck up outta here.

Dude offers an apology. Tells me no disrespect meant.

"Turn around," he says. "Let me see you."

I take a deep breath. Then face him 'n' the muhfucka's eyes bug out. I ain't gonna front. I know my body's right. Muscled and tatted with a long dick. So it is what it is. That's what I have'ta keep telling myself while I'm standin' here butt-ass naked in the middle of this muhfucka's bedroom.

"I want you to put your boots back on. Then climb up on the bed."

I stuff my feet back into my Timbs, then swagger over to him, lettin' the muhfucka get an eyeful of this dick. I'm good wit' him lookin' at it as long as he ain't tryna touch it.

He licks his lips. Goes in about how big my dick is. But I ig the shit. I know it's big. I climb up on the bed, then squat over him.

"Yo, where you want me to shit on you?"

"On my stomach. No, no, over my cock."

I frown, tryin' not to look down at his dick strainin' against his lil' panty-like drawz. *This muhfucka's real outta control.*

I pull open my ass, and start pushin'.

"Damn, you have a nice ass. I love the way your balls hang."

I frown. "Yo, my man. You gonna have'ta shut the fuck up. All this yappin' is makin' it hard for me to take this shit."

"I'm sorry. I can't help myself. You don't know how amazingly sexy it is to see a muscular, masculine man's ass pulled open over me. You're so sexy. The way your brown hole puckers when you strain. It's like it's winking at me. Seeing you squatted over me is such a turn-on."

"Well, no disrespect, my dude, but I'ma need you to keep the fuck quiet so I can concentrate."

"Okay. It's going to be hard, like my cock. But I'll try."

I close my eyes and push.

"Can I touch your balls?"

I shoot him a nasty look over my shoulder. "Nah, man. I ain't wit' that shit."

"Okay. Just asking. But I'll pay extra."

I ain't wit' havin' another muhfucka touchin' my shit. But, uh… it's all about collectin' this paper. So…

"How much more?"

"Fifty more dollars. I just want to touch them. Nothing else."

I hold my dick up in case the muhfucka tries to be on some slick shit. "Aiight, you can touch my balls. But don't squeeze 'em. And don't be tryna grab at my dick."

He moans, lightly grazin' my balls wit' the tips of his fingers in soft gentle strokes.

Oh shit.

I grunt. Fart. Then dump a pile of hot shit on his chest. And this nasty muhfucka nuts on himself without ever touchin' his dick.

I grab one of the big, fluffy towels he has on the bed and wipe my ass.

"Here," he says, holdin' a hand out. "I'll take that."

I hand him the shitty towel. Then grab my clothes and head into his marbled bathroom. He has a washrag and soap already up on the marble counter for me.

I reach for some toilet paper, wipe my ass some more, then run water over the rag, soapin' it up. I wash my ass out wit' the rag, then toss it up on the counter, catchin' my reflection in the mirror on my way out.

Muhfucka, you wild as hell.

I smirk, steppin' back out into dude's bedroom. I stop in my tracks. Dude's got my shit smeared over his dick 'n' he's jackin' off while sniffin' the towel I wiped my ass on. He stares at me, grunting as his nut spurts outta his reddish-pink dick.

"I couldn't help myself," he says all sheepish 'n' shit, grabbin' the other towel 'n' wipin' his hands on it.

He reaches for his robe. "Give me a sec to wash my hands, then I'll let you out."

A few seconds later, he's walkin' me down the stairs. "You seem like a really cool guy. Maybe we can make this a regular thing. I'm really a regular married guy who happens to have a weird fetish…"

Yo, shut ya shitty-ass up 'n' just show me to the muthafuckin' door.

"I love to be farted and pooped on. The smell turns me on."

I frown. But keep my thoughts to myself. I ain't hear to judge him. If that's his thing, and he's willin' to cough up that paper, then fuck it. I'll come through 'n' shit on the muhfucka. Hell, I'll even shit in his mouth if it shuts him the fuck up.

"You can smoke, drink, and watch porn if you want…"

"No ball touchin', though," I say, raisin' a brow. "And I want one-fiddy."

He opens the door, smilin' 'n' smellin' like shit. "Same time next week?"

"Yeah," I say, walkin' out. "I got you."

Nasty muhfucka!

TWO

"Ohmygod, bae! Dinner was soooo good," Nivia says, smilin'.
I lean over 'n' kiss her lightly on the lips. "Glad you liked it."
"Liked it? I loved it."

I grin, feelin' myself. I did my thing tonight. I surprised my baby wit' dinner 'n' flowers 'n' a card.

After I picked the kids up from school, then dropped 'em off over to her moms, I went to the grocery store, then came back here 'n' cooked one of her favorite meals. Shrimp scampi.

I ain't a Chef Ramsey or anything like that, but I watch mad cookin' shows 'n' I know how to put it down in the kitchen.

By the time Nivia walked through the door, I had the lights turned down low, candles lit all through the crib 'n' a Marsha Ambrosius mixtape floatin' through the surround-sound. And a place setting for two set at the dining room table.

"I can't believe you did all this for me."

"Why wouldn't I? You deserve it, babe."

She eyes me suspiciously. "Uh-huh. Since when?"

"Since I heard what you said the other day." I pull out the chair next to her 'n' sit, takin' her hand 'n' holdin' it in mine. "I heard you, baby. And you're right. I need to do more around here. I'm ya man. And I should be holdin' you down. Not the other way around."

"Don't say that. You're my man. I'm supposed to hold you down. It's just that sometimes…it's overwhelming."

"I know, baby." I put her hand up to my lips 'n' kiss the inside of her palm. "I love you. I know I don't tell you enough, but I love you 'n' I appreciate you holdin' shit down. You go hard for ya man. Always have. And I don't want you ever feelin' like I'm takin' you for granted."

"I don't feel like that," she says softly.

"C'mon, Nivia. Don't front. Yes, you do."

"Okay, sometimes I do. But I know you love me, Levar. And I know there isn't anything you wouldn't do for me. I know what kinda man you are when you have money. You've always taken care of me, and the kids."

"Shit's been hard, babe," I say, keepin' shit a hunnid. "Sometimes I feel like I'm becomin' a burden when you start comin' at me all reckless, like I'm some charity case 'n' shit."

She frowns, pullin' her hand away. "Don't even go there," she says wit' attitude. "I know you're not even trying to say I make you feel like that?"

"C'mon, babe. I don't wanna turn this into a fight. Let's enjoy the rest of the night, aiight?"

"I don't want to fight, either. And I'm sorry you feel that way."

I lean in 'n' kiss her on the lips again as "With You" starts playin'.

"I promise you, babes, we'll make it outta this storm; just don't give up on me. That's all I ask."

She kisses me back. Slides her tongue in between my lips. I let my baby in. Let her tongue swirl around mine. Savor her soft lips. Feel my dick brickin' up.

And when she pulls back, I can't front I feel weak. I love this fuckin' girl, yo.

I ain't into doin' some of the shit I'ma 'bout to get into, but if it's gonna keep a few dollars in my pocket 'n' help lighten the load around here, then I'ma do what I gotta do to make it happen until I can find something better.

But, until then…I'ma go hard 'n' make them tax-free dollars. Turn this dick into a business.

I stand up 'n' grab a bottle of her favorite wine, Sweet Bitch.

She grins. "Oh, you ain't slick. You trying to get some pussy."

I laugh. "Nah. I'm tryna get dessert." I wink at her, reachin' for a wineglass.

Nivia stares at me as I pour wine for her 'n' pass her the glass. "So are you going to tell me where you got the money to do all this?"

She eyes me as I take the bottle to the head, takin' a swig 'n' wipin' my mouth wit' the back of my hand. I can tell she wants to call me out on it, but she doesn't.

"One of my mans hit me up 'n' asked me to help this white cat he knows move. So I went out 'n' got that bread."

"Oh, okay. How much you make?"

"Three fiddy," I say coolly. In less than two hours, that is. After I shitted on dude this mornin', I went to my next appointment 'n' fucked the drawz off this older white broad. She was like fifty-five 'n' bored outta her head wit' hubby, lookin' for some excitement 'n' some hard, black dick.

I strapped up 'n' busted that old-ass pussy down. She started breathin' all heavy, shakin' 'n' clutchin' her chest 'n' shit. For a second, I thought I had fucked a heart attack outta her ass.

I ain't gonna front. That shit kinda had me shook.

But I walked outta there wit' two crisp Ben Frankies.

Nivia sips her wine. "That's great."

"No doubt." I set the bottle on the table. "I paid the cable bill, too."

"Ooh, look at my baby daddy. Go 'head, boy. You definitely getting some tonight."

I start laughin'. "Yo, you shot out."

"Lose Myself" starts playin'.

Nivia raises a hand in the air 'n' starts snappin' her fingers to the beat. "Ooh, this is my shit." She closes her eyes 'n' starts singin' 'n' swayin'. "Yasss Gawd. Sang Marsha, sang! I had to lose myself…"

I grab her by the hands 'n' pull her into my arms, grindin' up into her. I lean in 'n' whisper in her ear, "I wanna eat ya fat pussy real good. Lick you nice 'n' slow, then slowly kiss ya clit wit' my warm wet lips…"

She moans grindin' her pussy into my thigh.

"I wanna lick them sweet pussy lips 'n' kiss your inner thighs, then slide my tongue inside you, baby…I wanna taste you. Lick that wet pussy in 'n' out, suckin' on ya clit while ticklin' that shit wit' my tongue…"

Nivia moans again.

"I wanna make you come so good you start beggin' me to stop…"

"Oh, Levar," Nivia murmurs as I slide my lips back 'n' forth over hers. "You drive me so fucking crazy."

I smirk. "I know I do, boo."

She looks up at me. "You're all I ever need, baby. I'm so lucky to have you in my world."

"Nah, baby," I say, kissin' her. "I'm the lucky one. I'm all yours, baby…"

THREE

I'm up in my bedroom in my drawz goin' through another batch of emails on my laptop from the "Dick for Hire" ad I placed late last night. My shit's flooded with horny muhfuckas tryna get at some hard dick. Some of 'em about games, but there's a lot more tryna get it in.

It's been four days since my first two eps 'n' I'm already feelin' like I can really turn this shit into a money-maker.

Yeah, muhfucka, if the price is right…get that paper!

I hit up a few peeps that seem legit, then hit Nivia up on text to see what time she's comin' home. She 'n' the kids are up in Union City at her sister's baby shower and I'm here, relaxin'. But if I can fuck a few extra dollars outta some horny soul, then I'ma go make it pop.

I've already made two hunnid today fuckin' another old broad. She was in her sixties or some shit. Her pussy was dry as dust, but her mouth game was wetter than a muhfucka. Granny was all gums 'n' wet tongue. Them old jaws sucked my shit so good I almost let her suck my shit for free. True to life. Her head game was bananas.

I scan through my emails. Then open an email that catches my attention from Dicklover. I frown as I start to read the shit.

What the fuck?

On May 11, 2014, at 4:19 pm, Dicklover <dicklover4u@gmail.com> wrote:

Hi. Nice dick! no disrespect. I know you're only into women and couples.

But if you ever want to experience getting some good head from a guy, hit me up. What are your stats? Do you eat ass and like to 69? Do you fuck?
Sent from my iPhone

From: Dick4hire
To: Dicklover
Sent: Sunday, May, 11, 2014 5:22 pm
Subject: Re: Lickin this dick
31m in Linden n I'm straight yo
A few minutes later, my email chimes. I gotta 'nother email. It's dude again.
5:24 pm<<<<<Dicklover <dicklover4u@gmail.com> wrote:
I know. But I'm willing to change that.
Sent from my iPhone

I blink. Oh shit. I decide to see what's really good wit' this muh-fucka. I ain't checkin' for a nigga, but if his paper's right, I might let him suck on this dick. But it's gonna have'ta be mad dark. No lights. No TV. And I'ma have'ta wear a mask or some shit so he ain't seein' my face.

From: Dick4hire
To: Dicklover
Sent: Sunday, May, 11, 2014 5:35 pm
Subject: Re: Lickin this dick
U gen?

5:39 pm<<<< Dicklover <dicklover4u@gmail.com> wrote:
Yes. Very generous for the right dick. U host or travel?
Sent from my iPhone

From: Dick4hire
To: Dicklover
Sent: Sunday, May, 11, 2014 5:35 pm
Subject: Re: Lickin this dick
Na I gotta gurl. Travel only

5:39 pm<<<< Dicklover <dicklover4u@gmail.com> wrote:
Ok. I can host. Can we meet today? I am really horny. Can I suck your
dick more than once tonight if possible? Do you fuck?
Sent from my iPhone

I type back: *Wat u willin 2spend jus no kissin*

6:43 pm<<<< Dicklover <dicklover4u@gmail.com> wrote:
Ok, no kissing. that's cool. Like no more than 75. If you can give me
two rounds of dick then up to 100. How many inches is your dick?

This muhfucka crazy as fuck if he thinks I'ma let his nasty-ass get
two rounds of this dick for only a hunnid. I shake my head. All this
back and forth is starting to aggravate the shit outta me. But if this
muhfucka's tryna come up off that paper, then I'ma ride it out.

I type, *I'm only lookin for no lights no tv type of situation. Gotta be*
mad dark n ya crib. Let me know if you're down, then send.

On some real shit, I don't know if I'm really gonna let this muhfucka get at my dick, but I ain't gonna front, it's got me curious.

Another few minutes and I have another email.

5:45pm<<<< Dicklover <dicklover4u@gmail.com> wrote:
That's cool. I just want to feel good tonight. Let me suck that dick then
slow fuck me; turn my ass into a wet pussy for me. That's all I want.

I frown. *Yo, this nigga on some extra shit. I ain't say shit about fuckin' this muhfucka.* I spark another blunt. This is like my third one today. I take two deep pulls of the sticky, holding the smoke in my lungs until it burns, then slowly blow it out. A thick white cloud of weed smoke curls up from between my lips, then fills the air around me.

I reply back. *Yo im only n2 gettn head*

5:48 pm<<<< Dicklover <dicklover4u@gmail.com> wrote:
I know. But i wanna feel ur dick inside me. I'll pay for it. I love straight dick
Sent from my iPhone

I blink. Read the shit again, then type back, *yo bruh you wildin'. How much u payin for this dick?*

5:49 pm<<<< Dicklover <dicklover4u@gmail.com> wrote:
200$
Sent from my iPhone

I start goin' back 'n' forth in my head whether or not I should do it. But that paper sounds real right. Yeah, but what if this muh-fucka's some big, burly, lumberjack-type muhfucka? That shit ain't gonna work. I don't care how dark it is.

I type, *r u a fem dude? wat condoms u have*

5:52 pm<<<< Dicklover <dicklover4u@gmail.com> wrote:
Yes. Real girly. Heels n eyeshadow if that's your thing. I have Durex and Trojans. But if you need another kind, then I can get them. I hope you like tight ass. ☺

I glance at the time. Muhfucka and I been going back and forth for a minute now and ain't nothing been set up, yet. Pussy-ass nigga.

Na I can use those n listen im really nt in2 2much talkn ntg personal my dude itz bout business if itz real tight u mite make me nut qwik lol

He responds back. *6:02 pm<<<< Dicklover <dicklover4u@gmail.com> wrote:*

Who said anything about talking. I want good dick. AND if I'm paying for it, then I want to feel good, that's it. I'm not looking to be friends, bruh. I'm looking to ride some dick.

I type back: *Ok LOL now we on da same page*

6:06 pm<<<< Dicklover <dicklover4u@gmail.com> wrote:
I'm not looking to be fucked all rough and crazy. I'm looking to be dicked nice and slow and deep, and tip drilled too. IF you can serve me good dick, then maybe we can make this a reg thing

I shake my head. I can't believe I'm really about to do this shit wit' this muhfucka. I type, *If u got that bread then i got u.*

Word is bond, I'ma need to be high as fuck for this shit. Nivia finally hits me back as I'm takin' another thick pull off my blunt. *We'll be home around 8, 8:30. Love you!* I shoot her a quick text. Tell her aiight. That I love her, too.

6:39 pm<<<< Dicklover <dicklover4u@gmail.com> wrote:
U eat ass?

What the fuck?!
Yo dude. U doin' too much. Is we doin' this or not? U wastin' my time wit' all this back n forth. No I ain't eatin' no niggaz ass. Nothin' personal bruh. I told u I'm straight all Im tryna do iz get this bread

6:51 pm<<<< Dicklover <dicklover4u@gmail.com> wrote:

Oh let me get you right together, boo. Check this out, bruh. You know dam well your fake azz be on all fours sucking tranny cock nigga. U ain't straight. U straight frontin, yo. LOL. U the type of a cat who'll end up on the men section of a sex site hittin' up ads to get ya dick sucked. You already willing to fuck a nigga for paper. U are confused, bruh. And u sound crazy, yo. U might have a girl and kids, or whatever else. BUT truth is you ain't happy. Broke ass! U might not fuck with me, BUT you the kinda cat that will eventually be hittin someone else up tryna get your dick sucked by a nigga on the low. IF ya dick gets hard U ain't str8, dumb fuck! Maybe bi. But you def ain't str8. I know ya kind, pa. You'll bounce from nigga to nigga on da low when u start feelin' like u diggin' them, so U won't have to deal wit ya real truths. That you a frontin' ass fraud, yo. STRAIGHT niggas keep their ass off men's sections of sex ads. They on the female side tryna get pussy or get head from a chick NOT another dude, boo-boo. Soooo, get real...down low motherfucker! But it's all good. Keep on fakin like you str8. You gonna stay miserable in the process. I'm outtie. Fake ass pussy!

Sent from my iPhone

I blink.

What the fuck is he talkin' about?!

If this muhfucka came at me like this on the bricks, I'd beat the shit outta his muthafuckin' ass; word is bond.

I go over to where I posted my ad. *Oh shit!* Sure 'nough, my shit's in the men's section. *What the fuck?! How that shit happen?*

Now ain't this some bullshit, I think, quickly deletin' the ad, shakin' my head. I can't believe I was even considerin' that shit.

Yeah, muhfucka, ya ass trippin'!

I take another pull off my blunt. *You know you ain't about that life.* I delete all his emails. Then finish off my blunt.

Pussy-ass muhfucka!

FOUR

"Penelope, you cock tramp! You fucking bitch! You slutty white-trash whore!"

I blink.

"Yes, Peter, yes! Call me filthy names, you little dick fuck! Oh, God, yes! Mmm, mmm, mmmm…yes, yes, yesssss! I'm a slutty whore for big black cock!"

I slow my dick strokes. Blink again.

Yo, what the fuck…?

"Yeah, you filthy cunt-whore! Take that big black dick for me, you gutter rat whore!"

I frown. But then—as this broad beneath me starts to whimper 'n' moan—shit becomes clear. This is a part of some kinda sick game these two muhfuckas get off on.

Name-callin'.

Slut-shamin'.

Cock-shamin'.

I didn't sign up for this extra shit 'n' it's kinda fuckin' wit' my groove. But I have to keep remindin' myself that I'm here for this paper. So I keep strokin', keep thrustin', keep glidin' my dick in 'n' outta this broad's soft, wet hole.

I glance down at her clit peekin' through a patch of red pubic hair. This bitch's pussy is hairy as fuck, but surprisingly trimmed to perfection, almost like a well-manicured lawn.

She moans.

"You like that big dick, Penelope?"

"Yes, yes, yes…ohfortheloveofeverythinggoodandwholesome…
ohhhh, this dick feels so delicious, Peter. Mmm…Peter…oooh,
yes, yes…you did good this time, Peter, baby. Uhh, oooh…mmm…"

Dude grunts. "Yeah, fuck her good…aaah, yeah…fuck my wife's
sweet, tight cunt with your long, black dick. Uh, uh, aaah…my
cock's so hard watchin' you take my wife's pussy."

This Peter Pecker muhfucka hit me up this mornin' sayin' he
wanted a Cuckold-type situation. I'd never heard of the shit before.
But it's some shit he 'n' his wife get into. He likes watchin' his wife
get fucked by other muhfuckas. I wish the fuck I would sit back 'n'
watch another muhfucka run his dick up in my girl. But, hey, it's
whatever. His wife, her pussy, they can do what they want wit' it.

I cut my eye over at him. "Yeah, muhfucka," I groan, grippin'
his wife's milky white hips 'n' pushin' my dick up in her. "You like
watchin' ya wife take all this black dick?"

I ease in real slow, get half of my dick in, then pull out to the
head. Fuck her with the tip, then ease back in. I can't front, this
bitch's pussy is mad tight 'n' juicy. And she got some big-ass tits
wit' thick pink nipples.

"Oh Peter, baby," Pink Tits moans. "Look at how wet the masked
man's dick gets my pretty pink cunt. Mmm…don't you wish you
had a big cock like this?"

I'm wearin' a black ski mask, per this Peter muhfucka's request,
but sweatin' like a muthafuckin' racehorse in it. This shit got my
face itchin' 'n' shit.

He groans. "Yeah. I want me a big, shiny black cock to fuck all
up in your slutty walls. Penelope, my sweets, I can smell your wet,
slutty cunt way over here."

"Yes! Yes! My cunt is so slutty, Peter, my love…Oh, God, yes…
this sweet black bull is fucking me so good…"

Sweet black bull?

I pull out, slide my dick up 'n' down the front of her wet slit, then smack her clit wit' the head of my dick.

Pink Tits moans again.

"You want this dick?"

"Yes," she mutters, bitin' her bottom lip.

"Beg for it."

"Please. Give me your long, hard dick, you big black bull…"

Big black bull?

I keep tracin' my dick over her slit.

"Oooh, pretty please. Feed my pussy that big dick." She slides a hand down between her legs. Thrusts her hips up 'n' tries to get my dick to sink in.

I slap her hand away. Slap her clit wit' my dick. "Nah. Keep beggin' for this shit."

She begs for it. "Please, please…ohhh, please let me have that dick… oh, God, please…I beg of you. My pussy begs of you…fuck us!"

I glance at the time. It's 12:17 p.m. I've been here for almost a half hour. They're only payin' for an hour worth of dick. Four hunnid dollars' worth, to be exact.

The most I've made, yet, for servin' up this dick.

I plunge inside her, hard; amazed at how fuckin' wet she is, like a river.

"Yes!" she gasps as she lifts her legs 'n' bends at the knees, openin' herself to me, wider, allowin' me to go in deeper. "Fuck me! Hard!"

I slam in deep.

"Harder!"

I slam in harder.

"Harder!"

Her pussy grabs my dick.

"Oh yes, oh yes…faster! Fuck me!"

Aaah, shit, this bitch can take some dick…

Peter Pecker grunts, strokin' his dick. "Yeah, fuck my wife wit' that big, ole black nigga cock."

What the fuck?! Did this cracker muhfucka just call me a nigga?

I know these muhfuckas payin' for a service 'n' shit, but this muhfucka callin' me a *nigga* done took shit to a whole other level. But aiight. Since he wanna play those kinda games, I got some shit for his cracker ass. Real shit.

I stretch Pink Tits' shit open, then start slammin' her guts up, twistin' one of her nipples.

Her pussy starts gushin'.

"Oh, shit. You like that, huh, bitch?"

She cries out, clawing the sheets. "Oh, Peter, he's so big. Uhh, uhh, uhh…ohgod, ohgod…"

I keep twistin' her clit, tryna twist the muhfucka off.

She screams in ecstasy, her body shakin', her pussy pulsin' over the shaft of my dick.

"Shut the fuck up, cracker bitch," I say, slappin' her right titty, then her left.

Whap!

Whap!

"Aaaaaah!" she screams, archin' up. "Yessssss! Sweet heavens! Hurt me, Masked Man! Yessss! Whip my breasts!"

Whap!

Whap!

I slam into her. Pull out. Slam back in. Then speed-fuck her, poundin' into her wit' fast, hard thrusts, makin' her big-ass titties jiggle 'n' her pussy juice splash.

Peter Pecker groans, whackin' his dick all wild 'n' shit.

"Pinch my clit, you masked fucker!" Pink Tits snaps.

"Oh, shit. You wanna talk shit, huh, bitch?" I reach for her pink, swollen clit. It's all slick 'n' slippery from her juices. I pinch it between my fingers, then twist that shit.

I can't front, this bitch 'n' Peter Pecker got my head kinda fucked up wit' how raw they get down in the sheets. But the shit's got me turnt up. Got my dick harder than it's been wit'out tossin' back that Cuervo.

She shrieks, her head thrashes. "Yes! Yes! Oh Peter, Peter, Peter! Oh, how my pussy aches. It's on fire!"

Peter Pecker grunts again. His body starts jerkin'.

"No, no, no!" Pink Tits yells. "Don't you come, yet, Peter! Don't you dare let that little piggy sausage of dick of yours come before I do!"

"Uh, uh, uh, Penelope, my sweets, I can't help myself. I'm too far gone, my love. Watching that big, fat nigga cock all up in your sweet white pussy has me so fucking hot! Uhhhh! Aaah! Aaaah!"

Pink Tits cries out. "You worthless bastard, Peter! Don't you dare come, baby! I'll have your cock caged if you do."

He groans.

I cut my eye over at him again. He's stopped strokin' his shit 'n' is sittin' on his hands.

What the fuck?

Both of these freaky muhfuckas got me ready to bust. But I ain't ready to let loose yet. Not until I punish this freak-bitch 'n' her creamy white pussy. I pull out. "Turn the fuck over," I snap, yankin' her up.

I'm surprised when she leaps up all happy 'n' shit 'n' gets up on all fours. She tosses her red hair, rollin' her hips 'n' makin' her ass shake.

Damn, this bitch gotta fat ass.

I slap it.

She moans. "Ooh, yes, yes! Fuck me deep! Fuck me hard!"

I slap her ass again. It reddens 'n' she cries out some more.

"Shut the fuck up!" I bark. "That Peter Pecker muhfucka over there wanna talk that nigga talk, so now I'ma bust ya cracker ass open."

"Ooh, yes, Masked Man! I thought you'd never ask! Take my ass with your big black cock!"

"Get that muthafuckin' head down 'n' ass up, bitch!"

She does what she's told.

I pull open her ass cheeks 'n' my eyes pop open. This bitch gotta ass plug stuffed deep in her ass. And, word is bond, this kinky shit is sexy as fuck, yo.

She tells me to pull it out. Then calls out to Peter Pecker 'n' tells him to come suck it clean. I pull the plug outta her ass, starin' at her gapin' hole as Peter Pecker takes the dick-shaped plug from me 'n' licks it, then sucks it into his mouth.

I slam my dick into her ass. She yelps 'n' jumps.

"Nah, fuck that. Don't run from this dick now." I grab her by the back of the head 'n' snatch her neck back, ridin' her ass like she's a pony. And she's takin' all of me, every thick inch. I ain't no lil'-dick muhfucka, but this broad is takin' this shit like a pro.

"Yes, goddamn you! You, you motherfucker! Fuck me, Masked Man! Stretch my ass out so wide until my loving Peter's little piggy dick gets lost inside it."

She cries out for Peter Pecker. Calls him to her. Tells him to slide underneath us. Suck on her pussy.

The freaky muhfucka quickly hops up, practically runnin' over to the bed, positioning himself in front of her, then twistin' his body until he is on his back wit' his face underneath her juicy cunt.

He starts suckin' her while I'm poundin' her ass out.

Pink Tits screams. Her body jerks. Then the bitch starts sprayin' juices all over Peter Pecker's face.

That does it for me.

"Aaaah, shit, muthafuck...I'm gettin' ready to bust this nut...!" Peter Pecker groans.

"Aah, shit, Peter Pecker, this white bitch got some good ass... uh, aaah..."

He groans into Pink Tits' pussy.

She moans loudly, reachin' for this Peter muhfucka's dick—that ain't really all that lil' like she says it is, but compared to my shit, I guess it is—and starts strokin' it.

"Yes, you big, black bull! Come for me! Flood my sweet white ass with your big black cock cream!"

I groan. Grip her hips. Then fuck my head up when I start growlin' like some wild animal 'n' bite into her neck.

I nut...*hard.*

Pink Tits cries out 'n' starts cummin' outta her ass. I press my sweaty chest up against her clammy back 'n' squeeze her titties, still grindin' out the last bit of my nut into her hot ass.

I can't front. This shit was good.

When I finally pull outta her ass, my condom is soaked in her ass juices 'n' flooded wit' my nut.

I roll the condom off, then make my way toward the bathroom to flush it. But Pink Tits stops me.

"No, wait. Let me feed it to my darling husband."

I frown, glancin' over at Peter Pecker. He's still on the bed, on his knees. His face is wet, his lips glazed, from his wife's juices. He licks his lips in anticipation when I hand his wife the sticky condom.

I stand here, trippin' the fuck out as she walks over 'n' shoves the condom into his mouth. And the muhfucka chews it like she's just rolled a stick of cum-flavored gum into his mouth.

Goddamn. These muhfuckas are nasty...

FIVE

"Here, babe," I say, handin' Nivia three hunnid dollars. "It ain't much, but it's a lil' pocket change for you."

I don't tell her about the other five hunnid I got tucked away 'cause I ain't tryna explain no more than I have'ta.

She frowns. Eyes the paper in my hand suspiciously, before reluctantly takin' it. "Where'd you get this?"

I swallow. "'Member that cat I told you I helped move?"

She raises a brow. "Uh, yeah…"

On some real shit, I ain't wit' lyin' to my girl. But I know the shit I'm doin' to make a few dollars ain't somethin' she's gonna be down wit' 'n' I ain't beat for a buncha beefin' about shit she told me to get out 'n' do in the first place.

"Hell, go out and sling dick if that's gonna keep these bills paid…"

Maybe she ain't really mean that shit. Still, she said it. And, guess what? The shit's puttin' a few extra dollars in my pocket 'n' allows me to pay some'a these bills.

What I'm doin' isn't wrong. But it ain't really right, either.

Still, it's easy paper. And it's doin' somethin' I love to do. Fuck. And get this dick sucked. And, yeah, aiight…I might have'ta shit on a few nasty muhfuckas here 'n' there. Whatever. If muhfuckas are willin' to pay for a lil' pleasure, why shouldn't I be the one to help them fulfill some of their freaky desires?

Real shit…as far as I see it, it's a win-win situation.

My mind reels back to Peter Pecker 'n' his wife, Pink Tits. Now them two are some freaky muhfuckas. Do you know after that nasty muhfucka chewed up my nut-flooded condom, Pink Tits started kissin' him.

Then, right after he finished chewin' out my nut, Pink Tits told him to spit the condom out into the toilet, then flush it. He did. Then she started yellin' at him. Callin' him all types of fucked-up names.

"You worthless bastard! You lousy fuck! Look at you, you useless piece of shit! You let that Masked Man fuck my pussy, then tear my ass to shreds with his big horse cock and you did nothing, worthless fuck! You let him fuck me! Oh, how good he fucked me, you selfish bastard…!"

The muhfucka started whining like a lil' bitch, beggin' her for forgiveness.

"You want forgiveness, lil' piggy dick?!"

"Yes, my sweets. Forgive me, my love. Please…"

"Then you had better beg the Masked Man to stay 'n' watch what comes next."

Peter Pecker looked over at me. "Please, Mister Masked Man. Stay."

I frowned. "Yo, I ain't signin' up for this extra shit, yo."

"Please. I'm begging you. I'll double your fee. Plus throw in a bonus."

Enough said. The muhfucka had me sold. Even though I wanted to get the fuck up outta there, he had me with that "I'll double your fee" shit. Plus, on some low-low type shit, my nosey ass kinda wanted to stay 'n' see what else they were about to get into. And, word is bond, yo…them muhfuckas didn't disappoint.

"On the bed, you sad, pathetic fuck!" Pink Tits told him.

Peter Pecker eagerly did what he was told, practically droolin' as he spread out on the bed. Real shit, I though Pink Tits was about to fuck him or some shit until I peeped her walkin' over to the other side of the room 'n' yankin' Peter Pecker's thick leather belt from the loops of his khakis tossed on the floor.

Peter Pecker was stretched out on his stomach, grindin' his cock into the mattress, waitin'.

Pink Tits doubled the belt 'n' snapped it together, the leather crackin' loudly.

Oh shit! This bitch's about to whoop this muhfucka's ass...

"Get on your knees, you pathetic bastard!"

This muhfucka hoisted his ass in the air, then yelled out, "Yes, my love...whip my horny, white ass!"

Pink Tits slapped the belt across his ass.

Whap!

Whap!

Whap!

She whooped the shit outta Peter Pecker until his ass turned red 'n' bruised. Five, ten, twenty whacks to the ass wit' the belt, then the bitch dropped the belt 'n' started lickin' over his ass cheeks, pullin' his dick to the back 'n' strokin' it.

I couldn't believe the shit I was watchin'. But I ain't gonna front. The shit kinda made my dick hard 'n' I couldn't help but stroke my shit, watchin' as she made Peter Pecker nut, then licked his shit clean.

Pink Tits walked me to the door, then leaned in 'n' kissed me on the cheek. "Thanks for a fabulous time. Are you free next week? Same time?"

I smirked. "No doubt. I'll be back for some more of that sweet ass."

"It's all yours for the taking," she said, before shuttin' the door behind me.

Real shit, two hours of sex play 'n' I walked up outta Peter Pecker's crib wit' nine crisp Ben Frankies; eight hunnid for my company 'n' another hunnid as bonus for stayin' longer.

"I did some more work for him earlier today," I say, pushin' this morning's ep in the back of my mind. "Turns out dude's a butcher 'n' has a lil' butcher shop over in the city. One of his workers is out on some kinda medical leave so dude's gonna let me fill in until cat gets back…"

"Oh," she says, tryna decide if she wants to believe the shit I'm spittin' or not.

"I mean, it's only temporary 'n' the pay ain't much, but it's straight cash, feel me? And we can def use the ends until I can snatch up a job wit' some benefits 'n' shit."

A slow smile eases over her pillow-soft lips. "How many days a week are you gonna be working?"

I tell her maybe like two or three—maybe four, dependin' on how busy shit gets. "It's only for a few hours a day, so I'll be home before the kids get out of school."

She tucks the money into her bra. "Well, then, congratulations, baby. And thank you for the money."

I lean in 'n' kiss her on the lips. "No doubt, bae. You know I got you." I kiss her again, then turn to leave outta the kitchen.

"Um, baby…?"

I turn back to face her. "Yeah, wassup?"

"You never said what kind of work you're going to be doing for this guy? Unloading boxes?"

"Nah, baby. Meat-packin'."

I wink at her, walkin' outta the room, leavin' her wit' a smile on her face. My baby's just happy her man's gonna be bringin' home some bread.

I ain't gonna front, yo. The last few weeks have been crazy as fuck. My clientele list is growin' mad fast thanks to word of mouth. News of this good hard dick is spreadin' like fire.

When my paper was low Nivia made a slick-ass comment about me goin' out 'n' slingin' some dick. That stays stuck in the back of my head. So now I'm slingin' this dick e'ery which way to whomever is willin' to kick out that paper.

I don't give a fuck. It's whatever. Singles, couples, whatever…if that cash is right, I'm ready to rock. You want shit, you want piss, you want hard dick…I got you.

Don't get it twisted, though. I ain't tryna do this shit forever; just until I find me a legit job. Ain't no way I'm tryna let Nivia catch me out there wit' my dick out if I am bringin' that paper home to her.

It ain't cheatin'. But the shit still ain't something she'd be aiight wit', even if she was the one who put the idea in my head in the first place.

Nivia would be ready to leave my ass if she knew I've lucked up 'n' got four steady clients 'n' two couples—not includin' the muhfucka who likes me to come through 'n' shit on him—who wanna tag team their wives wit' me, or sit back 'n' watch me screw their wives solo.

I know Nivia ain't mean it literally when she told me to go out 'n' fuck for money, but still she put that shit out there 'n' hey…it is what it is.

Still, I know I'ma have'ta let this shit go in a minute.

But, word is bond, yo. In the meantime, I'ma sling this dick 'n' get that bread.

I'm only checkin' for them caked-up, freaky muhfuckas who don't mind comin' up off'a that paper, point-blank, period.

So until this job shit comes through, if you know anyone lookin' for a good hard fuck or freaky fun time, let 'em know I got some big, hard dick for hire.

ABOUT THE AUTHOR

Cairo is the author of *Between the Sheets, Slippery When Wet, Big Booty, Man Swappers, Kitty-Kitty, Bang-Bang, Deep Throat Diva, Daddy Long Stroke, The Man Handler,* and *The Kat Trap.* His travels to Egypt inspired his pen name.

THE PLEASURE ZONE

BY CAIRO

COMING SOON FROM STREBOR BOOKS

Hidden behind thick mahogany doors, a decadent sea of pleasure awaited everyone who stepped across its threshold.

The sign above the doors that opened up into the club's Italian-marbled foyer read: ENTER IF YOU DARE. LEAVE BEHIND YOUR APPREHENSIONS. SURRENDER TO YOUR DESIRES...AND STEP INSIDE THE PLEASURE ZONE.

Nairobia smiled wickedly.

The sweet notes of "Send Me Out" by Kelela played as flames swayed across the stunning fountain's water on the club's second level. The song was sexy. The artist's voice poured out of the speakers like warm honey. And it made the air around Nairobia thicken with sexual energy. She skimmed a hand down her neck, then allowed it to glide down over her pulsing body.

The club's grand opening had exceeded her wildest expectations. It was close to midnight, the bewitching hour—the freak hour, and the club was packed with hard-bodied hunks and curvaceously heeled women ready for a night of decadence.

Nairobia's tongue slid across her teeth as she gathered the drool that formed in her mouth, and swallowed. Salacious thoughts and forbidden desires bloomed into sinful realities right before her and she was…well, she was shamelessly wet.

Sweet pussies slid down hard dicks. Thick dicks pushed through swollen cunts; balls pushing against asses, while wandering hands skated up bodies to cup bouncing breasts. The music and the delicious sounds of orgasms echoed around the club. Permeated its walls.

And Nairobia was floating.

On lust.

On mounting desire.

Nipples peaked, her gaze swept around the sensual space, her arousal heightening. The luminosity of the flickering firelight from the gas lamps reflected beautifully off tiled mosaics of notoriously lusty satyrs and maidens. The walls illuminated by the fire's glow and its dancing flames gave the illusion that the satyrs were moving, their hips *thrusting*.

She felt herself growing lusciously wetter.

Not from the room's ambiance, but from the sight of a mocha-colored, mink-lashed vixen being ravaged by three delectable, broad-shouldered chocolate hunks. She was straddling the one with the braids, his long legs stretched out along an oversized burnt orange leather sofa as his hips thrust up in her, slicing into her cunt. Another, dark chocolate with dreads, was in back of her, his large hands on either side of her ass cheeks, the ring of her anus stretched around the head of his jumbo-size dick as he eased himself in and out of her, loosening the way inside her tunnel. The third hunk, bald, caramel-coated bliss, stood with both his hands on his hips, his legs spread wide, his balls dangling over Mr. Braids' face as Mink Lash licked the head of his dick.

Nairobia felt the urging need to squeeze her thighs together, and she did.

There was a deep throb, a sweet aching, spreading through her pussy as she watched the four lovers in the throes of unadulterated pleasure. Her cunt caught fire, enflaming her slickened lips. She could feel the flames quickly spreading through her asshole, swirling up and around her clit. Her whole body became engulfed in heat.

And she needed relief.

She needed something long, hard and thick to hose down the inferno raging inside her.

She needed to be...*fucked*.

And the hedonistic sounds of hot, raw, sweaty *fucking* only coiled her desires tighter and tighter, squeezing her soul helpless until she found herself nearly breathless.

Nairobia knew she needed to turn on her heel and flee to the comforts of her plush office and watch all of the *fuck*tivities from the safety of monitors that gave her a bird's-eye view of every wicked, every sordid, every salacious act performed in every part of her establishment before she broke her rule and joined in. Temptation was gnawing away at her resolve.

Yet, there she stood.

Fixed on the glorious sight before her.

Mink Lash opened herself to her three stallions, giving into the dick and the heat. She moaned loudly over the music. There was a delicious rhythm all three cocks found, thrusting and retreating, fucking into her holes. Pure bliss coated Mink Lash's face as she grunted and groaned and writhed around each thrusting cock.

Nairobia knew all too well the delicious feeling of being penetrated in all three orifices, pussy and ass and throat stuffed balls deep. She almost envied the busty vixen as she captured their meaty cocks in her greedy holes.

Bitch.

Watching the foursome was slowly uncoiling all her self-control, and Nairobia knew it. She felt it. But she wasn't ready to leave. No. Not yet.

So she prowled closer.

The voyeur in her wanted, no needed, to see more. They knew she was watching them and they fucked with wild abandon, wanting to be seen. Wanting to be heard. Wanting their wet, scented heat to be savored.

Nairobia seductively licked her lips, breathing in the aphrodisiac. She wanted to bite into the air and swallow up the musky heat. "Yes, my loves," she rasped, edging over toward the sofa. "Stretch her to the hilt. Fuck into her soul." She stalked around the sofa. "Fuck *haar ademloos…*" Fuck her breathless.

She found herself taking a slender, manicured finger and ever so lightly sliding it down Caramel-Coated's spine, then over the globes of his muscled ass. She reveled in its magnificence. Next to a long thick dick, a man's beautiful muscled-ass was another one of her weaknesses.

He thrust hard into Mink Lash's mouth and then slowed. "Open your fuckin' mouth," he ordered. She did what she was told, and he slid his dick gently over her tongue, rubbing the tip over her lips before plunging back inside the wetness of her juicy mouth. Mink Lash gagged. "Suck that dick," he growled.

Nairobia smiled. Mink Lash was a good, greedy bitch. She knew how to submit to the dick. Nairobia admired that. And obviously so did her three lovers. Her pussy and ass and mouth were spread wide with cock. Caramel-Coated feathered a hand over Mink Lash's cheek, then took her head and held it in place, thrusting, deeper, pushing every inch of himself to the back of her throat.

"Yes, my love," Nairobia whispered in his ear, "clog her throat with your hard cock. Crush her windpipe, my darling." Spit splashed out of Mink Lash's mouth, her eyes watered. Nairobia slapped Caramel-Coated's ass and he let out a groan.

The freak in her wanted to drop down, spread her warm hands over his sweat-glistened gluteus and reward him with a tongue lick or two along the crack of his ass.

But she resisted.

She preyed around him. Moved onto Dark Chocolate. She allowed her hands to stretch out across his thick shoulders. She stood in back of him, her body practically pressing into his, and marveled in the feel of his muscles as they fanned out. She ran her hands along his traps. Then caressed his delts, before spreading out over his back again. Her hands slid down to cup his ass and her mouth watered. Unlike Caramel-Coated's smooth, hairless ass, his was lightly covered with hair along the seam of his ass. Nairobia gripped it and he thrust himself deeper, his cock getting lost inside the warmth of Mink Lash's ass.

Mink Lash mewled, her big bouncy ass sucking in his dick as Nairobia glided her hands underneath him and cupped his low-hanging balls. She lightly bounced them in the palm of her hand. They were heavy. And hairy. As was his cock. And it looked scrumptiously heavy as it disappeared in and out of Mink Lash's ass; the thick, curly hairs at his groin brushing against her flesh.

Nairobia's own ass clenched in want. Desire settled in the pit of her cunt and spread along her inner walls, tightening viciously around her clit, spreading like a wildfire.

Her voice heavy with lust, she muttered words in Dutch. Told him to shove his cock deep in her ass, to fuck her shitless.

He groaned in response. She moved onto Mink Lash. "Yes, my darling," Nairobia whispered, leaning into her ear as she gurgled and clutched around a mouthful of cock. "Surrender to the dick. Worship it. Let it own you, my love. Or," she sweetly warned, "I'll put a crop to your ass, my darling."

She reached for one of Mink Lash's taut nipples, and pinched it. Twisted it.

Mink Lash screamed. Cried out as her three lovers impaled her with their engorged cocks. They fucked her mercilessly. She struggled for breath. Then cried out again. Her yell was sharp, echoing out across the room as they savagely shredded her throat and ass and cunt to pieces.

Arousal hummed through Nairobia's veins. She felt her entire pussy quiver and tingle with need. There was no way she would get through the night without clutching a dick into her cunt and orgasming around it.

Oh, how she would love the feel of a warm nut coating the walls of her pussy. The thought only fueled the fires of lust enflaming her.

She was ready to come. Not later tonight. Not tomorrow.

Right *now*.

And she would.